"Take a wild ride with Raymond Sheets and his friends Melon and Terminal, Iron Jack and Derry Berry and you're apt to discover a full range of emotions, laughter and lust and miserable loss. Ron Thomas has carefully selected his playlist, songs of love and longing cranked to the max, but you'll find the quiet contemplative moments equally engaging. Raymond is searching for nothing less than how to live in this world, how to trust, how to be, and Ron has left nothing in the tank."

—Daniel Coshnear,
author of *Occupy & Other Love Stories*

"Set in the era of Fats Domino and the Shirelles, *I Want To Walk You Home* wonderfully tracks the journey of Raymond Sheets from a young, idealistic Catholic seminarian, who meets the uninhibited Alice Derry, to a rebellious teenager who is goaded on by his equally rebellious friend named Melon. Only when Raymond nearly gets himself killed does he realize the message life has been trying to deliver all along."

—John Paine,
Professional book editor of many *New York Times* bestsellers

"Ron Thomas' book is extremely well-written and a finely crafted piece of work. The accolades I have for the novel appear to be endless. The writing style and story are wonderful. I especially like the way the contemplative Raymond Sheets, the uninhibited Alice Derry, and the trouble-maker Melon transport the reader from the edge of chaos to the saving grace of redemption."

—Bill McCausland,
author of *In the Mouth of the Wolf*

I WANT TO WALK YOU HOME

I WANT TO WALK YOU HOME

Ron Thomas

Palmetto Publishing Group
Charleston, SC

I Want to Walk You Home
Copyright © 2018 by Ron Thomas
All rights reserved

First Edition

Printed in the United States

ISBN-13: 978-1-64111-198-0
ISBN-10: 1-64111-198-4

No character is real or has ever existed except in the pages of this book. I attended two minor seminaries. The experiences depicted in these pages are not meant as commentaries on either of these two institutions, but only as broad fictional renderings of minor seminary life in 1959-1960. The incidents and occurrences portrayed in this book never happened and exist only in the author's imagination. Any resemblance to actual events or persons living or dead is entirely coincidental.

1

A LAWN RUNS LIKE A RIVER THROUGH scattered blue cedars. On the grounds of St. Jerome's seminary, little islets of white daisies dot sunny spots on the grass. I walk down a long drive toward an unruly snarl of vines like scrambled barbed wire. That's where a girl about my age is picking berries.

I really shouldn't talk to her, I'm studying to be a priest. I'm in my third year of high school at a Catholic seminary, but there she is, tasting the dark fruit of the blackberry brambles. Tanned face. Straight auburn hair curtained down to that soft spot where neck meets shoulders. A wild thing among vines. "Hey, who are you?" she asks like she owns the place.

"Raymond Sheets, and I'm trying to be quiet. We're having a day of meditation."

"What do you guys do up there, pray a lot?" The berries are small, second-growth, and she has purple stains on her fingertips. "My mom says you probably play with yourselves." She lifts barbed branches while she talks, like she's having a conversation with the underbrush. "Course, my mom's kinda crude. She drinks a lot."

"Sounds like your mom has a problem." I'm pulled. The rules forbid it, but I want to know, "What's your name?"

She studies me like I'm a person and not a thorny stem. "Alice Derry, and my dad's in the Navy."

The heck with the rules. "How'd you get so tan?"

"We just moved to California from Hawaii. You got a nice face. Come over on this side of the bushes so I can see all of you."

I feel a rush of red. I must be blushing to the roots of my blond crew cut. "Can't come over there. It's out of bounds."

"Out of bounds! Are you in jail? I'll show you all of me then."

"Look, I'm trying to be quiet, I have to leave now—" Before I'm finished talking, she's come around the end of the berry patch, holding a berry to my lips.

"Most of them are a little tart, but this one's soft. Should be sweet."

I front-teeth the berry, then push her hand away.

She brushes at a wisp of hair on her forehead. "What, are you afraid of me?" she asks.

She's medium height. Slim. Breasts budding under a white V-neck T-shirt. Blue pants cutting her leg at midcalf. I feel awkward in the presence of her soft beauty. I want to run my hand over the sheen of her hair, but I hold back. "No, I'm not afraid of you."

"Good. You ever been to a nude beach?" She's talking to the under-brush again. "Course not. You're trying to stay pure. Never could understand why priests couldn't marry." She's picking fruit on my side of the bramble.

I feel anxious and challenged by her direct manner. "You seem to know a lot. You Catholic?" I spit the words out, trying to match her boldness.

"With a name like Derry, what do you think, Raymond Sheets?"

I stretch my spine up to my full five feet nine inches. "Perhaps your family came from Northern Ireland. That would possibly make you Protestant." I can't believe I used the word "perhaps." In my attempt to get the best of this berry picker, I'm coming off like a prep school weenie.

"Perhaps you're wrong, Raymond Sheets. My ancestors came from Dublin." She pushes a berry to my lips. "Here's a nice plump dark one." I stand solid. Feel the brush of her finger on my tongue. "You look fit, Raymond Sheets. Play sports?"

"I run track."

She puts her hand on my wrist. "My aunt taught me how to read palms. Lemme see your hand."

Though I know I shouldn't, I let her take my hand. I haven't held a girl's hand since fifth-grade dance class, and this feels good. She tells me my palm says I wandered down to the boundary of the property because I'm thinking of breaking out of here. "How come nobody else is down here?" she asks.

I want to tell her it's none of her business, but she's so close I smell sun-warmth in her hair. "How come you ask so many questions?" I pull away from her hand and pick up a smooth gray rock. I fling it hard as I can toward the back of the metal sign that says "St. Jerome's Seminary." I put a small dent in the sign. I feel agitated. I should leave her, but I'm pulled by a tingling in my lower gut.

"You throw things like my dad. Why do you sound so mad?"

"Look, nobody else is down here because they're walking around in silence on the playing fields or doing the Stations of the Cross in the grotto along the creek. I'm down here trying to be alone so I can pray and think in silence, and you're not making it easy."

She stands, hands on her hips, and stares me in the eye. "My dad says pilots use this school as a final approach marker when they're landing at the air station."

"Yeah, Father Chuck tried to scare us about the planes. Says if one of these planes slams into the school some night and we're in the state of mortal sin, then we're headed for hell."

"Do you scare easy?"

"Heck no," I snap at her. I feel like I'm giving her too much ammunition. She's pretty, but irritating.

"Who's Father Chuck, and what kind of mortal sin could you possibly commit besides whacking off?" She's smiling again. Wide-teeth grin. Back to lifting berry branches.

I kick hard with my heel at a clod of dirt. She has a smart mouth. I'm really starting to dislike her. "Charlie Barrington. He's a priest, vice president of this place. Says it's possible to commit a mortal sin in our minds."

"So, if you think of me at a nude beach, you might be going to hell?" She's bent down from the waist, sucking on a finger of her right hand. I notice her pants stretched tight over her little butt. Mortal sin in the mind. I quickly look away. She must have snagged herself on a thorn.

"Look, I gotta leave."

"Sorry, why don't you take off, then? I was going to ask you over to my house. Too bad you're afraid to go out of bounds." She starts down the drive toward town.

I'm walking backward up the drive. It's against the rules, but I want to know more of her. "Where's your house?"

"Three blocks down," she calls over her shoulder. "On the right. Lots of roses out front. We're renting, and I'm tan all over, Raymond Sheets."

I continue up the drive toward the school feeling humiliation and anger. I'm trying to think of Christ on the Cross, but my mind keeps returning to Alice Derry, her effortless smile, her tan, and the way the tips of her hair brush that tender little reservoir of skin just above her collarbone.

I think of a letter my brother, Donnie, sent me: "I took Karen Ferris to the drive-in. I shouldn't be telling you this, little brother, but she was torrid." I decide I will pen a short letter back to my brother, telling him I met a girl, and I'm beginning to understand "torrid." Then I make a vow to talk to my spiritual advisor.

2

I LOVE THE BELLS. BELLS SET TO go off by a central great clock hanging on a wall in the office of the administration building. Bells demand order. A bell to roll out of bed. A bell to put you to sleep.

The regimentation of the bells envelops me like a safe mantle and keeps me warm.

I haven't seen Alice Derry in weeks, yet she flits in and out of my mind. Geometry class and she's among the triangles. Latin class, I silently mouth the word "puella," "puella." Only the compulsion of bells that demand the beginning and end of chapel, study hall, classroom, chases her away.

Nighttime's the problem. Nighttime and the Grand Silence. Nine o'clock and lights out. Ten-by-twelve-foot room, metal 1920s bed next to one wall. Chest of drawers, wooden chair, and a small closet. Washbasin in the corner with tiny mirror over it. Grand Silence. No one talks. Positively no one.

Tonight is Halloween. St. Jerome's celebrates this last night of October by lighting a giant bonfire. Old wooden pallets and timber scraps donated by parents, businesses, and construction companies make for a blaze fifteen feet high and twenty feet across. The fire burns for hours, and seminarians take turns performing skits and songs in front of the raging blaze in the middle of the playing fields. Tonight, I feel inattentive. The skits and laughter feel like a dream. My heart is out of bounds. "I'm tan all over, Raymond Sheets."

Halloween night. After the fire and festivities, I'm thankful for the solitude of my room, and I stare across the valley at scattered lights that stretch toward the air station. Alice Derry. Blue eyes. The touch of her finger on my tongue.

~

Father John Castaic, my spiritual advisor, can crush a softball, sometimes hits it far beyond the fence that edges the playing fields. He's built like a weightlifter, and behind his back we call him "Iron Jack." In the swimming pool, he reaches up, with hands on either side of the diving board, and does endless chin-ups. I need to talk to Iron Jack.

My thoughts about Alice become more obsessive. While I pray at Mass, run track, and try to concentrate in class, she's on my mind.

Iron Jack knows my history. I think back to my first year at the sem. I was homesick and thinking of quitting after the first month away from home. I climbed the stairs to Iron Jack's living quarters, rapped on the door, and was seated in front of his neat but busy desk.

"So, what brought you here in the first place? What made you think you wanted to be a priest?"

"I dunno, Father, I always admired priests. I like the ritual, the vestments, power to save souls. My mom would like to see me a priest." I was rattling off the top of my head. I took a deep breath and held it for a second, then let out a deep, exasperated exhale. "And I guess to tick off my father. He bet me a hundred dollars I wouldn't last in the sem."

Jack fingered the upper edge of his Roman collar. I wondered if it made his neck itch. "Did you take him up on that bet?"

"Yeah, I did. We got in shoving match at the dinner table. He was drunk and took a swing at me—"

Jack was quick to interrupt. "And your mother, Mr. Sheets, you mentioned your mother."

"She's Italian Catholic. Big-time Catholic." I spit the words out. I didn't like being interrupted. "Her favorite book is *The Sacred Heart of Jesus,* the one with Jesus on the front cover, and he's pointing to his burning heart."

Jack leaned forward, arms on the desk. "So, your mother wants you to be a priest?"

"She's constantly asking my brother and me, 'Which one of you would like to be a priest?' My brother answers, 'Sure as heck won't be me, Ma.' My brother's got Italian good looks. Girls call him up for dates."

Jack glanced at his wristwatch. "What about you, Mr. Sheets, how do you answer her?"

"I tell her, 'Maybe, Ma,' just to keep her happy. Seems like I'm always trying to keep her happy. It's like her happiness is my responsibility. Ever since I was a kid, I felt like it was my fault if my mother was sad."

Jack sank back into his chair, elbows on the armrest, fingertips touched in a basket shape in front of his chin. "Seems like a big burden for a young man. Seems like it would be your father's job to comfort you mother."

"My father's angry. The whole damn family's depressed since my sister died."

"When did that happen?"

"A couple of years ago." I felt my body tense, soles of my feet pressed into the carpet. "She went to UCLA on a dance scholarship. Riding with her boyfriend in his Austin Healy. He rolled it at night on the Pacific Coast Highway. Killed them both."

Iron Jack got up from his chair. "I'm sorry, Mr. Sheets, and I hate to cut you short when we're talking about the death of your sister, but

I'm afraid we'll have to take this up another time. I have an appointment to keep."

I left Iron Jack's quarters feeling rushed, irritated, shortchanged. I left without telling him my father has cursed God ever since: "Elana, your God is an asshole!"

Without telling him that my olive-skinned, starlet-looking mother shrieked and turned into a woman possessed. "Walter, stop it! That's sacrilegious! A terrible thing to say!"

"It's the truth, Elana. Only an asshole would steal my daughter!"

Without telling Jack my mother would stomp from the room with her hands in the air, her fingers stretched tight as steel.

"Go ahead, Elana, run away to church!"

"Better than the bottle you run to."

Without telling him my father stood spread-legged, in a rage, clenching and unclenching his fists because he missed his only daughter.

I missed her too. Anne, my sister, fabulous dancer. The musical notes of her body cells wired for combustion. I missed my whole family, but I missed my sister most of all.

I came close to calling it quits in those early days, but I hung on. Talked to Iron Jack. Played sports. Became friends with an irreverent knucklehead named Melon. Melon, a cajoler, deceiver, and trickster who might lead me down a very bumpy road.

3

THE WAKE-UP BELL RINGS AT 5:55 the morning after Halloween. Immediately after the bell, a single knock on each door along the corridor. A knock and a greeting: "Benedicamus Domino." The greeting, the refrain echoing from each room: "Deo Gratias." "Deo Gratias" from each room except from Phillip Chantelope's room next door. We call him Melon. Through the open transom I hear: "Up your asias."

The student doing the wake-up knock ignores Melon and moves on to my door. "Deo Gratias," I answer.

Melon borders on blasphemy. He loves to agitate with his pudgy, round-faced sarcastic humor. He loves to grin and brag that his parents shipped him off to priest school just to get him out of the house.

Fifteen minutes to wash and dress. At 6:10, the bell sounds again. Like a shepherd it guides 450 seminarians out into the corridors, and we flow silently down stairwells to the outer porticoes, manicured lawns, and walkways of a great quadrangle of buildings. At the east end of the quad, the sun begins to wedge up through pink mist behind the fortress of the chapel.

Wednesday morning, in uncertain light of a new day, while we walk down the last set of brick steps from the porticoes to the quad, I spot Alice Derry's face peering up between clipped bushes of mock orange. Only her tanned face shows above the green camouflage of stems and leaves. Her blue eyes stare up at me. "Psst, Raymond Sheets," she whispers. I ignore her, quickly glance away, and walk hurriedly toward the chapel where shafts of yellow light slant out from tall open doors.

Alice. Her angelic face in the shrubbery once again ignites the tingling in my gut. The more I try to put her out of my mind, the stronger her presence becomes in my thinking. I want to be with her.

Everyone else is either too sleepy or pretends not to notice the face flowering among shrubs. No one seems to notice except Melon, who walks beside me. "Sheetsy, who's the girlie? That better be your sister hiding in the bushes." Melon breaks the Grand Silence. Get caught doing that a couple of times, and you get the boot. You're out of here.

Melon won't let up. "Sheetsy, the Cat's going to get you." The Cat is Father Skillen, prefect of discipline. The Cat can appear out of nowhere. He seems to be all over campus, for his walk is a silent glide, white socks flashing beneath his black cassock. The Cat can walk through walls.

I brush Melon off, hurry through the chapel doors, and slide into my place in the pew. Charlie Barrington begins the rumble of morning prayers. This morning I do my own kind of silent praying. I pray to Jesus like I'm a boxer and He's in my corner: *I'm trying to back away from her, but she comes out of nowhere.* My mind wanders to home. The bet with my father. *You'll never make it, sonny boy.* My mother, the way she looks with smiling pride on her seminarian son.

In the middle of my thoughts, Melon turns his head from the pew in front of me and grins, slowly slides his finger horizontally across his Adam's apple. He mouths a word: "Cat."

The morning prayers drone on followed by early morning Mass. I keep turning over arguments in my mind. *Not sure if I want to be one of your priests. This girl is slowly changing my thinking. And, you'll not only owe me money, sonny boy, you'll deeply disappoint your mother.*

After Mass, we file out of chapel, move toward the refectory still maintaining the Grand Silence. As we cross the quad, I see Alice Derry walking way out in front of great clusters of seminarians. I plunge my hands in my pants pockets and drop my chin to my chest. *Damn, what is she doing?*

She walks with Pop Stiles. Father Stiles is old, bald, and gentle, the kind of guy any kid would want as a grandfather. He leads her toward the administration wing, probably directing her out the door. She must have given him quite a story to let her stay around this long. I hope the story didn't include me.

Melon nudges my left arm. "Sheetsy, your girlfriend is talking to Pops. You think she's telling him about your wild love affair? You're a goner now. Before the sun sets, you're probably going to get the boot," Melon whispers and gives me one of his diabolical grins.

Breakfast in silence. We sit at rectangular tables, one upper classman as table head and four younger seminarians down each side of the table. We say "pass the toast, bread, or jam" with sweeping hand signals. The priests sit at a long table at the side of the refectory. Their table is up on a dais, ten priests at breakfast, and they all face the student body. I look up at Pop Stiles, try to read his face, but he just spoons his oatmeal and maintains his benevolent, smiling composure.

After we finish eating, Father Barrington rings a hand bell, and we all stand, say a prayer, and file out of the refectory. The Grand Silence is over. This is the first time we can talk. Melon is on me. "What's the story on Little Orphan Annie? How do you know her? What's up with her and Pop Stiles?"

We climb the stairs to our rooms to make beds and clean up. I take the stairs two at a time, trying to get away from Melon. The chatter is loud in the stairwells. "There is no story, Melon, I hardly know her," I shout.

Thoughts of Alice Derry twist my insides all day long. Finally unable to stand any more, I excuse myself from evening study hall, tell the study hall prefect I need to talk to Father Castaic, then climb a flight of stairs to the second-floor corridor. The corridor echoes when it's empty, and my rapping on the door of Iron Jack's small three-room apartment feels like a barbaric intrusion on the silence. "Come in," Jack bellows.

He stands behind a large desk, looking down on papers lit up by a black goose-neck lamp. The rest of the room is washed in a dim yellow light from a table lamp in the corner. Dark bookcases line the walls. Iron Jack raises his head and juts his chin. He wears an unfriendly scowl. I feel disturbed like maybe he doesn't appreciate a distraction. Jack barks, "Mr. Sheets, what can I do for you?"

"I'm thinking about quitting the seminary."

He motions to a high-back reading chair. "Sit down."

Jack looks casual in his white T-shirt and black clerical pants. He lowers into a swivel chair behind the desk, shuts off the desk lamp, and leans back, locking his hands behind black hair on his massive head. He looks so relaxed, I wonder if he thinks I'm here to talk about the World Series.

"Your father bet you a hundred dollars you'd never finish high school here, Mr. Sheets. Are you homesick once again, or are you having a crisis of faith?"

I scoot up on the edge of the chair. "More like a crisis of the body, Father."

"Sit back and breathe, Mr. Sheets, and explain, please."

I push deep into the chair, feeling annoyed every time he says "Mr. Sheets," but that's how they do it here. Everybody's "mister."

"It's the celibacy issue. There's this girl."

Jack drops his beefy hands on top of the papers on his desk. "A girl. That's a tough one, Mr. Sheets. I've seen you run. What's your time for the mile?"

"My time for the mile, Father?"

"How fast do you run the mile?"

I sit up again, stretch my back. The backs of my knees are tight against the edge of the chair. "Five oh three."

"Not exactly a world record, but not too bad for this place. You looking to drop under five minutes?" He stares at me. I feel like a specimen.

"I'm trying, Father." Still uncertain where the questions are going.

He's up, paces the room, and talks evangelist thunder. "In other words, Mr. Sheets, you know how to push your body. You understand discipline, and that's what celibacy takes, sheer discipline." Then he goes quiet. "Mr. Sheets, you've got to have transcendence, you've got to see the bigger picture."

"You mean like heaven and hell and the afterlife?"

"No, I mean what's in your heart." He stops pacing, stares down at me. "The bigger picture in your heart."

I can't hold his gaze. I look down where one leg of the desk meets the carpet. *This guy doesn't get it. It's not my heart that's the problem.* "I don't know what you mean. I don't know what's in my heart."

He paces again. "It all comes down to pleasure or pain, Mr. Sheets. Short-term pleasure can bring long-term pain that can mess up the big picture. Short-term pain can give long-term pleasure for the rest of your life."

He reaches up and adjusts a volume perched in the deep shadows of the bookcase. The books, the entire room seem obsessively neat. "Mr. Sheets, I've been where you are. I struggle with the celibacy problem every day. I keep battling because the pleasure of serving God's people and teaching young men like you mostly outweighs the pain of battle."

He stands over me like an imposing Neanderthal. I scan his face for some consolation. "This feels like too tough a fight, Father."

"Chosin Reservoir."

I shake my head in irritation. "What—"

"Korean War. Chosin Reservoir. Now that was a tough fight. I was two or three years older than you are right now. I quit the seminary to enlist in the military. I was not Father Castaic back then, Mr. Sheets, I was a Navy corpsman, and every man in my unit called me 'Doc.' It was my job to save wounded Marines." Jack has his hands on his hips. He turns away and stares up at the bookshelves, talks quietly as if to someone else, not to me.

"In that battle, we had a Corporal Jessen that I found on his back in the snow and mud. His insides spilled across his hip bone. He's sobbing, 'Doc, Doc.'

"Jessen took up a collection for me when we were on R and R...R and R, Mr. Sheets, means rest and recuperation." Jack makes sure I'm paying attention. "He took up a collection to pay for Doc's beer and girls, and now Jessen's on the ground moaning. It's nighttime with a wind chill way below zero. We get hit with wave after wave of North Koreans and Chinese. They're blaring bugles. Bullets and shrapnel flying. Wounded Marines scream, 'Corpsman! Corpsman!' They want me to fix them. Save them. Patch them up. Tell them it's going to be okay. We're bearded, ragged, and dirty. I'm scared and crawling on my knees and elbows in the snow and filth. Now that was a battle."

Jack's eyes fill with tears. This time, I hold his gaze, unsure of what to feel or how to react. "I had to leave Jessen, Mr. Sheets. I had to make a decision to treat the less seriously wounded so they could continue the fight. But I dream about Corporal Jessen to this day. Some nights I wake up with the shakes and drenched in sweat."

As he paces the carpet, my hands dig into the arms of the chair. The dim light of the room feels foreign. I want to run from this man's confession. My gaze settles vaguely on the books that stand shoulder to shoulder in the shadows of the shelves, but the books have no answers.

"I made another decision at Chosin," Jack goes on. "I made a deal with God. I said if He got me out of there alive, I would rededicate my life to His service. My toes were frostbitten, and I took a bullet through my right calf, but here I am, in one piece and finding God's service greater than all the girls and beer. Yet I'm human, Mr. Sheets; some days, the temptation is strong."

Jack returns behind the desk. "Not a soul in this school, outside of some faculty, has heard that story. I like you, Mr. Sheets; you're a seeker, a warrior who understands pain. You will find your own answer."

My emotions spin and rattle like a lopsided centrifuge. I came to tell him about my secret obsession with Alice Derry, and instead Iron Jack unloaded his secret on me.

My father, owner of W. N. Sheets Mechanical, would not be proud of me. *Afraid to spill the beans, tough guy? What's the matter, can't say her name? Afraid to say she lives down the block? You're not priest material. You should have listened to me, sonny boy.*

Iron Jack is not my father. Iron Jack doesn't seem to give a damn about a name, yet I feel deceitful, like I'm holding a great weight as I stand. "Thank you, Father."

Jack comes out from behind the desk. "Kneel for a blessing."

He raises his hand over me. The same hand that patched wounded Marines at Chosin, the same hand and arm that can send a softball hurtling far beyond the reaches of the fence line, now moves over my head in benediction.

After the blessing, I stand and feel a mix of confusion and resolve as I open the door. Before I step outside, before the echoes of my footsteps begin to break the silence of the corridor, Jack puts his hand on my shoulder. "Run fast, Mr. Sheets. Don't be afraid of the pain."

4

THE FOLLOWING MORNING AFTER MY TALK with Iron Jack, Melon's still at it. I grab a small dust mop from the closet for a quick run over the floor before I make my bed. Melon stands outside my doorway, the corridor loud with opening and closing doors. "Sheetsy, you're in deep doo-doo." Melon looks smug in his button-down blue shirt, hands in his khaki pockets. "The Cat's coming for you. You're gonna be history around here."

He won't leave it alone. I swipe at the bottom corner of the door with my mop, slam the door in Melon's face. He yells over the transom, "Bye-bye, Sheets!"

At 7:55, the bell rings for study hall. At eight o'clock another bell, and we are in our assigned desks in study hall for a half hour of preparation for Latin class. Melon's desk is two rows to the right of mine.

Twenty minutes into study hall, Melon relays me a piece of paper with a pencil drawing of a large black cat wearing a roman collar. The cat has one paw raised, dangling a little human from a single claw. The human looks a lot like me. Melon's an artist. He frequently pencils women in evening gowns, calls them his dream girls.

Eight twenty-eight a.m. Bell sounds. We walk in silence to Latin class.

Eight thirty a.m. We stand by our assigned desks. The Cat enters the classroom, kneels on a raised dais in the front of the room. In unison, we pray in Latin and end with a resounding "Amen."

We sit at our desks. The Cat stands, and without wasting a breath, he shouts, "Mr. Sheets, recite the passage from Caesar."

I stand and begin, "Quod si non hic tantus fructus ostenderatur—"

"I can't hear you, Mr. Sheets."

"Quod si non…!" I feel my face go red. I yell the lines like they're vile syllables and I need an exorcist.

"Thank you. You may sit down."

I sit and worry. The Cat's picking on me. He knows something. Maybe he's talked to Pop Stiles. Maybe Alice Derry's going to get me kicked out of school.

More bells. Classes. Study halls. Silent lunch. Melon keeps it going all day, passes me notes that say "meow, meow." I'm on edge. By the 3:00 p.m. recreation period during a pickup softball game, I lose it.

Melon's behind home plate. In spite of his round, chubby body, as a catcher he has a rifle arm. I take ball one; all the time Melon chatters, "Hey batter, hey batter, you're out of here!" I swing at the next pitch and catch it too low. The ball pops up above the backstop. Melon flips off his mask in a fluid motion like Yogi Berra and fields the fly. He tags me hard for drama, then shouts, "You're outta here, Sheetsy!"

I turn and push him all the way to the backstop. He still holds the ball as I shove on his chest, grind him into the wire mesh. Two guys from the track team grab my arms. One of the guys is Lankin, the team captain. Lankin wears a gray sweatshirt with the sleeves cut off. "Sheets, what the heck are you doing?"

I stare at Melon as I yank my arms free of my teammates. "He's been on me all day. I just lost it."

Lankin's five inches taller than me, wearing cutoff jeans that show his knobby knees and ostrich legs. He's redheaded with long, bony arms. "On you about what?"

Melon's red-faced and thumps the ball into his catcher's mitt. "Sheets, tell them what I'm on you about." By now even the outfielders have come in to see what's going on.

I'm not confessing to a big circle of guys in dusty jeans and baggy gym shorts milling around home plate. "It's nothing. I lost it over nothing." I walk off the field beyond the third baseline.

I count on Melon not to rat on me. Although seminarians try to outwit the faculty, they never backstab or spread rumors about one another.

There's an unwritten code at St. Jerome's: nobody rats. Spot an infraction, keep it to yourself. I'm counting on Melon's fear of being ostracized and maybe getting a "jake shampoo."

With a jake shampoo, someone going against the code is snatched from the corridor by vigilantes and carried to the bathroom, where someone lifts a toilet seat and the offender is dunked head first into the toilet.

At 5:40 p.m., the bell rings and we head to the locker room for a shower and a change of clothes. Melon avoids me, yet I hear him in front of his locker. Above echoes of the showers and the clang of locker doors, he shouts to a couple of guys his theory about how to make hard liquor by letting a piece of potato ferment in apple cider.

Dinner's at six o'clock, another silent meal with an upper classman reading from a lectern. This semester it's Thor Heyerdahl's *Kon Tiki*. As I eat Swiss steak, mashed potatoes, and canned peas, my mind is not on the meal or the epic voyage across the Pacific. It's on Alice Derry. When dinner is over at 6:30, I'll have exactly thirty-five minutes to make it to her house and be back at my desk in study hall by 7:05 p.m.

After dinner, during free time, Lankin and some of the guys are throwing a small rubber football across the courtyard. I break free from them, saying I need to hit the jakes because of stomach trouble.

I jog up to the porticoes and through the building to an outside door. As a shortcut, I run hard across the lawn. The stands of cedar trees provide some cover as I move toward the paved drive just before the berry patch. I have to slow a little at the slight downslope of pavement, for the leather soles of my dress shoes feel slick on the asphalt.

Past the berry patch, I'm officially in town and "out of bounds." The road outside the grounds is called Seminary Way. Three blocks down at the corner of Seminary and Euclid I spot a house with roses. The roses are pruned like miniature trees on both sides of the entry walk. As I knock on the front door, I recall the way Alice's hair frames her blue eyes and delicate face, but I resolve to be firm. She needs to stay away from me.

The house is small, well cared for. I knock again, and someone peeks out from the edge of a curtain at the large front window. Seconds later, Alice Derry opens the door. "Raymond Sheets, you're out of bounds!" She wears an apron and has what looks like white flour on her hands.

"I know I'm out of bounds. Look, you need to stay away before I get in big trouble." I have one hand on the doorframe, trying to catch my breath. "What the heck were you doing? I saw you walking with Father Stiles."

"I wasn't talking to him about you," Alice informs me. "I lied to that nice old priest so he wouldn't throw me off the property. I told him I was thinking about becoming a nun, told him I wanted to see how a religious community lived. He let me sit with him in the back of the chapel."

This is unbelievable! I shake my head as a thought strikes me. *While I'm praying tormented near the front of the chapel, my tormenter is sitting in the back of the chapel with Pop Stiles?*

"Today's my birthday. See, I'm trying to bake a cake. My dad's got night duty. My mom's a bartender at the NCO club, and she'll be dead drunk by the time she gets home…" Alice Derry has her floured hands out in front of her like she's holding an invisible beach ball. "I just wanted to feel like I had a friend on my birthday. I'm sorry, Raymond Sheets."

I knew Pop Stiles was easy, but for this girl he was a pushover. "You lied to a priest?"

"That's all I could think of."

I'm stunned. Nearly out of time. "Alone on your birthday? Don't you have brothers and sisters? What about friends?"

Alice swipes at her left eye, smears flour on her cheek. "My brother's in the army at Ft. Leonard Wood, Missouri. I haven't lived here long enough to make friends." God, she's cute. "This will be the third school I've gone to in eight years. My dad keeps getting reassigned."

I check my watch. I have twenty-two minutes to get to study hall. I take out a penknife and look for a decent bloom among the fading roses. I cut a red rose. "Happy birthday, Alice Derry. How old are you?"

She takes the rose in her powdery hands. "Seventeen. One plus seven equals eight, and eight represents infinity. Infinity means I haven't had a good birthday in forever. At least my dad left me a card today. The card says he has a gift for me, so maybe the cycle will be broken."

I need to start back toward the school, but I'm hesitant to leave. I want to stay close. This girl has a hold on me. I want to know more about her. "What are you talking about?"

Alice places her hands on her hips, looks more confident. "My aunt who taught me to read your palm also taught me numerology. How old are you?"

I move out of the yard toward an Irish setter standing in the street. The dog ambles over to a parked car and lifts its leg. I shout from the street, "Same as you!" I start to jog away.

She shouts back, "Do you have a room number?"

"It's 317," I call out. I shouldn't have done it, but the school's on lockdown at nine thirty at night. No way could she get in, but to be on the safe side, I give her Melon's room number.

"Three plus one plus seven," I hear her on the street calling after me. "Your room number means courage, but eleven also says you may be living in the space of a dreamer. Do you dream, Raymond Sheets?"

"Never!" I call over my shoulder. "Happy birthday, Alice Derry!"

Now I run with a chest-heaving tempo up the drive. The tip of a cedar branch brushes my arm as I cross the lawn. Up the stairs and through the door, the building briefly swallows me into its womb, then it spits me out. I slow to a fast walk and tag on to the last group of seminarians as they pass through the open doors of the study hall.

5

A T 9:05 P.M., THE BELL RINGS for lights out. Except for using the jakes, no one is allowed out of their room after lights out. Most nights, sleep chases consciousness from my mind within minutes and leads me into dreams. I lied to Alice Derry. I do dream, and for the past few months, my dreams have been soft and biblical. I'm pressed against Salome, and she has me wrapped in the folds of her long, sheer gown. Sometimes I wake blinking with a deep spine-jolt rush that sticks to my legs and hardens by morning into white crusty ropes.

Tonight, sleep stalls in the corridor outside my room. I think of Iron Jack and his devotion to discipline, chin-ups, and a bullet through his leg. Iron Jack, sweaty nightmares. Shakes. Battlefield memory of a dying Marine.

In the middle of my thoughts, I hear three taps on the wall from Melon's room. I'm still angry with him, but I kneel on the bed and quietly slide open the window. I check the pavement below for any sign of movement. I give three taps for all clear, and Melon hangs out his window, reaches toward me with a binocular case suspended by a strap on the end of his mop handle.

I get my mop from the closet and unscrew the handle, return to the window to retrieve the binoculars. There's a note in the case that I read by window light: *Sorry, full of myself today. Very un-Christlike. Take a peep. Marilyn Monroe at the El Monte. Who's the girl?*

I rest my elbows on the windowsill, raise the binoculars, sweep the lens across the valley of lights to the little screen where I squint and see fuzzy images of Tony Curtis and Marilyn Monroe.

My eyes tire of the movie and the lights. I knock three times on the wall and smuggle the suspended binocular case along the mop handle transmission lines. I insert a note: *Un-Christlike jerk. Tell you about the girl when I'm ready.*

The heat of Indian summer ends, and in early November, rains begin. Bells chime their litany, and we respond, moving to classrooms, chapel, sleep, and muddy touch football games that trample new shoots of green. The mammoth school with its eighty-foot bell tower sits at the base of foothills. The angular buildings, lined with rows of windows that look out on the world like dull cataract eyes. Cattle graze on rises beyond the barbed wire of the playing fields, and along folds and napes of hills, green leaves of live oak slake their thirst for rain.

With the end of sunny days, thoughts of Alice Derry diminish, and the bone-ache cold of winter sets in. I pass her house during St. Jerome's Thursday afternoon once-a-month walk to town. Curtains drawn across windows, and roses along the entry walk depleted with a fleshy confetti of petals on the ground. The road to town lined with small front yards and graceful liquidamber trees with towering sky banners of red, purple, and gold. The day, heavy gray, with no promise of sun.

We're bundled up, this brotherhood of seminarians who live in punctual order directed by the rhythm of the bells. We walk out of sync with the outside world. Thursdays are for sports, cleaning our rooms, extra study if we need it, and the monthly walk to town. We must look odd to the inhabitants of Loyola Corners, scattered rabbles of young men and boys who laugh, talk, and punch each other in mock battles, joyous with this sudden burst of freedom.

I walk with Lankin, Melon, and Georgie Thurmond. Lankin's ambling, long-legged cadence sets the pace, and Thurmond and Melon struggle to keep up.

"Slow it down, big guy, we're not all track stars." Melon emphasizes "track stars" like the words signify some genetic aberration.

Lankin picks up the pace. "Melon, lose ten pounds, and maybe you could actually walk to town instead of rolling."

Thurmond laughs like a toady, and Melon gives him a shove. "What are you laughing at, Terminal, I see you huffing and puffing." Thurmond, also known as Terminal or sometimes Terminus, continues to grin. He's small and slight with large black-rimmed glasses and prominent upper cheekbones. He looks like an owl.

Melon and I have made our peace. Occasionally, he asks about the girl in the bushes, but I keep stalling him. I'm tempted now to tell him that she lives in the house with the roses and she's madly in love with me, but I keep it to myself.

Loyola Corners is a village of shops, a small grocery, a soda fountain, two stoplights, and a gas station. Seminarians scatter through town to shop and call home from pay phones. Our group stands in a long line that snakes out the doorway of Togwell's Soda Fountain. Streets are damp where buildings and trees shadow the pavement. Traffic is sporadic along Main Street; cars sizzle through a large puddle that forms around a clogged storm drain.

Lankin is in the middle of telling Melon to order a single scoop instead of his usual triple when I spot two girls on a small motorcycle.

"Hey, Raymond Sheets!" The silver and black BSA pulls to the curb. The engine gurgles low and stops with a pop as Alice shuts it down. She takes off her helmet. Her hair falls longer, framing her blue eyes and the delicate canvas of her face.

Damn, how am I going to explain this? What do I say to jackass Melon and the rest of the guys?

Melon lets out a whistle. "All right, Sheetsy, it's truth time!"

I walk to the curb; Melon trails behind. The girl on the back of the bike takes off her helmet. She has a freckled face and long brown curls. All the guys in line have turned toward the motorcycle. Alice wears a blue wool sweater that deepens the color of her eyes. "Raymond Sheets, this is my friend Melinda."

Melinda smiles, sticks out her hand. "Hi, I'm Melinda Garret."

Melon clears his throat and pokes me in the ribs.

"Nice to meet you," I say. "This is Phillip Chantelope. We mostly call him Melon."

"They call me Melon because I'm a sweet and juicy hunk of humanity." Melon stands with his arms folded and wrapped in his brown windbreaker with his collar up, like he's a pudgy, slightly balding James Dean. He grins excitedly like he's about to be clued in on a secret stash of lemon meringue pies. "Nice bike, is it yours?"

Both girls smile at Melon. Alice Derry's voice becomes animated. "My dad used it to go to work when we lived on Oahu. He doesn't use it now. He gave it to me for my birthday."

"Well, what a nice present and a nice dad, and a happy birthday to you." Melon has taken over the conversation, and I feel like I want to melt and dissolve into the street puddle. "And where do you know my friend Raymond from?" With his hand on my shoulder, Melon beams, enjoying himself.

Alice Derry quickly scans my face. "Oh, from the berry patch."

Melon digs his fingers into my shoulder. "Ah, yes, of course, the berry patch."

I remove Melon's hand and turn back toward the line of onlookers. Lankin and Terminal are inside now and staring out the big window. Right above them, lettered in red: "We'll make you scream for ice cream."

Alice Derry redirects the conversation. "Would you like to try the bike?"

"We'd love to try the motorcycle," Melon chimes in, "but unfortunately, my friend Raymond is a little clumsy with machinery. Maybe we could meet you in the parking lot just past the Chevron station, so my buddy doesn't fall over in front of the peanut gallery. Also, we're not supposed to consort with females."

The girls put on their helmets, and Alice Derry kicks the starter. "See you in the parking lot." She twists the handlebar throttle, and the BSA speeds away. Melon waves with his forearm raised like he's brush-stroking whitewash on the side of a building.

I'm furious. "Melon, what the heck are you doing?"

"Sheetsy! The berry patch!" Melon chuckles wildly. "You been flirting with Satan, you little devil."

Lankin and Terminal come back on the sidewalk. Lankin licks a vanilla cone, and Terminal's up to his eyeglasses in rocky road. Melons chuckles like he's so glad to see them. "Guys, can you believe that the young lady driving that motorcycle was actually a next-door neighbor of our buddy Raymond? They grew up together in San Francisco. What a coincidence meeting her way down here."

The guys in line along the sidewalk have crammed themselves three deep inside the soda fountain, and I'm stunned by Melon's capacity for fabrication. He continues: "Lankin, I think you're right, I'm getting a little pudgy. Sheets and I are going to forgo the ice cream. We're going up to the grocery. I'm going to eat an apple."

Lankin looks up from his cone. "That's good, you'll be eating something that's good for you and just as round as you are."

Terminal snickers into his rocky road.

Melon flashes Terminal a mean stare, then breaks into a smile. "Lankin, Lankin, always the wit. Come on, Sheetsy, let's get some health food."

I want to punch Melon. I'm angry he found out about Alice Derry. I wanted to keep her as my own warm secret. I'm embarrassed about the way he dominated the conversation. I felt tongue-tied. We walk fast toward the grocery and the Chevron station beyond. "Damn it, Melon, I didn't even want you to know about her. This has gone too far. Forget the motorcycle. You're out of your mind."

"Sheets, relax! We're both out of our minds. If we get caught, we'll plead insanity."

I know nothing about how to operate a motorcycle. I'm going to embarrass myself even more. What if one of the other guys sees us? Riding a motorcycle is one thing, but girls are against the rules. "Melon, we're breaking rules."

"Of course we are, but just think about a ride on a motorcycle with a little minx on the back and her arms holding on to you for dear life. The heck with rules." Melon grabs two apples off the fruit display in front of the grocery and ducks in to pay.

We approach the parking lot and its scattered cars, sink our teeth into the sweet taste of our apples. Alice Derry and Melinda stand next to the motorcycle at the far end of the lot. "Who's first?" Alice radiates joy, not the same girl with flour on her hands who answered the front door on her birthday.

"I think I'll pass," I stammer into the apple.

"Ray, Ray, it's time you got over your fear of mechanical objects." Melon sounds like a guidance counselor for driver's ed.

"Melon, I don't have any fear of machines. I just don't think it's a good idea."

Alice Derry takes my hand. "Come on, get on the back." With that electric touch, she draws me like I'm a needle and she's magnetic north. I toss the apple and sit on the back of the bike with my hands on the edge of the seat. We're speeding away from town along Foothill Expressway. "Hang on," she calls back, "this thing can fly."

She moves through the gears, and I tentatively place my hands on her waist. Holding on to her is a wild thrill, and it anchors me to the bike so I won't slide off the back. The speed picks up, and I grasp her waist with my arms. The back of my hand brushes the underside of her breast, and I quickly move my arm lower down.

"Two fifty cc's, Raymond Sheets! I've got it wide open!" I press the left side of my head into her upper body just below the edge of her helmet. I suddenly wish I had a helmet. I'm holding on to a crazy lady, and in the rush of cool November air, she feels warm. I don't ever want to let her go.

Alice maneuvers around and between cars at the forty-five-mile-per-hour speed limit. We head north for a couple of miles, until she slows the bike and we bump and rumble over the dirt median and speed south again.

We enter a left-turn lane, wait for northbound traffic to clear, then cross over the expressway into the parking lot. I turn loose of Alice Derry and sit up straight, return my hands to the edge of the seat. I've never touched a girl that way. I loved holding her, pulling her tight against me. Maybe Melon has a point. The heck with the rules.

Melon smiles like he's a politician about to glad-hand some con-stituents. "Have a good ride, kids? How about letting me take a spin?"

I step off the BSA. "Melon, we're running late. We'll never make it to four o'clock study hall on time."

Alice hands off the motorcycle to Melon. "Just a short ride; we've got to get going too. You know how to ride this thing?"

"I've ridden my cousin's Doodle-bug. Not quite as powerful as this little speedster. A quick trip around the parking lot. We'll be back in plenty of time." Melon straddles the machine and revs the throttle like he's Marlon Brando in *The Wild One*.

The motorcycle leaps forward just as an elderly woman pulls out of a parking place in an old powder-blue DeSoto. Melon swerves to avoid her and clips a concrete curb on a parking lot planter. He releases the throttle as the machine tips and sends him sprawling into a thick planting of ivy. He snaps off a tree stake with his shoulder on the way down. The bike's on its side half in and half out of the planter. The motor sputters to a stall.

The DeSoto chugs away. The old lady must not have noticed. Melon sits up and appears dazed when I get to him. Alice Derry and Melinda stand the BSA upright.

Alice sounds shaky. "Are you okay? I thought you knew what you were doing!"

I help Melon to his feet.

"A slight mishap. Is the machine okay?"

"Small scratch where it grazed the curb." Alice straps on her helmet. "We have to go. We ditched school this afternoon, and Melinda's got to get home. Sure you're okay, Melon?

Melon gives a cavalier wave of his hand. "No need to worry about the Melon."

Alice jump-kicks the starter; the engine catches. "I hope to see you again, Raymond Sheets!"

The girls and the motorcycle are gone from the parking lot. Melon staggers out of the ivy. "Sheets, my shoulder feels like I been kicked by a stallion."

"How about a jackass? A motorcycle with a jackass on it that went flying into a tree stake. You got as much coordination as a one-legged kangaroo."

"Sheets, if I wasn't a severely wounded semi-invalid, I'd break your jaw right now."

I grab hold of Melon's good arm to hurry him out of the parking lot. "Come on, we're not gonna make it back in time, and speaking of jaws, what were you talking about with that Melinda girl when I wasn't there?"

Melon pulls his arm free and massages his shoulder while we walk. "I told her I was an orphan, and I had hopes of becoming a priest in order to start a home for waifs like Father Flanagan did with *Boy's Town*. I also told her that you're probably a homo and you were becoming a priest to please your mother."

The anger I've been feeling toward Melon boils over. He's hit a nerve, and I want to wrench his other shoulder. "You're not a real orphan, your parents just don't want you, and I'm not a homo, and don't say another word about my mother!"

"I take back the orphan and homo part, all bald lies, but your mother has a hold on you, and I wonder what she'd say if she found out her little Jesus is messing around with Our Lady of the Brambles."

The low sun steals away any traces of warmth and replaces it with a damp November chill as it drops behind the liquidambers. We're stragglers, and I feel dwarfed by the trees along Seminary Way. The trees and the chill air temper my anger. "Who cares what she'd say? I'm my own person."

"You haven't been your own person since the day you were born." Melon massages his shoulder. Falling leaves punctuate the air. "You're mama's little Jesus, and you do everything the priests say, and you love rules and bells because you don't have to think, and now you have to think because Our Lady of the Brambles has you all mixed up."

"Look, Sigmund Freud, your parents abandoned you. They don't come down on visiting Sunday because they think you're repulsive and an abject moron who used to run their grocery bill into triple digits."

We pass Alice Derry's house, and I purposefully don't look toward the doorway. Melon walks with his head down; he holds his left forearm with his right hand. "Sheets, my parents don't come down because my dad is a big-city cop who works on Sunday, and my mother doesn't drive. That's why I hang around your family and listen to your father verbally knock you around while I delicately nibble at your mother's picnic food. Little deviled egg sandwiches she made for her squeaky-clean little Jesus she fawns over because he's so darn pure of heart and doing God's will, and meanwhile her other dago-looking son undresses every girl who walks by."

"Enough mother stuff, Melon."

"Sheets, I see what I see. If your mother raises a good son who becomes a priest, then she's a good mother. Good mothers get to heaven. That's a heavy load, Sheetsy; you're Mama's ticket to heaven."

I want to hammer him. "Where do you get this mother stuff from?"

"I get it from the deviled egg sandwiches. I eat those little triangles and notice things. Your mom and dad are at war, and you've taken sides. You want to please your mother, but now this little Derry berry has your brains scrambled."

"That's enough, Melon, you're over the line." I feel mad enough to bust his face. "We're two different people, and you have no idea what's in my head or what I'm about."

"We're different, all right, and the difference between you and me is you like the rules and routine of St. Jerome's, and I love rebellion and chaos."

We pass the berry patch and enter the grounds. "What are you doing here if you like chaos?"

"It's safer here, Sheets. My father's a drunken cop. Remember visiting Sunday last spring, the county sheriff cruising the grounds looking for me?"

I do remember that Sunday. Blue sky, sun warmth, cloud shreds floating over blue cedars like wind-driven parachutes. A sheriff's deputy got out of his patrol car and strolled to the eucalyptus grove where Melon, Donnie, my mother and father, and I were enjoying a lunch on the grounds.

"Afternoon, folks, I was told Phillip Chantelope might be in this group."

Melon stopped eating his egg sandwich, looking like he didn't know whether to smile or run. "I'm Phillip Chantelope." He chose a smile. "Am I under arrest?"

"No, son, but I need to talk to you over by my car." The deputy walked away, his brown uniform shirt struggling to contain his belly.

Melon stood with a half-eaten sandwich in his hand. He turned toward us and looked perplexed. "What'd I do now?"

Melon and the deputy huddled by the squad car. Donnie chose to make light of the situation. "My little junior priest brother is hanging out with felons." My father pressed his lips into a simper, and my mother looked like she'd rather run to church or be home feather-dusting her antique furniture.

Melon returned, brow knitted into furrows. "The police picked up my father in Loyola Corners. He was driving down to see me. His car has a big gash on the passenger door where he sideswiped the back corner of a flatbed truck. Sheriff's trying to smooth it over because my dad's a cop. My dad's incoherent, and he was holding an open bottle of Jim Beam on his lap.

"I need to get permission to leave the grounds. Mr. Sheets, any chance you could go with me? I may need someone to drive my dad and the car back home." My father rose slowly, with the reluctance of a plumber called away from his dinner table to unclog a sewer line.

I never brought up the incident of Melon's father to anyone. We never spoke of it again.

Melon continues to knead his injured shoulder. "That day was my father at his best. At his worst, he likes to use me as a punching bag. He once slammed my head into a wall heater. Another time, he threatened me with a meat cleaver."

As a rule at St. Jerome's, we limit our talk about home, what our brothers and sisters are like, what kind of work our fathers do, or how our parents treat us. That kind of talk could bring on forbidden attachments and homesickness. The world inside St. Jerome's and the road ahead are all that matters.

However, as I listen to Melon, I'm drawn in by darkness, meat cleavers, and the slamming of heads. "What about your mother?"

We walk fast toward the imposing fortress of buildings that were designed like bulwarks against the outside world. Bulwarks to keep the world out and the spirit of the inhabitants locked in. Whoever designed the place must have specialized in penitentiaries.

"My mother sips wine all day." Melon's voice is resigned, without jokes or sarcasm. He's turned the dark pockets of his soul inside out. "And I think she pops pills."

I suddenly feel the same discomfort I felt when Iron Jack revealed the weakness of his night sweats and fear. I don't want to hear anything else from Melon. I feel like a coward, and I only want to run.

6

MIDTERM EXAMS FILL THE LAST DAYS of November, and December arrives and drags toward the Christmas holidays. The days weighted with ponderous skies and the endless slash of rain. The raucous student body seems to turn inward, embraces an abnormal lassitude of silence within classrooms and study halls, and even the athletic fields seem to succumb to a quieter slosh of feet as bodies romp and slide through slippery games of mud. Sometimes chapel, and always deep sleep in the monastic harbor of our rooms, feels like relief from the daily incessant drone of learning.

Melon, too, seems to yield to a sullen call. Perhaps he dreads Christmas break and the abusive atmosphere at home, and although he angers me at times, I miss his jokes and derisive, cutting banter. I'm like a boxer who has lost his sparring partner. I stand in the ring alone, punch at shadows. The memory of my sister. She enters the ring and dances. Arms upraised, she twirls and smiles at me.

A week before Christmas, a cold, deep blue sky banishes the clouds. I think of Alice Derry's eyes. I remember her alone on her birthday. A single rose. Silver motorcycle. "Do you dream, Raymond Sheets?"

Yes, I dream. My arms around her waist. I bend into her. Hang on, full speed ahead. Side of my face pressed into her back, into the blue wool sweater that covers the carnal softness of her body.

The litany of prayers to Jesus, the beautiful repetition of Latin phrases have lost their influence. Only the thrumming of the motorcycle calms the muddled chaos of my mind.

~

Christmas break comes, and I'm back in my parents' house, a magnificent home of heavily troweled stucco and a Spanish tile roof, with a wide brick stairway leading to the front door. The house sits on a street lined with manicured eucalyptus trees in exclusive St. Francis Wood in San Francisco.

Three shuttered windows on the ground floor and three on the second story, look out to the street. A manicured ensemble of impressive camellias and broad rafts of rhododendrons now out of bloom enhance the front yard.

My mother loves her gardens, and I watch her now through the front window as she rakes leaves with Mr. Sako, her gardener. They seem absorbed in conversation as they rake. My mother's probably telling the little Buddhist man that he should convert and maybe pray the rosary every night. Mr. Sako doesn't need the rosary. I've never seen a man so methodical and happy; he rakes, prunes, and tip cuts Ma's rhododendrons like he is performing the most important job in the world.

My mother's big on everything Catholic. She used to tell Donnie and me, when we were toddlers: "So-and-so's a good person, she goes to our church." Her words flew by Donnie, but they stuck with me.

As I watch her out the window, I want to tell her, "Ma, Melon goes to our church, but he's an idiot." I want to tell her this, but truth be told, lately I enjoy the company of the idiot.

Mom is also big on saints and martyrs. She used to say, "St. Martin was roasted on a spit like a turkey rather than worship false idols," and, "St. Agatha had her breasts ripped out rather than give in to her tormentors." Martyrdom is a free ticket to heaven in Mom's book. I sometimes picture Donnie and me in front of a Russian firing squad ready to be shot full of holes because we won't renounce our faith and accept Communism, and Mom leads our cheering section and yells, "Shoot! Shoot!"

Mom told us all these things in our tender years. Then we started Catholic grade school, where nuns taught us the soul was a milk bottle and mortal sin turned the bottle black. The soul only had three choices: heaven, hell, and purgatory. The fires of hell and purgatory were hotter than Mom's steam iron, hot enough to boil our blood. "And you'll feel this heat for eternity, boys and girls, and eternity is longer than it would take one of God's little birds to remove all the sand from all the beaches in the world, one grain at a time."

The nuns rode herd on us, and guilt and fear were stamped on my forehead. Donnie laughed it off, saying, "The Devil has all the fun," as he tried to catch glimpses of girls' panties under those plaid Catholic uniform skirts.

Crucifixes. Statues. Scapulars, those itchy little pieces of sacred material that the truly devout wear against their skin. Catholic fear hangs on me like a coarse shirt made out of scapular material. The fear of mortal sin and an eternity in hell still can make me itch.

The fear the nuns taught seemed threatening yet remote, but Ma's fear seemed personal, close, and real. I don't know where Ma learned her fear. Perhaps from the church, or maybe from her mother, who always seemed creepy and superstitious to me.

Ma and my Italian grandmother, Nona Siracusa, were tied together in my mind by a room in the house we called the bookroom.

It's down the hallway on the first floor. Dark wood paneling, lush carpet the color of grizzly bear, and shelves and shelves of books. Many of the books were inherited from Nona. She lived with us until she was eighty-eight, but in spite of her readings, she never quite mastered English pronunciation. In the creepy bedtime stories she used to tell Donnie and me as we sat in the bookroom, "snakes" were always "sneks," and crawly things like giant spiders always sounded like crawly "tings."

The bookroom, a solemn place where our weird Nona's ghost haunts the shelves and where Mom retires in the evening to pray. After dinner dishes have been cleaned and stashed in the cupboards, after the kitchen is wiped down and spotless, you can find Mom at her kneeler in the shadowed corner of the bookroom, hands clasped to her chest, eyes closed, head tilted over the right shoulder like she is witnessing some sort of beatific vision.

On a small linen-draped walnut table in front of Ma's kneeler stands a hefty wooden crucifix on a solid wooden base with one of poor Jesus's outstretched plastic arms slightly detached from the cross. Next to the crucifix rests Mom's well-thumbed book, *The Sacred Heart of Jesus*. Beside the book stands a porcelain statue of St. Therese. It used to hold a tiny bouquet of flowers and a miniature crucifix, until one day I busted them out of her hands and detached poor Jesus's arm in the process.

I was ten years old and alone in the house when I placed a chair next to Ma's kneeler. I stood on the chair and stretched over the kneeler, reaching for a volume of the encyclopedia. I leaned far to the right to retrieve the volume that contained the picture of the headless, bare-breasted Venus that Donnie had showed me. I slid the book back with my fingertips, and it launched from the shelf, grazing Jesus on the cross and sending Therese face down on the carpet.

The intensity of Ma's wrath was matched only by the intensity she displayed when she had her beatific visions. "Which one of you tore loose Jesus's arm?" she screamed. "Which one of you broke the blessed statue of St. Therese?"

Anne and Donnie stood back, dismayed, while I studied polished dark grains of kitchen flooring. Later, Anne whispered in my ear, "I know it was you, Little Prince, because you bit your lip and looked at the floor."

Anne took our secret to the grave, and Ma never tried to glue Jesus's arm to the cross.

The old memory of Jesus and Therese makes me smile, and the loss of my sister, Anne, feels sad and sobering, yet it's fear that surfaced my first year away from home. It's fear that branded me.

My first year in the seminary, I missed Donnie. I missed my father; I even missed his anger. I missed my pious mother but was determined to stick it out and bask in the favor of her smile. Gone was the boy who rose to the challenge of a hundred-dollar bet. My first year in the seminary, I was one homesick little Jesus, and I never told a soul except Iron Jack.

I held down homesickness, and fear stepped in to fill the void. I became convinced I was a sinner, I began to take to heart the words of the Mass: *I confess to almighty God…through my fault, through my most grievous fault. Lord, I am not worthy…* The Eucharist became a white wafer of terror, and I was unworthy to receive. Then I met Melon.

Melon, the class clown, took me under the wing of his laughter which loosened me up.

Lately, I feel like I've become Melon's coconspirator. Momma's little Jesus gives up the fight, abandons the rules, trades discipline for chaos, forgets about his mother. Maybe Alice Derry's a little preview of heaven.

I leave Mother to Mr. Sako and wander this house of arched windows, hefty walnut tables, cumbersome antiques, and ominous dark

curtains that hang like robes of those grammar-school nuns. My father, president of W. N. Sheets Mechanical Contractors, has done well. The house is 3,200 square feet of paneled rooms, alcoves, hallways, and chandeliers.

The basement is a large recreation room with pool and ping-pong tables. This room is haunted by the ghost of my sister, Anne. Slender Anne bent over a pool cue and smiling into her next shot. "Six ball, right corner."

Anne, toes pointed, calf muscles flexed, practicing her dance moves in front of the mirror at the far end of the room. "Raymond, look at me, don't you think I'm a beautiful sister?"

"No, but your father's a contractor. Maybe he could solder in some new body parts and get you looking acceptable."

My mother hides from Anne's death. My father is angry at God. I miss my sister's banter and the fluid magic of her dance.

On Christmas Eve, I serve midnight Mass with Renato Fogli as the other server. Renato is three years ahead of me at St. Jerome's. He's a tall, angular, bookish sort who looks like a great bald bird talking with nasal inflections as he peers down his beak.

It's a high Mass in a packed church, all candles, choir, and sweet smell of incense. I love the pageant of the Mass, and tonight, I can't help but think the spirit of my sister is kneeling between Donnie and my mother out in the congregation.

My father refuses to attend church since he began to view God as an asshole, and I have to admit as I ring bells, answer Latin prayers, and pour water and wine out of little glass cruets, I sometimes have doubts about God myself.

Monsignor McCoy, the pastor of St. Emidyus, is the celebrant of the Mass tonight, the same priest who buried my sister. I wish he could explain it to me. *Why my sister?* I want to grab him by the ears on each

side of his florid face and scream: "Why?" Instead, I think of my sister doing a graceful dance to "Silent Night" like she's explaining the meaning of this holiest of nights with movements that flow from her shoulders down the curves of her arms to the tips of her delicate tapered hands.

After Mass, I return home with Ma and Donnie. My father is silent but pleasant when we get back to the house. He's had a scotch or two and is slicing prime rib and tending to the roasted potatoes and vegetables Ma left for him to oversee in the oven. "How was church?" The question is casual. I can see my pop is doing his best to be polite and at least a little festive.

"Oh, Walter, the Mass was wonderful. I said a prayer for you." My mother's effusive manner usually sets Pop off on one of his rants, especially if the effusion was about religion.

Tonight, my father doesn't take the bait. "That's good, Elana, at least somebody's praying for me."

Donnie picks a piece of roast potato off a serving platter and inhales it. "Yeah, and my pretty-boy brother did a good job on the altar."

"Who's the pretty-boy?" I chide. "At least I don't stand in front of the mirror for two hours combing my hair."

The Christmas Eve meal is not only tasty, but peaceful. My father is on good behavior, either by sheer determination or because he caught the mood of his two sons. Donnie and I are trying to keep it light. For one night, God is not an asshole. It's good to see my father smile.

When God became an asshole, my sister ceased to exist. Dance trophies and awards hidden away. Her picture gone from the mantel. Not one of us mentioned her name. In a war with Russia, my family would make great stone-faced secret agents. All except me. Once in a while in my room at night, I crack. My eyes tear up when I think of her. Other times, I feel anger and want to punch someone.

On another night over three years ago, the night Donnie refers to as "The Great Spaghetti War," we were at the dinner table twirling pasta and savoring the taste of Mom's special tomato sauce. She'd simmered it all day with red wine, chopped celery, mushrooms, and carrots.

My father scowled, drunk and belligerent, and I was spoiling for a fight. "Pop, I'm thinking about entering the seminary to be a priest."

My father drilled me with his eyes. His black chest hairs seemed to bristle over the collar of his blue denim shirt. He dropped his fork and stared at me. "No son of mine is going to be a priest."

I sat on his right and leaned into him. "Well, this son might."

From across the table, Donnie eyed me like I was a madman. "Easy, Ray…"

My mother stared down at her plate. Her auburn hair reflected the soft light of the crystal chandelier above the dining room table.

My father's round and balding head pulsed red. "Elana, you and your commie brother been working on this son of yours to be a priest?"

My mom's brother, Tulio, was a priest, an assistant pastor at a parish in North Beach in San Francisco. He loved to play the guitar, sometimes crooning and strumming folk songs while another priest said Mass. Tulio drove a blue-and-white '56 Ford with dual pipes, and when he took his foot off the gas, twin glass-pack mufflers roared like tigers at feeding time. We called him Uncle Tool, and I think he worked out a deal with my mom to get Donnie and me away from our godless father once a week.

Most Thursday evenings, we either went bowling or to the ping-pong and pool tables at the CYO club. Once Tool took us cruising in North Beach with rock 'n' roll bass-thumping at a low volume on the car radio.

Tool was relaxed behind the wheel and used a lot of Brylcream in his thick Italian hair. That night at a stoplight, the tallest and widest man I'd ever seen yelled out at my uncle: "Hey, Padre, what's the cloth doing out here?" The big man had a broad smile. I bet he weighed over three hundred pounds.

With the windows down and Fats Domino purring "Blueberry Hill," Tool waved. "How you doing, Eric?"

"Who's Eric?" Donnie asked as he eyed a bleach blonde hanging on a sailor's arm.

"Eric Nord. Big Daddy Eric Nord started the Hungry i Nightclub, then sold it."

The blue-and-white Ford moved slowly in traffic that reflected night lights of Broadway. Tool had his right hand on the wheel, left elbow on the open window frame. I was in the back seat watching Donnie turn away from the blonde and stare at Tool. "You mean the beatnik? How do you know him?"

Tool was tapping on the steering wheel to the rhythm of the music. "I like to get out. Meet people in the neighborhood. Jesus was a street guy."

Tool lifted off the gas, tailpipes rumbled. Fats Domino ended. The idea of Jesus walking North Beach felt impressive, and the word "beatnik" had a foreign, organic feel, and I couldn't get enough of the street. Girls, lights and shadows, two guys arguing on a corner, the bouncers in front of clubs.

The Hungry i, Purple Onion, Bimbo's. On the way home, Tool and the priesthood were high on my list, and Donnie and I and even Tool sang along with the Platters, "My mind is such, I pretend too much…" I sang so loud I thought my throat was going to bleed.

My father thought all beatniks were communists, and Uncle Tool the head of the party.

"No, Pop, this is my idea to be a priest."

My father reached for me, grabbed the front of my gray sweatshirt. "I'll bet, sonny boy." I ducked my head, straightened my arms, wiggled out of the sweatshirt, and stood up.

My father backed out of his chair and came to his feet. He was unsteady when he swung at me. I clasped his arm, buried my head in his stomach, and he landed backward on the platter of spaghetti. Silverware scattered to the floor.

"Raymond, stop! The two of you, stop!" My mother was screaming, and Donnie jumped up and pulled me to the front door.

The Great Spaghetti War. Next morning, no apologies. My father groused into his bacon and eggs. "Listen, tough guy, I got a hundred bucks that says you won't be in that place long enough to finish high school."

I still felt combative. *Just watch me, old man,* I thought. *Just watch me.*

7

CHRISTMAS DAY. THE EMOTIONAL EXTREMES OF my parents. My father makes an attempt to bridge the chasm. He gives my mother a pair of diamond earrings. The earrings act as a small band-aid, but the days between Christmas and New Year's are like tinder sparks of spoken and unspoken skirmishes, and always the shadows of God and Anne haunt the edges.

On New Year's Eve, I call Melon. "You want to spend a couple of days with my family?" He lives close-by on Twenty-Seventh Avenue at Ulloa in the Sunset District.

"Sheets, I'll be there. Anything to escape this crazy house."

Melon comes for dinner. My father has had some early evening scotch; he's jovial and seems to enjoy Melon's good-natured chatter at the dinner table. "Mr. Sheets, don't you think you're contributing to my delinquency with this dinner wine?"

"Melon, you can call me Walt, and I think you're a delinquent without the wine. How come you hang around with my choirboy son?"

"I enjoy keeping him loose. He's wound so tight I'm afraid he's going to cut off the blood supply to his brain."

My father grins, and my mother does a quick change of subject as she sets down her fork. "Do you boys have any plans for this evening?"

Melon grabs a dinner roll off a platter. "I thought we might go down to Market Street or Union Square, or wherever the festivities happen and mingle with the crowds. Or if Adonis Donnie wants to take us to a party, that would be good too."

My brother's almond-colored eyes fix on Melon. "You boys are gonna take a vow of celibacy." My brother points his fork at Melon. His olive face muscles are taut like he's a school principal or some type of junior godfather. "Besides, you might hamper my style with the ladies."

"We'll stay out of your way." Melon's undaunted. "And as far as the celibacy thing, we're not gonna have sex; we just want to meet people."

My mother clears her throat, and my father has a grin that I haven't seen in quite a while. My brother's back to cutting his prime rib. "How about I drop you off at the trolley line?"

"That'll work." Melon smiles the way a first-grader waits for dessert. "Or better yet, drop us off at my house—I want to get my heavy parka—then me and Sheetsy can walk to the trolley." I marvel at Melon's comfort with my father and my family, and I feel a pang of jealousy. Dessert arrives, and Melon seems oblivious as I watch him dig into a generous slice of homemade cheesecake my mother places in front of him.

An hour later, I'm waiting in front of Melon's house under the starlit cold of the last night of December. Melon comes out the garage door and offers me a stick of gum. "Sheetsy, save the tin foil from the wrapper; we're going to borrow a car."

We hunker down in our jackets and scuttle up Twenty-Seventh Avenue toward Taraval Street. "Whose car are we borrowing?"

"We're borrowing Lester Sage's '48 Studebaker. He owns Atlas Heating Company up on Taraval."

"And this guy said we could borrow his car? You got the keys?"

"We don't need keys, and he won't know it's gone. It's parked in front of Atlas, and Lester won't be back at work until after the holiday."

We round the corner onto Taraval. A green streetcar screeches along the tracks; autos creep by the streetcar. I see an old Studebaker parked along the curb. The whole scene is illuminated by the golden cones of avenue lights along Taraval. "You mean we're going to steal a car?"

"Borrow, Sheetsy, we're just going to borrow it for a few hours."

"No way, Melon. Count me out of this one. Let's grab a streetcar and head downtown."

"Sheets, you worry way too much." Melon works a pocketknife blade between the frame of the wing window. The Studebaker's tan with two red and white "For Sale" signs plastered on the inside of the windows. Melon gets his arm through the wing window and unlocks the door.

I move away from the car. I stand back on the sidewalk in front of Atlas Heating. Melon opens the passenger door. "Come on, Sheets, get in."

"You're crazy, Melon. What if somebody sees us and calls the cops?"

"Hey, we're just a couple of guys checking out a car for sale. Besides, my dad's a city cop; don't worry about it."

I shouldn't get in the car, but I do. "How you going to start it?"

"Give me your gum wrapper." Melon opens two sticks of Juicy Fruit. "I'm gonna jump the ignition wires to the starter wire." Unruffled, like he's opening a quart of milk or plugging in a toaster. He twists the tin foil and sprawls on the seat with his legs out the driver's door and his head under the dashboard. The engine grinds twice, then starts. Melon's all smiles as we pull the signs off the windows.

"Melon, where do you learn this stuff?"

We pull away from the curb. We are now car thieves, and my thumping heart is about to punch through my chest.

"I been hanging around cops all my life, and I listen to their stories. I actually tried the tinfoil on my parents' car when I was in eighth grade. The first time took me a while. After lots of practice, I got good at it."

"You drove your parents' car in eighth grade?"

"Never drove it, just started it." We circle the block, then head down Ulloa toward the beach. "I phoned Terminal when I was in the house. He wants to come along."

"Along, where?" I sink into the seat like I want to disappear. Melon checks every intersection as we cross the avenues. "Where in the heck are we going in this stolen car?"

We make a right turn and head north on Fortieth. "How many times do I have to say it? It's not stolen, we're going to return it. I thought we might go to Mel's drive-in for a burger."

We pick up Terminal on Fortieth. He gets in and perches on the back seat, leaning forward like the big-eyed barn owl. "Whose car?"

We're heading east on Geary toward Mel's. Melon has the radio going on KYA, Keely Smith and Louis Prima belting out "That Old Black Magic."

"Car belongs to one of my neighbors. He has it up for sale, said I could try it out while I'm home. I'm thinking about buying it."

"He stole it, Terminal."

"If I stole it, then you're an accessory, Sheets." Melon wheels us into a parking place in front of Mel's.

"That makes me an accessory too." Terminal goes along with what he thinks is a joke. Taking his thick glasses off, he wipes the lens with a handkerchief. The parking lot must look like a blur to his naked eyes.

All around us, teenage testosterone groans from tailpipes of souped-up Chevys and bright metallic Fords. The tattered Studebaker stands out like a rag picker at a debutante ball. "Hey, you guys drive that thing straight from the junkyard?" four guys in the car next to us jeer. The drive-in lights reflect off the hood of their candy-apple-red two-door sedan.

Melon's unruffled as he leans out the window. "Careful, this old baby belonged to my grandmother. She willed it to me, and just before she passed away, she made me promise I'd take good care of it."

One of the guys shouts, "You should have buried it with Granny."

Melon gives an ingratiating smile just as a carhop sidles up to the Studebaker. "What can I get you boys?" Her white blouse has an open collar as she leans in. I glance at the secret valley of her breasts.

Melon's hungry eyes go back and forth from her face to her collar. "Three burgers and three shakes. You guys tell her what kind of shakes; I'm buying." Melon orchestrates the order like he's a tuxedoed social ringmaster in a limousine.

The waitress walks off, and her rear end dances a cancan under the stretch of her red pedal pushers. Inviting, seductive curves. I know I shouldn't stare, but the attraction is overpowering.

"My father handed me fifty bucks for Christmas. He's trying to make amends." Melon gives me a side glance. "He's been sober for over three months. Say, Sheets, I'm reading your mind, and we better find a priest so you can go to confession."

"Yeah, well, you better get in line ahead of me, car thief. Your penance will probably be the rest of your life in reform school."

"Sheets, we're already in reform school."

"You guys knock it off." Terminal joins the banter. "You're making fun of my priestly calling, belittling the Sacrament of Penance."

"Terminal, you talk like you been reading too many encyclopedias." Melon adjusts the rearview mirror to get a better look at Terminal. "And don't ever stare into the sun with those glasses on. You'll probably set your lashes on fire."

We get our order, and Melon has me hold his shake and burger while he feels under the dash with the tin foil. The hungry songbird in the backseat is too busy inhaling his milkshake to notice.

We head east on Geary, and Melon's driving with one hand and eating his burger like he's a taxi driver used to a meal on the fly. It's a little after seven o'clock when he makes a quick turn onto Gough

Street toward the freeway ramp. He turns so quickly that Terminal dumps milkshake all over the back seat. "Nice going, Hoot Owl." Melon coasts into a gas station where we try to clean up the mess. "Fill it up," Melon shouts at the attendant. He sounds like a swaggering prince instead of a guy trying to sop up milkshake with a wad of newspaper he pulled out of a garbage can.

"Melon, we got a half a tank of gas. Let's get this car back where it belongs."

"Sheets, it's New Year's Eve. The night is young. We're gonna take a ride."

"To where?"

Terminal walks to the trash can with the paper dripping milkshake; Melon's back behind the wheel. "How about Loyola Corners? We could look up your little girlfriend."

"That's forty-five miles from here. I don't have a girlfriend."

Terminal piles in. Melon pays the attendant, and we roll toward the freeway. "Sheets, your mind is like the back seat, only instead of milkshake, you got little Derry Berry spilled all over it."

Terminal's leaning forward. "Who's Derry Berry?"

Melon checks the side view mirror as the Studebaker merges onto the freeway. "Sheetsy's got a girlfriend. He's no more priest material than I am."

Richie Valens croons "Donna" on the radio. The freeway's a red ribbon stream of taillights. "Knock it off, Melon, let's get this car back where it belongs."

"Will somebody tell me what's going on?" Terminal cranes his neck, his face between Melon and me, until he's nearly in the front seat. "Where does this car belong?"

Melon brings his elbow up toward Terminal's face. "Sit back, milkshake breath, let the night unfold. All will be revealed."

We drive south past San Francisco Airport, past Millbrae and Burlingame and all the towns beaded together like a rosary of lights. "Sheets, you know where she lives, don't you?"

I close my eyes and press into the seat. I breathe deep and exhale. *Maybe he's right, I'm not priest material.* "Yeah, she lives in the house with the roses." I want to punch Melon; I feel he has a power over me.

"House with roses, that doesn't tell me a whole lot."

"Shut up and drive, Melon. I may or may not show you where she lives."

Melon changes lanes, passes a mail truck carrying letters and packages into a new year. "Do I sense Mama's little Jesus getting perturbed?"

Melon wears his suave smile. I'm mad enough to stomp a hole in the floorboards, but instead I keep silent. Chuck Berry's on the radio belting out "Johnny B. Goode". I settle back and soak up the sound.

We pass the air station and leave the freeway, turn south on Foothill Expressway where I first rode on the back of Alice's motorcycle and felt the softness of her sweater against my face.

At an arterial just opposite the Chevron Station in Loyola Corners, Terminal breaks the silence. "Look, there's Iron Jack."

Iron Jack Castaic stands next to a white and coral '56 Chevy. He wears a tie and tan sport coat, and there's a woman in the car. Melon yells, "Whoa," and makes a quick right turn onto a side street and spins the car around facing the Chevron station. We park in the darkness and watch.

Iron Jack pays the attendant and gets in the car. Melon pulls away from the curb, and we follow the Chevy north on Foothill. "Shit, Iron Jack on New Year's Eve with a blonde." Melon's flushed with excitement, and my heart pounds as we turn up a narrow winding road into Los Altos Hills. My first thought is betrayal. Jack's been bullshitting me.

"Melon, not too close." Terminal sounds a voice of caution. "We don't want him to spot us."

The Chevy turns right into a cul-de-sac. There are cars parked everywhere along the dead-end street. All of a sudden, Terminal becomes the backseat man in charge. "Melon, don't go down there."

Melon pulls to the side of the road. We watch the Chevy make a three-point U-turn and back into a vacant spot on a driveway. Iron Jack and the blonde get out of the car. Terminal shouts, "Damn, get down," and before I duck below the dash, I see Iron Jack kiss the blonde full on the lips.

Melon peeks above the steering wheel. "All clear, they got their backs to us." Iron Jack and the blonde disappear into a house where there appears to be a party going on.

Korea, discipline, celibacy. I feel like I've been stabbed in the stomach. Iron Jack's a fraud. "Let's get out of here, Melon."

"Get out of here? Are you kidding? We got the goods on Iron Jack. Let's stay until he comes out."

I've been personally lied to by my trusted spiritual advisor. *Run fast, Mister Sheets. Don't be afraid of the pain.* "Melon, start the damn car."

"No way, Sheets."

I grab Melon by the shirt front and shove him up against the driver's door. I lay into him with the intensity I used when I shoved my father into the spaghetti platter. "Melon, I've had enough. Start the car now!"

I grind my fists into Melon's chest. I take out my rage for Iron Jack on Melon. *Transcendence, my ass!* I won't be able to look Jack in the eye again without thinking *liar.* I come close to punching Melon.

Terminal has his hand on my shoulder. "Raymond, easy. Melon, he's right. We've seen enough. Start the car."

"All right, all right. Sheets, what's the matter with you?"

I let go of Melon and sink into my seat. "I don't like sneaking around. Start the car, and I'll show you the house with the roses."

We ride narrow roads down out of Los Altos Hills. The black night, heavy with betrayal, and cold flint-sparks of stars scratch at the darkness. Paul Anka sings "Lonely Boy" as we pass under canopies of leaf-barren trees.

I direct Melon to Alice Derry's house on Seminary Way. The porch light illuminates the two steps to her front door. The roses are leafless in the shadows. "Sheetsy, she's almost our next-door neighbor. Why didn't you tell me?"

"Lots of reasons. Melon, park this thing, and you two wait in the car."

The street around Alice's house is crowded with parked cars. Melon finds a spot, and I step out and walk toward the house. The strength of my anger toward Melon frightened me. It's a relief to be away from him. I need to cool off. Besides, I want to talk to Alice alone. I hear loud music and pound hard on her front door.

The door opens and a gangly redheaded guy in his thirties fills the doorway. "Hey, pard, happy New Year. What can I do for you?" His voice a gravely Texas drawl.

I notice another guy at an old upright piano pounding out "Great Balls of Fire." "I'm a friend of Alice; is she here?" I shout to be heard. People are walking around with drinks; one couple dances shoeless and wild on the hardwood floor.

"Hey, Lee," the redheaded cowboy yells. "There's a young buck here to see your daughter."

She appears out of the smoke and noise. "I've got it, Dad." Alice Derry ventures out on the front entry stoop and pulls the door shut behind her. "Raymond Sheets! Happy New Year!" She kisses me hard on the lips and pulls away. "What are you doing here?"

Before I can stammer out an answer, Melon scuttles up the walk. "We're taking a ride in my grandmother's Studebaker. Thought we'd look you up and wish you some holiday cheer. Sounds like quite a party in there."

The door opens, and Melinda Garret sticks her head out. The noise increases a few decibels, and Alice shouts, "My dad's having a few people over from the air station." Alice grabs my hand and pulls me up the steps and in the front door. I brush by Melinda and turn to see a smiling Melon and a curious Terminal follow me inside.

The guy at the piano is huge and cheerful as he pounds and wails out the songs. The rest of the evening blurs in smoke and music. Melon learns to fast dance from Melinda. "Dream Lover," "La Bamba." Terminal's glasses half off his face as Alice's drunken mother squeezes his head to her ample bosom. During a lull in the music, Alice's mother says to Terminal, "You're irresistible." Someone drops a drink glass. More music, I slow dance with Alice, hold her in tight. If Iron Jack can have a woman, why not me?

Midnight. We all hoist champagne; other than a little red wine at dinner, my first drop of alcohol since I pilfered one of my father's bottles when I was twelve. Scotch. How could my father stomach the stuff? I spit it out as soon as it hit my tongue.

Midnight. Melon holds a glass and weaves around the room tooting a plastic gold horn. Midnight. "Auld Lang Syne," Terminal blows a paper horn that curls and uncurls like a snake's tongue. Midnight. Alice clings, her swells and indentations galvanized hot and tight against me. Once or twice her tongue flicks electric in my mouth.

By twenty minutes to one, I steer Alice toward the door and yell over the big man hammering the keys and belting out Fat's Domino's "I Want to Walk You Home," "Melon, it's late; we got a long drive." Melon waves me off with a cavalier flick of his left hand, and the party swirls around him. Through the smoke I see him wear his ingratiating smile, his right arm extended in front of Melinda Garret like he's trying to sell her a new Electrolux vacuum.

I break away from Alice and grab Melon by the back of his blue button-down shirt. "I hate to interrupt, but we need to get going."

"Easy old buddy, jhush splaining facts of life to my new friend."

"The car, Melon, and I'm driving. You can't even talk right."

Melon gives Melinda a shrug as I spot Terminal and wave him toward the front door. Terminal turns to Alice's mother with one last blast from his curling snake horn. Mrs. Derry leans against a wall, glass in hand. "You're irresistible." She laughs like she thinks Terminal's a real hoot.

Maybe I need a few drinks to see the humor, but all of a sudden, I want back in the Studebaker. I snag two jackets off a chair and toss one to Melon. Alice clings to my arm like I'm her last friend on earth. I gather her in for a quick hug. "Thanks, Alice, it's been a blast." Then I move out the door.

Alice Derry and Melinda Garret follow us out onto the front porch. Alice wears tiny gold earrings that shine in the light. "Happy New Year, Raymond Sheets!" I wave as we meander down the walk, three confused seminarians intoxicated by life and celebration, stumbling toward a stolen Studebaker in the first cold rush of a new year.

Darkness crackles with stars. Melon, in the passenger seat after doing his magic with tin foil, beats his chest with one fist and howls, "Whoo-weee!" We slide through neighborhood streets, and I'm not a passenger. Melon's no longer in control. I'm in the driver's seat, and I feel a surge of confidence.

Near the freeway on-ramp, I spot a hitchhiker with a bedroll near his feet. I'm feeling goodwill in the New Year. Goodwill and a sense I want to get this guy's story. How does it feel to be so free and your only possession is a bedroll? I skid the car to a stop along the shoulder. "Melon, get in back; I'm gonna give this guy a ride."

"St. Raymond, the guy's a bum. Let him find his own ride."

The hitchhiker jogs toward the car with his arms around his sleeping bag.

"Melon, get in the damn back seat. If the guy pulls anything, you and Terminal can take care of him. We're practicing holy charity by giving a traveler a lift."

As Melon steps out of the car, the hitchhiker slides in. He wears a military fatigue jacket and rimless glasses. I notice a crazed intensity coming from his eyes. He looks a little unbalanced. I have second thoughts about picking him up. "Trying to get to Daly City." Melon climbs into the back of the car without acknowledging the new passenger.

"Happy New Year, buddy." I check the mirror and merge with the fast river of taillights that stream north toward home.

The traveler keeps his arms wrapped around his bedroll. He rocks back and forth in little movements. His hair is white and plastered back like he's been scared by a wild vision of the Holy Ghost. "Going to Daly City to see my kids. Love them kids. Got their names tattooed on my back. Do you guys have anything to drink?"

I adjust the volume on the radio. The Kingston Trio's sings "The Tijuana Jail." Suddenly Melon becomes animated from the back seat "You're reading my mind, pal. We'd love a beer, but unfortunately, we're just a little underage. Possibly you could buy for us if I give you a little money?"

"Find a liquor store, and you got a deal."

Terminal exhales a loud, "Jeeez!"

"No more booze for you, Melon."

"What are you my mother, Sheets? Find a liquor store. Our new friend's been dry for too long."

The newcomer hugs his bedroll. "That's right. I'm about spittin' cotton."

Against my better judgement, I turn onto the Holly Street off-ramp into San Carlos as the Kingston Trio croons, "Just send our mail to the Tijuana Jail…"

"I'm spittin' cotton too, Sheets; all that dancing left me dry. Where you coming from, traveler?"

"State prison down in Los Angeles. Most of the time in a cell block for psychos."

"…a man in blue said, señor, come with me, I want you…" The radio plays as I wheel into a parking spot in front of Bi-Rite Liquors on Holly and ask, "If you don't mind telling me, what were you in for?"

The man passes his bedroll to the back seat and takes some cash from Melon. "Don't mind at all. It's public record. Was a little down on my luck, so I robbed a liquor store."

All quiet in the car. The convicted felon with the plastered white hair slams the door. We watch him walk into the brightness of Bi-Rite Liquors. Melon says, "Sheets, let's go, we're in a stolen car giving a ride to a felon who's buying beer for minors. How do we know he's not going to rob this place?"

"Well, look who's going to implode with worry. The guy's a little intense, but basically a pussycat. He needs a drink to settle his nerves. Nothing for you though. You'd probably be passed out if I hadn't dragged you out of Alice's. Take a deep breath and relax like Terminal."

I check Terminal in the rearview. He looks like somebody's bewildered little brother. He wants to know if the car is really stolen. I tell him it is, and Melon keeps repeating it's borrowed.

The hitchhiker gets back in the car with a brown paper bag and a six-pack of Olympia in his hands. Melon is all holiday cheer. "My favorite brew. What's your name, my friend?"

"Lucas," he answers as he pulls a stout little can of Country Club out of the bag, punctures two holes in the top. He reaches over his shoulder and hands the opener and a beer to Melon. "That church-key's been with me for years. Cops took it from me when I got arrested, and then on my release they hand it back along with my empty wallet and thirty-two cents that was in my pants pocket."

"I'll guard it with my life. Lucas your first or last name?" Melon opens the beer and hands it to Terminal. "Here, four-eyes. Mama Sheets says I better not drink." I crane my head around toward Terminal. He holds the beer like it's radioactive.

"First name. Last name's Foyt." Lucas Foyt sets the can of Country Club on the dash and pulls a half pint of bourbon out of the bag, unscrews the top, and takes a long pull. "Glad I hooked up with you boys; been thirsty for a long time."

The car's warm with the engine still running and the heater going full blast. I shift into reverse and start to back out of the parking lot. "Hold up a minute if you don't mind." Lucas Foyt is raised up in the seat and fishing through the pants pocket of his greasy jeans. "Got to take my pill."

The Studebaker's idling. "What's the pill for?"

"A little Thorazine for the voices."

I catch a glimpse of Terminal in the rearview mirror. He clenches his lips together, drills a hole through me with terror-stricken eyes, and shakes his head in disbelief. My heart pounds for the second time tonight. For once, Melon is nearly speechless. "Ah, yes, the voices…" We move east on Holly and merge onto the freeway heading north. I have Lucas open me a beer, and I take some sips to calm myself, holding it between my legs so it doesn't slop out of the can. We're silent in the car except for Lucas Foyt as he punches holes in a new can of Country Club. He alternates the malt liquor with the bourbon. I notice the bourbon bottle is nearly empty.

By the time we reach San Bruno, Duane Eddy's guitar hammers out "Cannonball" on the radio, and Lucas breaks our silence: "That little fella in the back thinks he's got me fooled with those glasses."

I'm in the fast lane; the freeway's a glare of oncoming headlights. "What are you talking about, Lucas?"

Lucas has a hand on my right arm. "You need to let me out. That little fella in the back is transmitting to the Russian Embassy. You can't fool me. He's letting them know I'm back on the street."

"Easy, Lucas. That's Georgie Thurmond in the back seat. We call him Terminal. The other guy's Melon. They're both friends of mine." I check the mirror, change lanes. I shake free of Lucas's grip on the sleeve of my jacket. I pull into the slow lane, ease back on the speed.

Lucas's voice is nasal and hysterical. "You need to let me out now! Or we need to get rid of the little guy. He's transmitting through his glasses."

Terminal mouths, "Shit," and I try to concentrate on the road. Melon attempts to calm the hitchhiker. "Lucas, we can't let you out on the freeway; you'll get hit."

Lucas grabs the steering wheel, holds it in a death grip. "Better to die here than at the hands of the KGB."

As I fight for control of the wheel, beer slops onto my pants. Melon reaches over the seat and slaps his hands on the hitchhiker's shoulders. He head-butts Melon, and Melon yells as his nose spurts blood.

I roll the Studebaker to the shoulder of the freeway. "All right, Lucas, how about we just get rid of the glasses?"

"No way!" Terminal yells. "No way do I give up my glasses. I can't see a thing without my glasses."

Melon slumps in the back seat, tips his head back, nose in the air, the front of his shirt streamed with blood. "I told you not to pick this guy up, Sheets."

Lucas opens the door. "They're gonna be after me. I gotta run for it."

"Damn it, Lucas, you're safe with us. Get back in the car!"

"The little guy. The little guy's KGB!"

Lucas slams the door. Bolts away from the car. Melon has the back window down. Traffic screams by. I yell above the noise. "You be careful out there, Lucas. Don't do anything foolish!"

"You sound like a father dropping his son off at boarding school, Sheets." Melon still has his nose clamped. "What the hell were you thinking, picking up that nut?"

I chug the rest of my beer. Toss the can on the floor. Terminal stares out the back window. "Geez, he's crossing the freeway." We hear a screech of brakes. "He made it to the median strip," Terminal's yelling. "He's stepping over the guardrail!"

Melon pinches his nostrils and turns. As we watch Lucas Foyt, he gets hit as he steps into the fast lane of southbound traffic. For a second, his upended body forms a silhouette in a blaze of light. Then all I see is the sudden red of braking taillights. "Sheets, we need to go back. He got hit."

Moving slowly, I maneuver the car along the shoulder. "Sure, Melon, I'll make a U-turn right here on the freeway."

Terminal shouts in excitement and concern, "Look, he's up and stumbling. I think he fell on the other side of the road."

"Sheets, double back at the next exit. We need to see if he's okay."

We merge with traffic. "He just got hit by a car doing sixty miles an hour. He's not okay, okay? What are we going to do, stop traffic and administer first aid?" I'm shouting like a wild man.

Terminal gulps some beer. "It's illegal to leave the scene of an accident."

"Where'd you get your law degree, Four Eyes." The sarcasm streams out of my mouth.

"Damn it, Sheets, he's right. We could be in big trouble."

"All right, all right." I yield to the protests and pull off at the Grand Avenue exit. We cross the freeway, use the overpass, and clover-leaf down into southbound traffic, which is now at a dead stop because Lucas Foyt had it in his head to run across six lanes of traffic.

It's two in the morning, and the freeway's jammed because of the accident. We're stuck in stop-and-go traffic for the next forty-five minutes. Melon keeps verbally whipping me. "Sheets, have you lost your mind, picking that guy up? What the heck is the matter with you? You're pressed into Derry Berry in a slow dance, so close you might as well been screwing her, and now you pick up some psychotic who's probably lying dead by the side of the road."

"That's a mouthful coming from Mr. Trouble himself, Melon. We wouldn't be in this mess in the first place if you hadn't stolen this damn car, and we have no idea if he's dead."

Finally, a highway patrolman waves a flashlight in big arcs and directs us off the freeway and up San Bruno Avenue. I open the driver's-side window. "Hey, what happened out there?"

The cop is all business. Pretends not to hear. His flashlight beam dances between the pavement and the sky. "Keep it moving. Just keep it moving."

We reach a consensus that we won't tell anybody about Lucas Foyt. Melon's nose has stopped bleeding. My sister enters my thoughts. Is this the way she died? Among anonymous witnesses in the midst of flashing lights and sirens? My sister. Dead on a freeway. A tear courses down and over the bump of my right cheekbone. I wonder how long it took her to die. The coroner's report said instantly. I wonder at her last flicker of thoughts. I miss my sister. I slap the steering wheel. *Goddamned Lucas Foyt.*

Terminal tries to calm his nerves. He gulps down a beer, sets the empty can on the floor, then punches a hole in another can using Lucas's church key.

"Enough, Georgie, we don't want you passing out." Traffic is still slow. I reach back, and Terminal hands me the beer. I drink like I'm stranded in the Mojave. I'm trying to drown my sister. Get Lucas Foyt out of my head.

We're north on Skyline Boulevard. Off to the east, San Francisco Bay forms a dark expanse ringed with a great swath of flickering lights. Ricky Nelson croons "Lonesome Town." I carry the dark image of Lucas Foyt's upended body like a deep gash that throbs near the front of my brain.

I pull into a rest stop that overlooks the lights of South City. I leave the engine running and step out of the car. I breathe in the scent of eucalyptus in the air. To the south, a green light from the airport strobes the night sky.

Melon gets out of the car and stands next to me. "Sheets, what are you doing?"

I tip my head and scream at the stars: "Damn it! Damn it!"

Melon stands in front of me. Grabs my shoulders and shakes me. Tries to joke with me. "What's the matter with Mama's little Jesus, using words like that?"

I bat Melon's hands away. "We left that poor bastard to die out there." I'm nose-to-nose with Melon. "And don't you ever talk about my mother again! You got that, Melon?"

I feel Terminal's hand on my arm. "Easy, Raymond. Lucas ran out of the car. There was nothing we could do." He peacefully takes charge. "Let's get back in the car. Melon, you better drive."

I slump into the passenger seat. We're silent all the way into the city. Fats Domino moans low and melancholy in this deep hour of the morning.

With a streak of crusty blood on his face and his shirt a mess, Melon remains quiet until he checks the rearview and mumbles, "Oh, shit."

I look out the rear window and see flashing lights of a black-and-white patrol car. Melon turns off Sunset Boulevard onto Ulloa and pulls to the curb. The cop car is tight behind us, red and blue lights flashing.

"You guys leave this to me. Don't say a word." Melon rolls down the window. A tall, stocky policeman approaches the car, fingers of his right hand poised above his holstered pistol. "Evening, officer. Happy New Year to you."

"License and registration, please." The cop, in freshly pressed blues, peers in toward Melon.

Melon fishes in the back pocket of his khaki pants. "License coming right up. I'll have to check the glove compartment for the registration." Melon opens his wallet and shows the cop a driver's license encased in plastic.

"Just the license. Remove it from the wallet." Melon hands the cop his license and reaches across the seat for the glove compartment. That's when the cop shines his flashlight onto the beer cans and empty bottle of Jim Beam on the passenger side floorboards. "You're underage. Have you been drinking?"

Melon pretends not to hear as he rifles through papers in the glove box. "I don't seem to have the registration, officer."

"Beer cans, empty bottle, and no registration. You gentlemen remain in the vehicle." The cop returns to the patrol car. Terminal squirms in the seat. I notice I'm holding my breath. A strong spotlight beams into the Studebaker. I can't shake the image of Lucas Foyt.

"Shit, Melon." Terminal's up on the edge of the seat. "We're in deep now."

Melon grips the top of the steering wheel and stretches his arms. "Just stay calm. My father is one of San Francisco's finest."

Time ticks off minutes that seem like hours. Melon jumps as a second cop pokes his head in the window. He's red-faced, not wearing a hat, and has a thick mane of gray hair. He's chewing the end of a stubby unlit cigar, and he appears as wide as the first cop was tall.

Melon exhales, "Geez, Gruff, you scared the hell out of me."

"Chantelope, I got a rookie with me on his first night out. He's ready to call for backup units because he thinks he's onto the crime of the century. Does your old man know you're out carousing? I thought you were in priest school. I want you to hand me the cans of beer and any other booze you got in here, and then the three of you step out of the car. And Ace, for once in your life, keep your mouth shut and do exactly as I tell you, or we'll both be in hot water."

The cop orders Terminal and me to face the Studebaker with our hands on top of the car and our legs spread. He has Melon assume the same position over the hood. "Wong, turn off that goddamn spotlight before you blind me, and get over here and pat down these two whiz-bangs."

The starched and freshly ironed cop comes running, slides his hands over me and then Terminal. "They're clean," he says in official cop talk.

The old cop jerks Melon up by the back of his shirt. "We ran the plates on this car, punk, and it don't belong to you."

"It belongs to my grandmother, sir."

"What's your grandmother's last name, Ace?"

"Sage, sir. Mrs. Lester Sage."

"You passed that test. Now stand on one foot with your arms out like you're an airplane, bend your head back, eyes up toward the stars." I look over at Melon; the old cop nearly has the cigar stump in Melon's face. "You wobble even slightly, and we're hauling the three of you to the station."

Melon completes the task. I look under my armpit and see an older man and a silver-haired woman in a white Lincoln slow down to gawk at us. "Wong, shut off the flashers before we draw a crowd. I'll finish with these punks."

The old cop herds us back into the Studebaker and then cranes his burly neck through the driver's window, the cigar inches from Melon's eyeballs. "Of all the damn cars out here tonight, we gotta pull *you* over. I know your grandmother on your mother's side is not named Sage, and I don't know where you got this old junker or what you're doing with the booze, and I don't want to know. Get this heap back where it belongs, and get on home."

Melon draws back from the cigar. "Whatever you say, Gruff. What'd you pull me over for?"

"Your right taillight's out. We should give you a citation, but I'm letting it slide."

"One more question, Gruff. Do you ever smoke those things or just chew 'em?"

The cop moves his red face even closer to Melon. I notice a slight smile around the cigar. "Don't push it, Ace. I'll haul you in for being a smartass. Now get the hell out of here."

Melon inserts the tin foil, and we chug up Ulloa toward Nineteenth. I look back at Terminal, and we both shake our heads in relief and disbelief. "Melon, who was that cop?"

"Gruff Ramage. My old man calls him the Polar Bear."

"How do you know him?"

We roll to the curb in front of Atlas Heating. It's three thirty in the morning. I feel wired up and shaken. Lucas Foyt won't go away.

Melon curbs the front wheels, shuts down the Studebaker, rubs his eyes, and stretches like he just woke from a long sleep. "He's my godfather."

8

JANUARY 4, 1960, SECOND NIGHT BACK at St. Jerome's after Christmas vacation. The low night sky seethes moisture, and wind-driven rain slashes against the window. I feel secure beneath the blanket in my room on the third floor. I feel insulated and warm, protected from the gnashing teeth of the rain.

Sleep has been restless since New Year's Eve. Tonight, a distorted film strip in my mind shows the upended body of Lucas Foyt caught in headlights. Landing on his head, his crushed skull shape-shifts into my sister. My father laughs, shakes hands with Iron Jack. Iron Jack kisses the blonde.

And then Alice Derry. I dream she holds my right palm up toward the sun. The hand is translucent and detached from my arm. Alice has pulled the thumbnail off my hand. She holds my thumbnail in the air like the priest holds the host at the consecration of the Mass. My thumbnail glistens and radiates a small blinding light. Alice Derry wears white vestments. She is shouting: "Behold the Lamb of God, Raymond Sheets!"

I startle awake by the morning bell, and I'm drenched in sweat. My heart thumps, a raging animal behind my rib cage. The knock on my door: "Benedicamus, Domino."

"Deo Gratias," I answer. My voice cracks, and I'm breathing hard. I swing my feet to the hardwood and stand, feeling light-headed. Alice Derry. Only a dream.

In tin morning light, the rain has withdrawn its wind-driven armies, and only a vertical drizzle sifts through still branches of cedars down on the big lawn. I turn from the window and leave my room, pad down the corridor alive with sleepy seminarians and the flushing of jakes. Melon stands next to me at the urinal. "Careful, Sheetsy," Melon whispers. "Shake it more than three times and you're playing with it."

I ignore Melon and slam down the lever, flush the urinal. Back in my room, I dress and put on a heavy wool sweater, a Christmas gift from my mother. The sweater is tan with brown silhouettes of reindeer running across the front and back. It feels snug against the damp morning chill as I walk in silence along the porticoes toward the chapel's wooden doors, which funnel 450 seminarians into yellow vaulted light.

The Mass begins. "Et introibo ad altare Dei. I will go unto the altar of God." The vigil of the feast of the Epiphany. I kneel and stare at the translation in my missal: "And at that time, when Herod was dead, behold an angel of the Lord appeared in sleep to Joseph in Egypt..." My mind wanders. Mama's little Jesus. I think back to when I was eight years old. My mother's stirring spaghetti sauce. "Would you like to become an altar boy?"

"No, it would take too much time to learn the Latin." I'm chomping on a mouthful of pink bubble gum. "Besides, I'm in cub scouts, and that takes up a lot of time."

She lays down the wooden stirring spoon and gives me an icy stare. "If there's anything I can't stand, it's a cub scout who smacks his gum."

The look. The words. I'm disappointing my mother. Letting her down.

"Kyrie eleison. Christe eleison." Father Chuck's words fly out like the darting of bees in the candlelight air, and suffering Christ looks down from the great cross above the altar. His arms spread wide like He wants to envelope us. I think of Alice Derry. The concave of her body. Her arms draped around my back. My mother's sad, disapproving eyes.

"Gloria in excelsis Deo…Pater noster…" The gothic chandeliers bathe the student body in flickering warmth. Altar candles alternately burn straight up and then waver. Father Chuck raises the chalice amid reflections of light and candle fire. Like Lucas Foyt, airborne in the stream of headlights. "Hoc est enim corpus meum. For this is my body." Father Chuck genuflects. Raises the host. *I'm tanned all over, Raymond Sheets.*

The raised host. "My Lord and my God." I'm having difficulty breathing. The words in my missal are slightly out of focus: "My daily thought from the following of Christ—Forsake all, and thou shalt find all; relinquish desire and thou shalt find rest." I reread the passage over and over until my breath settles into slow, long exhalations.

"Domine non sum dingus…" Lord, I am not worthy. I really *am* not worthy. I abandoned Lucas Foyt to die alone on the freeway.

I leave the pew and join the stream of students moving slowly toward the communion rail. *Domine non sum dingus.* Alice Derry. Slow dancing. Lord, I am not worthy. Receive communion in the state of mortal sin, and I further compound my sins. I left a man to die. I'm drenched in sweat as Father Chuck places the host on my tongue. My tongue. Alice Derry's tongue. *Hell is real, Raymond.*

Alice Derry. The more I try to forget her, the stronger the memories. I'm in the state of mortal sin. *But what was my sin?* I let a man die, and I can't erase Alice Derry, her arms, her breasts, the flick of her tongue. I can't shake her. I'm in the state of mortal sin, and by receiving communion, I commit a sacrilege. I remember the words of scripture and soothe myself: *Relinquish desire and thou shalt find rest.*

End of Mass. Breakfast. The day damp with low, breeze-driven mist that swirls past classroom windows. Trigonometry. Greek.

Cat's Latin class. Father Cullen's Shakespeare class. We're studying *A Midsummer Night's Dream*, and Melon sneaks up behind me as we enter the classroom. He grabs the back of my collar and whispers: "Lysander, my son."

I bat his hand off my neck. "Better Lysander than Oberon, king of the fairies." Melon grins big as he takes his seat. He loves it when I come back at him. My mood is dank as the outside air. Melon lifts my spirits, parts the mist like the sun.

At three thirty, religion class with Father Robert Gibbs. We call him Bobby Beam because he keeps a half-pint under his cassock. Our religion text is *The Way, The Truth, and The Life*, but Bobby rarely uses the text. Today, he starts talking about the Epiphany. "Gentlemen, an angel of the Lord appeared in sleep to Joseph in Egypt, saying, 'Arise and take the Child and his Mother…' Excuse me, boys, I've got to see a man about a horse." Bobby gets up from behind his desk and hurries out the classroom door. The collective whisper among the students: Bobby's taking a swig.

Bobby bounds back into class in big strides, black cassock flowing like bat wings, his cheeks redder than the hair on his head. His rimless glasses accentuate the glow of humor in his green eyes. "Boys, we'll get back to the Epiphany, but first let me tell about a parrot and a canary sitting on a windowsill watching a naked lady take a bath…" The jokes start. Bobby's like a warm breeze blowing pink petals off a plum tree. "Boys, a salesman from Cleveland needs to break wind…"

Four fifteen. Another bell ends the guffaws and laughter and signals it's time for the playing fields, but instead of the locker room, I climb the stairs toward Iron Jack's quarters. I tap on the door. Iron Jack grumbles, "Come on in." I open the door, and Jack stands in the middle of the room in his black clerical pants and white T-shirt. He holds a fly swatter and scans the ceiling. "Flies bother you?"

"Not especially, Father."

"Can't stand 'em myself. Close the door before this little pest escapes." The fly lands on the binding of *Progressive First Algebra* near the top of the bookshelf. Iron Jack swings at the books, and the fly sticks to the green face of the swatter for a second, then tumbles to the carpet. Iron Jack snatches a piece of paper off his desk and bends like an infielder shagging a hot grounder. Sliding the fly onto the paper, he turns and tosses the remains into the wastebasket all in one quick motion. "Never could figure out why God put flies on earth. Sit down, Mr. Sheets."

"Sorry to barge in—"

"Not a problem, Mr. Sheets." Iron Jack's in an effusive mood, like killing a fly made his day. "What's on your mind?"

"I committed a sacrilege."

"How so?" Iron Jack leans back in his chair behind the desk, his hands behind his head, muscled arms and elbows sticking out like wings.

"I received communion in the state of mortal sin."

Iron Jack has a trace of a smile like he's trying to soothe me, or maybe he thinks I'm joking. "What was your sin?"

Suddenly, I feel foolish. What's with his smile? "I let a man die on the freeway on New Year's Eve…" I blurt it out, and foolish or not, saying it feels like relief.

Jack sits upright in his chair, hands folded on top of some papers on his desk. His forehead's furrowed, and he's staring at me. "You mean you left the scene of an accident?"

"Sort of…"

"Start from the beginning. Let's explore this sin of yours."

Without naming anyone, I tell him I was with some guys and we picked up this hitchhiker. I tell Iron Jack about Lucas Foyt and the beer. I leave out the other events of New Year's Eve, about Alice Derry, and following Iron Jack and the blonde to the party.

"Sounds like Mr. Foyt wanted out of the car…"

"Sure he did, but we should have stopped him."

"How, Mr. Sheets?" Jack's dark eyes bullet through me, and he shrugs. "How do you stop a stranger from getting out of your car? You kidnap him?"

"No, Father."

"And you don't read minds, do you? You didn't know he was going to run across the freeway. Where's the sin, Mr. Sheets?"

"We left him to die." I white-knuckle the arms of the chair and nearly jump up in frustration. Why can't I get this priest to believe I'm a sinner? "We didn't identify him for the police…"

"You did double back toward the scene of the accident, and you were detoured off the freeway. It sounds like you had a car full of beer, which is illegal, and yes, there may be some illegality in not contacting the police, but maybe under the circumstances, it's more prudent that you didn't. I see a possible error of judgement, but no sin. Were you drunk?"

"No, but the car was stolen…"

Jack leaps up from behind the desk and hovers over me with his arms folded. "Stolen car? Who the heck are you hanging out with?"

"Just some guys I know, but we returned the car."

"Okay…" Jack sighs. He pulls back and half sits on the edge of his desk. "Mr. Sheets, I told you about Korea, that I had to let a man die. You didn't let Mr. Foyt die, if in fact he is dead. You had good intentions mingled with a stupid teenage blunder headed error of judgement that may have in fact served you well."

"Then why does it feel like a sin?"

"Feelings and facts are two different things. When did this feeling start?"

"After I woke up from a dream."

"What dream?"

"About Alice Derry."

Jack straightens over me like a perplexed lion. "Who's Alice Derry?"

The bell sounds to clear the playing fields. "She's this girl I met. Can't get her off my mind."

"Mr. Sheets, we'll have to continue this another time. I need to clean up for dinner. Take it from a cleric who knows. I see no sin in spite of what you may feel, and it's pretty normal to think about girls at your age. If you'd like to talk more, I can see you Wednesday evening during study hall. Now scram."

I stand and head for the door. Iron Jack stops me as I turn the knob. "And…"

"Yes, Father."

"Don't try to be so squeaky clean. Lighten up on yourself. And try not to steal any cars between now and Wednesday."

I only half understand Iron Jack. He says to lighten up on myself, but after seeing him with the blonde, I question his judgement. I guess the blonde is his version of not being too squeaky clean. After lights out, I toss and turn in confusion. I wish I were a kid again.

My father used to call me a beanpole. From my bed, I think back to when I was young and scrawny. It was all so simple. I knew who I was. I wanted to be a priest. Beeswax and incense. Stained glass and shadows. Blessings and forgiveness. I felt at home in church.

I can still see myself. A beanpole on my tiptoes, my arms reach high above the altar. I use a thin brass pole with a wick at the tip, extend my body full length to light six tall candles, three on either side of the tabernacle. By the time I reach the last candle, my arms are tired and heavy from so much stretching.

Above me, Jesus hangs on the cross. He's been up there for many years. My arms ache even more just thinking about how long Jesus has been hanging. I have thoughts of getting a ladder, taking Him down, and laying Him on one of the pews for a good long rest.

I'm twelve years old and full of thoughts about rescuing Jesus. With the last candle lit, I extinguish the wick, genuflect as I cross in front of the tabernacle, trying to be careful not to trip on the hem of the cassock. I have thoughts that it might be better if girls worked the altar. Girls are better at dealing with long skirts. When I become a priest, I might look into turning the altar-boy jobs over to girls.

I want to be a priest like Father Riordan. I return to the sacristy and watch him dress for mass. Father Riordan is a big-knuckled, raw-boned guy who looks like one of the cowboys on Saturday morning television. Put him on a horse, he'd be a drover on the Bar-7 Theater. He places the amice behind his neck, a linen cloth that reminds me of a scarf that a cowboy wears around his throat.

Saturday morning cowboys. The comics on Sunday. Prince Valiant and King Arthur's Court.

After the amice comes the alb. The alb is a long white gown that looks like a cassock. Like the linen Prince Valiant wears under his armor. Father Riordan is preparing for spiritual battle. One day I'll dress like a priest. Heathens and devils will shrink away from my armor and Godlike gaze.

The cincture, which looks like a fine white rope, wraps around the waist of the alb. My mind is full of thoughts. I'll bet if Father Riordan did have that horse, he could use the cincture to hog-tie a doggie.

When he puts on the stole, a long strip of colored cloth that goes around the back of his neck and crosses over his chest, I remember a news photo of an army chaplain in Korea saying Mass on the hood of a jeep. He was wearing a stole draped over his uniform.

One time I was alone in the sacristy, I lifted a stole out of the drawer and put it around my neck. I pretended there was a jeep in front of me and I was saying Mass. The stringy tassel ends of the stole hung from my twelve-year-old body like a pair of floor mops. A janitor instead of a chaplain.

My favorite vestment is the chasuble, a two-sided poncho. The chasuble is made of the finest cloth, and it comes in many colors. Red. Purple. Green. Or even gold. It fits like a piece of armor embossed with crosses of silver or gold. The chasuble feels like a banner of allegiance, a shield, a final coat of armor. I imagine myself a future priest among a legion of priests all wearing chasubles, marching en masse to confront the armies of Satan.

With a nod from Father Riordan, I stand at the door of the sacristy prepared to march into the lighted pageant of the Mass. "Are you ready, son?"

"Yes, Father," I answer, proud that he deferred to me for readiness. At that point, we enter the sanctuary.

The packed congregation stands like troops coming to attention as we walk in time to the music from the thunder-pipes of the organ. The chasuble glitters, a festive banner under the sanctuary lights, which hang from links of black chain like they would in a castle. Father Riordan turns and bows to the altar. I kneel on the step beside him, readying myself for the Latin responses.

"Introibo ad altare Dei," he intones. "I will go into the altar of God."

I take a breath. "Ad Deum qui laetificat juventutum meum. To God who gives joy to my youth." I answer in Latin, trying my best to sound like a drover, a worthy knight.

As is the custom, I bend forward from the waist to recite the Confiteor in Latin. "I confess to Almighty God…" I don't know if

God listens to my rambling prayer, but I hope the man next to me hears it. Cowboy. Knight. Priest. I'm going to be him someday.

Tuesday's cold sunlight chases the fog and mists of January. The afternoon air is crystalline, and green hills loom close beyond the playing fields. Vales between the hills are creased with the deep-rooted assurance of coastal live oaks.

Trees soothe me. I often daydream of escape into the protective shadows of muscled limbs, but today as I stare out the windows of Bobby Beam's religion class, my thoughts are not of trees. Today, I'm fraught with guilt about a tawny girl I first met among the thorny bramble of the berry vines. I try to loosen up, but Alice Derry spins in my head.

Morning Mass. Instead of meditating on the Body of Christ, I think of Alice's body. At the communion rail, I sweat with fear, and when the host is placed on my tongue, I have another thought: *What if the host isn't literally the Body of Christ? What if Jesus was talking in metaphors? What if when He broke the bread at the Last Supper and said, "This is my body," He meant, "This represents my body...."*

All of a sudden, I feel like a heretic. I'm receiving the Body of Christ, but I don't really believe it's His actual body. I'm a heretic receiving communion...

"Yoo-hoo, Mr. Sheets, are you with us?" Bobby's got his hands up to his eyes, his fingers and thumbs curled like he's looking at me through binoculars.

The class breaks out in chuckles.

"Sorry, Father."

"Ah, Mr. Sheets, I'll bet you're not half as sorry as the truck driver who gave a lady a lift outside Cincinnati. She talked with a lisp and had a battleship tattooed on her right forearm…" Bobby's got a glow on, and I smile along with him, all the time wondering why most of his jokes take place in Ohio.

At four fifteen, the bell rings. A summons to the playing fields. On the way downstairs to the locker room, Melon appears at my shoulder. "Sheetsy, this place needs some laughter and intrigue. We need to pull a caper."

"Not now, Melon."

"Sheets, you walk around here wearing the face of a depressed undertaker. I feel obligated to levitate your mood."

"Levitate my mood?" I work the combination on my locker. I half wish Melon would shut up. "What kind of caper, Melon?"

Melon voices a whisper of conspiracy close to my ear: "I'll let you know as soon as I get hold of a crescent wrench."

9

IFIND DELIVERANCE FROM MY DARK FEELINGS in the mud ruts and tramped grass of the playing fields. Running, kicking, and catching footballs soothes me. In the wind-sprint rhythm of games, I breathe with deep, lung-searing abandonment. Running is my savior. In breathlessness, I sweat out my obsessions until my tired limbs feel heavy and my mind steeps itself in meditative calmness that feels like prayer.

Today my prayer is interrupted by the grunt-rush of expelled air as Melon collides in the back field with the solid two-hundred-pound bulk of Tommy Zane. Melon's down and doubled up, clutching himself as if he's trying to keep his insides intact. We form a silent circle around him.

"I didn't try to hit him. We just crashed into each other." No one doubts Tommy's words. Tommy could pound any one of us into the ground, yet the truth is, unlike Iron Jack, Tommy would feel bad if he killed a fly.

Melon moans and writhes in the suck of black mud, his glasses twisted crooked on his forehead, the left side of his T-shirt smeared and caked with black ooze. His eyes clutch tight in a grimace of pain. Lankin enters the circle and bends down. "It looks like what happened to my brother once. He just got the wind knocked out of him."

Unsure of what to do, we stare at Melon until he quits squirming and tries to sit up. Tommy enters the circle and helps scrawny Lankin hoist Melon to his feet. Melon looks dazed. I hover around the outer edge of the circle of guys, my heavy-limbed tiredness punctuated with a giddiness that Melon, the instigator and mix-master of my troubles, got what he deserved.

Dinner, study hall, evening prayers, bedtime all orchestrated by the reliable music of bells, and then I dream of Alice Derry. She's nailed to a cross and wearing layers of white gauze. Lightning strikes the base of the cross, wood splinters, and the cross falls toward me. Tiny pieces of Alice's gown shred and flutter like wings. I startle awake as Alice touches a piece of white fabric, light like a moth, to my tongue.

I shudder, with a lint-dry taste in my mouth; I've dodged a falling cross, and my breath pumps fast and shallow. Alice Derry terrorizes my sleep. I inhale deeply, then empty my lungs with a long, slow exhalation. I sit up in bed and look out the window as the first tinsel light of morning begins to comb darkness from the cedar trees.

An hour passes, and a new day begins with footfall in the corridor and the flushing of jakes. The day moves forward, measured by the insistent trill of the bells. By evening study, I'm back in Iron Jack's room. I tell him about my dreams of Alice Derry.

"Interesting dreams, Mr. Sheets. You know, when I was young, I was a thug." Iron Jack leans forward in his chair behind the desk.

"Hard to believe, Father, but what's that got to do with my dreams?"

Iron Jack pins me with his eyes and touches the fingertips of his hands together on his desk. "Maybe nothing, Mr. Sheets, and maybe everything."

I sink back in my chair and glance away toward the bookshelf for a brief relief from his stare.

"I shot up the windows of my grammar school with a pellet gun. My mother hauled me off to a psychiatrist."

Jack's got my attention now, and I'm on the edge of my chair. "You think I need a psychiatrist, Father?"

Iron Jack chuckles. "Relax, Mr. Sheets, let me finish."

I take a couple of silent breaths.

Iron Jack rambles, "The woman psychiatrist pointed out all my hoodlum pranks seemed to gravitate around wanting to be a tough guy, and inside of every tough guy there's a gentle soul needing to be developed. I only saw her twice and thought she was full of baloney."

"I still don't get it, Father."

"At first, I didn't get it either. Then I came home from Korea with the shakes. You see, Corporal Jessen wasn't the only one in my unit to die. There were others with blood loss and wounds so severe I couldn't save them."

"I'm sorry, Father…"

"Nothing to be sorry about, Mr. Sheets, that's war." Iron Jack's speaking softly now. "After I returned from Korea, I suffered from battle fatigue. I saw another psychiatrist, a wise old man from the VA hospital who had studied under Carl Jung. Have you heard of Carl Jung?"

"No, Father." I'm keyed up and tapping my foot, wishing Iron Jack would get to the point.

"Jung's theory is the masculine and feminine live in all of us. Your dreams might possibly be trying to release you from the male-dominated seminary into the world of the feminine."

"This feels creepy, Father. You mean I'm part woman? You think I'm a homo?"

Iron Jack smiles. "You ever look at a flower, Mr. Sheets?"

"Yeah, probably…"

"You ever help your father do heavy work?"

"Sure, my dad's a mechanical contractor. I've helped him lots of times."

"Opposites, Mr. Sheets; both your mother and father live in you. I know your father doesn't like the idea of his son in the seminary. How does your mother feel? Is she happy for you?"

"Of course she is, but I'm here because I want to be." My fists are doubled, and I'm shouting now. "Not because of my mother."

"Easy, Mr. Sheets, I didn't mean to pry. I seem to have touched a sore spot. By the tone of your voice, you seem a bit irritated."

"Sorry, Father, Melon thinks I'm in the seminary to please my mother. I thought you were going to say the same."

"And why would Melon say that?" Jack stares at me, his forehead an accordion of wrinkles.

"Because of the egg sandwiches."

Jack tilts his head. "Egg sandwiches?"

"My mother brings egg sandwiches on visiting Sundays. Melon says my mother fawns over me and feeds me egg sandwiches. It's stupid, Father. Melon's an idiot. Besides, it's not my mother in the dream, it's Alice Derry, and she lives down the road. I can't stop thinking about her."

"Your mother aside, Mr. Sheets, Alice may be a symbol."

"Of what?"

Iron Jack picks up a little brass cannon he uses as a paperweight. He turns the cannon over in his hand. "Not sure. What comes to your mind?"

"Maybe she *symbolizes* the Devil and she's trying to get me to quit this place."

"I doubt the Devil harbors much interest in you, Mr. Sheets." Jack places the cannon back on his desk. "How about Alice may be a part of yourself?"

"I'm feeling confused, Father. You just said my mother was a part of me, not Alice."

"Let's forget about your mother for now and concentrate on Alice. She may represent a gentle part of yourself. Maybe Alice in the dream is trying to get your attention, trying to tell you not to be so hard on yourself."

This talk feels crazy. I catch myself clenching and unclenching my fists. "Father, there was nothing gentle about my dream. There was lightning and a falling cross that nearly crushed me."

Iron Jack rises up from behind the desk. He examines some books on the shelves and pulls out a weathered paperback. He thumbs some pages then snaps the book shut and stuffs it back on the shelf. He stands over me and leans against the edge of the desk. "Where does lightning originate, Mr. Sheets?"

"The sky."

"What can the sky symbolize?"

"I dunno, maybe stars, the moon, sun." I start to get a headache. "Where you going with this, Father?"

"Suppose the sky symbolized heaven in your dream. Heaven sends a lightning bolt to cut down the cross. Suppose the cross represents a link between heaven and earth. Suppose the dream is telling you to get down to earth, walk softly, disconnect from heaven for a while."

The bell rings for the end of study period. "What about my tongue? Both dreams had something white like the host landing on my tongue."

"Know what litmus paper is, Mr. Sheets?"

"Kind of, Father, I think it has to do with chemistry."

"Exactly. Lick litmus paper with your tongue, it turns either red or blue. Red is acid. Blue is alkaline. Two opposites, Mr. Sheets, just like masculine and feminine. I don't know for sure, but I think your dreams may be putting you to a litmus test."

My headache gets worse, but I try to listen. Iron Jack hardly ever lets me down. "What, to see if I'm acid or alkaline?"

Iron Jack folds his arms and grins, and I wonder if old Carl Jung whispers some happy secret in his ear. "Possibly, but more likely the test has something to do with where your life is heading on this journey between heaven and earth."

My head feels like it's about to split open from this confusing talk. "I better get to chapel, Father."

"Relax, Mr. Sheets; try being late for chapel this time. When we're being tested, we need to go easy on ourselves."

"Why you telling me all this?"

"I'm not sure, but as your spiritual advisor, I sense something in you, Mr. Sheets. I've told you before, you're a seeker, a searcher. I hope to help you along the journey."

Out in the corridor, I feel dizzy and off-kilter from too much hazy thinking. I resist the temptation to run; I walk alone across the courtyard toward the chapel doors. I wonder about Iron Jack and his blonde on New Year's Eve. Maybe she's acid and he's alkaline. I'm confused but lighthearted as I bound up the stairs into the muted light of evening prayers.

By mid-February, Melon is back to his antics. "Sheetsy, you getting your little girlfriend a valentine?" Apparently running into the two-hundred-pound bulk of Tommy Zane did not knock any sense into Melon. We're in the rec room in the basement, and I'm whipping him at ping-pong. Outside, a wind snarls, and torrents of rain punch away at the somber walls and crying windows of the towering old school.

I slam back a high lob from Melon. The little plastic ball nicks the edge of the table and bounces away across the hardwood floor. Melon chases it down and returns to the table, tries to catch me off guard with a fast spinning serve that has too much muscle behind it.

"She's not my girlfriend; she's a symbol."

Melon delivers another serve, we volley back and forth in a strong rally, and I see sweat on his balding, porky face. "That's a good one,

Sheets. I guess I saw you on New Year's Eve pressed in a slow dance against a figment of your imagination."

I smack the ball hard, and it hits the net. Score one for Melon. "I told you before, Melon, knock it off."

Melon serves, and I whack back a fast return that catches the right corner on Melon's side for a game-ending point. I charge around the table and into Melon's face. He senses the fire in my eyes and pulls off his glasses and rubs the lenses against his T-shirt. "Easy, Raymond, I'm joking with you."

The room vibrates with shouts and loud conversations. Pool balls clack, and silver discs stream along the hardwood length of shuffleboard.

I toss my paddle on a table and walk over to a speed bag. "You don't know when to quit." I punch a two-fisted rhythm. I imagine Melon's face on the tight leather.

I give the bag a final wallop and turn toward Melon. He wears his unctuous smile. "Sheetsy, I confiscated a crescent wrench from the boiler room."

My knuckles sting from the slam of the punching bag. The pain feels like sweet release, the way pain from a dentist feels right after he's cleaned your teeth. "And what are you going to do with a wrench?"

"We're going to use it to pull a caper."

"Whatever you're going to do, Melon, leave me out of it." I head to the door of the rec room and out into the cold basement corridor that leads to the locker rooms.

Steam pipes line the concrete ceiling of the corridor. The pipes thud and clunk as they send warmth into the building's old veins.

Melon tags along, pleads his case over the noise of pipes and musty smell of lockers. "Sheetsy, I'd never involve you in anything that would jeopardize your good standing in this institution. Your dad's a big-time contractor, and you know pipes. I just need a little technical assistance."

I don't bother to tell Melon that a plumbing job might require a pipe wrench, not a crescent wrench.

February rolls into March with no more talk from Melon about a caper. Mid-March brings scattered clouds and unusual warmth, as streams of sunlight begin to tickle up emerging blue swaths of lupine on the nearby hills.

In early spring, the student body blossoms along with the flowers, shouts of joy herald track and field workouts, and slaps from fungo bats send hardballs up toward the sun. Intramural sports make up a big part of seminary life, but our first big event of the year is a Catholic school all-comers track-and-field meet on the first Saturday after Easter.

This year, the meet is to be held at San Jose City College, and the members of the "house" track team practice muscled heaves of the shot put, hammer out wind sprints, and run distance with long, loping strides.

Ours is not a cinder track, but a hard, trampled clay path inaccurately measured around the perimeter of weedy soccer fields and makeshift baseball diamonds. For exact times, I run the Lincoln high school track over and over when I'm home on vacation.

Today, Iron Jack stands along the sidelines, shouting both encouragement and criticism. "Pick it up, Mr. Sheets, you look like you're sauntering to the grocery to buy your momma a loaf of bread." I push harder, both to silence Jack and silence thoughts of Alice Derry. Feelings of guilt about Lucas Foyt also clutter my mind.

I confess these feelings weekly. The sacrament of Penance is a Friday evening ritual, but my real penance occurs on the makeshift track. I push myself daily into exhaustion. The Wednesday before Easter, I have a good feeling, and I convince myself I can drop my mile time to under five minutes.

My hair's still damp from the shower, and I'm tying my dress shoes in the locker room when Melon leans down and whispers, "Sheets, I need to talk to you."

Lockers slam, towels snap, steam from the shower room mingles with shouts and echoes of horseplay and laughter. "Melon, whatever it is, the answer is no."

I stuff my gray sweats into my locker. Melon puts his hand on my arm. "Raymond, I want to know how to shut down the water supply to the college dorms."

I shake loose of Melon's hand and duck out into the basement corridor. Melon's on me like a bull terrier as I climb the stairs that lead to the porticoes. They are empty except for old Pop Stiles reading his breviary and walking back and forth in the distance.

"C'mon, Sheets, the water, I just want to have a little fun."

A gaggle of students heads from the locker room to the refectory. I reluctantly give in to Melon's badgering. "A pipe feeds the building probably on the north side," I tell him. "The pipe will come up out of the ground and elbow into the building. The pipe likely will have a large gate valve on it. Just turn the valve."

"Sheets, you're a genius. I'll knock on the wall after midnight."

"Melon, you're an idiot. Leave me out of this."

Sleep does not come easy. It happens sometimes when I push the limits of my running; my body feels too amped for sleep. I twist under the covers, trying to get comfortable, when I hear Melon's three taps on the wall.

I ignore his signal, and in the silence, he taps again. No way am I going to let him get me involved in this. I hear a click in the corridor. Melon has shut his room door, and the click sounds loud as a gunshot. Melon is out of his mind. He knows the Cat has insomnia and sometimes prowls the darkness. My heart races. If Melon gets caught, the faculty will boot him out of here as soon as tomorrow.

From three stories up, I study the main drive. Melon will have to cross in front of the building to reach the north side of the college dorms. I slide my window up and lean out into a night tinged with dampness. Minutes pass; then two figures dressed in black cassocks hug the building and edge along behind bushes that separate the building from the drive.

When they reach the lit-up entry steps to the administration building, I see that Melon has recruited Terminal. Georgie Thurmond. I want to break the Grand Silence and yell, "Georgie, get back to your room."

In less than ten minutes, Melon and Georgie return from their mission. They sprint across the lighted exposure of the entry steps and once again hug the building. I rest easy when I hear Melon's door click shut in the corridor.

Thursday of Holy Week dawns with cold clarity, and the student body crosses the courtyard in silence. As I walk toward chapel, I can almost hear angels sing in the cobalt blue of the sky until Melon breaks the spell as he furtively nudges me. With his fingertips in his armpits and his elbows out like wings, he whispers, "Cluck, cluck, Sheetsy."

Holy Thursday. The day of the Last Supper. Jesus breaks bread with his disciples. "The Lord, Jesus, after He had supped with His disciples, washed their feet and said to them: 'Know you what I, your Lord and Master, have done to you? I give you an example that you may do likewise.'"

Holy Thursday. "Gloria in excelsis Deo..." Bells ring throughout this prayer, and then the bells go silent, not to be heard again until Holy Saturday. After the morning service, we walk in silence to the refectory.

We stand behind our chairs, waiting for Father Chuck's words from the faculty table: "Gentlemen, take your seats."

Today, those words never come. Instead, we hear the push-button bell at the faculty table get smacked with a fury. "Gentlemen," Chuck's voice explodes, "During this holiest time of the church, one or more of you has pulled an untimely prank. Someone shut down the water supply to the college dorms and removed the handle from the main valve. Luckily, maintenance will soon have the water up and running, but I expect the guilty party or parties to return that handle to my office before noon today. Until that handle is returned, except for classroom and chapel, I am imposing a rule of silence on this student body."

Terminal is one of my tablemates, and I don't dare look at his face when I give him a hand signal to pass the butter. I don't expect Melon to come forward and give up the handle to the water valve, but Georgie might crack and confess, although he may be more afraid of Melon than Father Chuck.

Noon comes and goes, we eat lunch in silence, and the afternoon recreation period is canceled. We are confined to more silence in the study hall.

At dinner, Father Chuck once again hammers the bell. "Gentlemen, I can wait as long as you can. I don't care if this community stays in silence until Easter Sunday. I'm still waiting for the valve handle."

C. C. Mullins, the high school student body president, a tall and broad-shouldered athlete, unfazed by Chuck's threats, dares to speak out. "Father, what makes you think it was one of us?"

"Mr. Mullins," Chuck roars, "do you think I'm an idiot?"

"No, Father."

"Well you'd better believe someone in this room knows what happened to the water system."

"Yes, Father."

Good Friday arrives with sunrise reflecting off a thin layer of cloud. Walking to chapel, Melon keeps his eyes straight ahead. No grins or nudges this morning. I wonder how Georgie Thurmond slept last night.

In honor of Good Friday, the altar in the chapel is bare of any linens, the Tabernacle is open, and the Blessed Eucharist has been removed to a side altar called the Altar of Repose. Father Chuck begins the Passion of Christ according to St. John: "At that time Jesus went forth with His disciples over the brook Cedron, where there was a garden which He entered with His disciples. And Judas also, who betrayed Him, knew the place…"

Judas. One slip of my tongue, and I could betray Melon. Secrets. Iron Jack with the blonde, and now Melon. Keeping secrets saps my energy.

Like a furtive Judas with things to tell, I carry my secrets into Good Friday morning study hall where an old priest we call Jimmy O is the prefect. Jimmy O has a habit. He marches back and forth at the rear of the study hall while he reads heavenly words from his breviary. His hair is cut in a gray flattop, and his feet are big when he marches. With his nose pointing down to the black book, he never looks up from his round-trip circuit.

Even under punishment of silence, the collective humor of community prevails. Today, an irreverent prankster has poured a large

box of cornflakes over the worn hardwood floor where Jimmy marches. We're getting stomachaches from stifling our laughter as Jimmy
marches and crunches across the carpet of corn. Good Friday. The
Crucifixion. In the tedium of our punishment, we're nearly hysterical;
we bite our lips with tears in our eyes.

When the bell rings for the end of study hall, Jimmy closes his book
and pauses. Leaving heaven behind, he stares downward. "What is this
mess?" We howl. We howl more when a sudden expression of recog-
nition floods his face. Jimmy O stands stable on his oversized feet. He
stands, an aging boxer coming back into focus after too many punches.
An aging boxer whose smile soothes like an antidote to Father Chuck's
harangues. "You got me, boys." Jimmy O grins. "You really got me."

Good Friday. During the three hours Jesus hangs on the Cross, I
wish I could say I'm thinking of Christ's agony, but I'm really thinking
of Alice Derry. I walk in silence down to the berry patch where I first
felt her red-stained fingers place a blackberry on my tongue.

Alice Derry. How easy it would be to step out of bounds and keep
walking to the house with the roses. Instead, I stop at the unkempt
scramble of vines. Alice Derry. I remember the scent of her. Her cocki-
ness on the day we met: "Are you afraid of me, Raymond Sheets?" The
motorcycle. My arms around her waist. "Hang on, Raymond Sheets."

I turn away from the berry patch and head back up the long drive,
my thoughts tangled by the solemn silence of the day and the contours
of Alice's body draped against me as we danced on New Year's Eve.

Friday evening. The sacrament of Penance. One by one, students
drift in and out of study hall, taking turns to meet with their spiritual
advisor and confess their sins. Tonight, I need some levity, and I wish
Bobby Beam were my confessor. After absolution of my sins, he might
pull out his half-pint bottle and tell me a joke about a salesman from
Cincinnati.

Instead, I'm weighted with secrets, and the stairs to Iron Jack's quarters feel steep. Alice, Lucas Foyt, Melon and the plumbing caper, Iron Jack and the blonde. "Bless me, Father, for I have sinned. It's been one week since my last confession." I'm on a kneeler, and Iron Jack is seated off to my right. He wears a purple stole draped around his neck. "Father, Alice seems more than a symbol. She's flesh and blood, and I'm having trouble getting her out of my mind."

"Time will tell, Mr. Sheets. Meanwhile, keep fighting the good fight."

"Just like you, huh, Father?" I spit the words out like my head's going to burst.

"Is it sarcasm or anger I hear, Mr. Sheets?"

"Both. I saw you on New Year's Eve with a blond lady." I've turned my head toward my confessor, my damn spiritual advisor, and I feel my face flood red with anger.

"Mr. Sheets, this is the sacrament of Penance, not a sounding board for what you may or may not have seen on New Year's Eve."

"Okay, Father, my sin is anger. I'm angry you lied to me. All that stuff about Korea, and how you made a promise to God. How you'd dedicate your life to His service."

"Korea was not a lie, Mr. Sheets, and I did make a promise to God. Now let me absolve you of your sin of anger which, in view of the circumstances, may not be a sin at all." Iron Jack waves his big bear paw of a hand over me and makes the sign of the cross. "Ego te absolvo…" The Latin tumbles from his lips, and in the midst of confusion about this priest, I feel lighter, less burdened.

Smug and righteous, I rise and stand before him. "Why did you say my anger may not be a sin?"

"Easy, Mr. Sheets, I understand your confusion. Before you accuse me of anything, did you happen to think that wasn't me you saw on New Year's Eve?"

"It was you, Father, and you had on a tan sports coat."

"What if I have a twin brother?"

"Do you?"

"No, Mr. Sheets, I do not, and the blond lady was not my sister."

"Why are you messing with me, Father?" My anger is up. "Why are you messing with my head?"

"I'm trying to get you to think, exhaust all possibilities. I'm trying to get you to think instead of react."

"Yeah, well, how is being with a lady on New Year's Eve the same as doing God's work?"

"Watch your tone, Mr. Sheets. I don't feel I need to explain my actions to you or anyone else, but in your case, I will have an answer for you. Right now, I want you to return to study hall. Cool off, weigh the possibilities."

The man talks in riddles. On the way back to study hall, I stomp down the stairs. Good Friday is coming to an end. Iron Jack is two-timing God, and Melon has the whole school locked down in silence. I'm mad enough to punch walls.

10

SATURDAY ARRIVES DULL, GRAY, AND OVERCAST. Christ's in the tomb, the entry secured by a large boulder, but Melon refuses to unlock the vault of silence. Tomorrow starts a weeklong Easter vacation, and the community moves in a quiet rush from study hall to classes as if the faculty and students want to hurry into the needed respite that follows Easter Sunday.

Recreation time has been canceled for days because of the water-pipe caper, and I'm frustrated that I'm unable to practice my running in preparation for the Catholic school all-comers track meet that will happen in a week. I want to grab Melon and shake him.

By evening lights-out bell, I fume, restless and unable to sleep. I lie awake until eleven thirty, and again a bell rings calling us to a special midnight service in the chapel. We file out of our rooms and down the stairwells, crossing the courtyard like sleepy ghosts.

The chapel lights are dimmed to a yellow glow, and as we enter, we each receive a small white candle. When the student body is seated, the lights are turned off, and the great high structure of the chapel is immersed in darkness.

"All stand." A voice from the rear of the congregation booms a command. In silence, we stand waiting for the Resurrection, waiting for the Angel to move the boulder from the entrance to the tomb. Suddenly, the great doors of the chapel swing open and a procession of priests and acolytes led by a single candle enters the chapel. Iron Jack's deep bass voice rings out in the night: "Lumen Christi," he sings.

The procession stops, and fire from the main candle is transferred to a candle in the last row of the chapel. The fire is passed to the candle of each seminarian. Slowly, the light of Christ moves from back to front through the community. Iron Jack continues his chant, and the community answers in unison. "Lumen Christi," we sing, and in the dancing light of candles, 450 male voices chorus out of the darkness. The hair on my neck stands up and tingles.

"Resurrexi, et adhuc tecum sum...I arose and am still with thee." The Mass of Easter proceeds, pipes from the great chapel organ thunder in unison with surging male voices as the Mass is punctuated with chorus after chorus of mighty "alleluias."

By 2:00 a.m., we are back in our rooms. Sleep comes shallow and restless, my dreams filled with running. I'm running a tree-lined drive, the school behind me. I'm past the berry patch, and rose petals from Alice Derry's house fly in my wake. Alice floats in the air ahead of me; she's now blonde and, her body draped in thin wings, her arms stretch toward the sky. She balances a crescent wrench on her fingertips, and she laughs as she sings: "I can fix you, Raymond Sheets."

I awaken with Alice's voice in my ears, and sweat pours from my forehead. The eight o'clock bell clangs. We've been allowed to sleep in, yet the ring of the bell feels harsh and annoying. It's Easter Sunday, with the drama and pageant of the midnight Mass worn off, the day clear and blue out my window, yet I still feel I want to punch someone.

We stand behind our chairs in the refectory, and after we recite the prayers before meals, Father Chuck presses the button on the chrome bell next to his place setting. "Happy Easter, gentlemen, the rule of silence has been lifted. However, on this most holy of days, I have sad news. The person or persons responsible for interfering with the water pipes has not come forward. Therefore, I am canceling this school's participation in the all-comers track meet next Saturday."

The chatter of the student body in the refectory reverberates extra loudly this morning. Plates, silverware, and metal serving trays clash with the sound of voices. The pent-up silence has been released. Whether the chatter is about the upcoming week of vacation or about the cancellation of the track meet, I'm uncertain. What I do know, my anger won't allow me to look Georgie Thurmond in the eye.

After breakfast, I wait outside the refectory door. Melon and Georgie are the last ones out of the dining hall, and they have their heads together, talking in low tones. I stand and lean against one of the columns that supports the porticoes. Melon shakes his head and points at Georgie. They fail to notice me.

From the porticoes to the flower beds below is a four-foot drop. On impulse, I rush Melon from behind and plant my hands hard on his lower back. He expels a groaning rush of air from his lungs as I push him off the ledge. He hits hard. I hurry away like a coward in the grip of a frightful anger. I leave Melon painfully moaning among the spring flowers.

In my room, I use my toothbrush, brush hard until my gums bleed. I spit blood and flecks of oatmeal into the sink, then hurriedly finish packing for vacation. I toss a comb and the toothbrush into my battered brown suitcase. The room, a haven sheltering me from the consequences of my anger.

I can't stall any longer. The buses are waiting. I step into the corridor, which hums with voices and slamming doors. I take quick notice that Melon's door is open, but in his empty room remains only an unmade bed and an unfastened overnight bag stuffed with clothes.

I lug my suitcase downstairs and out the side of the building, where two chartered diesel buses idle their engines. One bus will carry seminarians to San Francisco and towns along the peninsula; the other bus services the east bay. Lankin wanders over from the side of the east bay bus. "Got any ideas who shut off the water, Sheets? I'd like to pound him."

Like a guilty Judas, I don't meet his gaze. "I have no idea who shut it off, but I'd like to pound him too."

Gaggles of students crowd around the buses, and luggage piles up. The east bay bus gasps as its door opens. The driver steps out and tosses excess baggage in compartments beneath the bus, while students begin to board. Lankin wanders away. I spot Georgie Thurmond as he walks toward me. "How's Melon?" I ask.

Georgie sets his bag down and slides his glasses up on his nose. "I went with him to the infirmary. The nurse thinks his right arm is broken, and she's taking him to the emergency ward."

"What did he tell her?"

"Said he was horsing around with some guys and he fell off the portico. He's in a lot of pain."

We board the bus, and I share a seat with Georgie and stare out the window. We glide up the highway past peninsula towns. I cringe when we near the place on the freeway where Lucas Foyt got upended on New Year's Eve.

I don't hear from Melon during vacation. I know I should tell him I'm sorry I broke his arm, but missing the track meet sits hard on my gut.

"What's the matter with you?" My dad is grousing over bacon and eggs at the breakfast table. "You look like you lost your last friend."

"A little tired, Pop."

"Tired? You don't even get out of bed until the day's half shot." He forks some egg into his mouth. "Come on and work with one of my crews. They're running a two-inch water main. I'll show you tired."

God, I hate it when my dad talks with a mouth full of food.

I'm tired because I'm not sleeping well. I toss and turn, feeling guilty because I pushed Melon and busted his arm. What kind of a priest can I be if I can't control my anger? I'm supposed to practice compassion and forgiveness. Instead I lose my temper and hurt my friend.

My father leaves for work. I'm alone at the table. Ma's in the kitchen cleaning up the breakfast mess. "Raymond, can I get you some orange juice?"

"No, Ma. I'm going to go back to sleep."

Ma stands in the dining room doorway wiping her hands on her apron. "Why are you so tired, Raymond?"

I push away from the table and stand. "I don't know, Ma. I just am."

I leave her with a perplexed look on her face. I climb the stairs and flop on my bed. I remember years ago, Donnie gave me a bad time about wanting to be a priest. Maybe he was right, the priesthood's not for me.

I remember when we were young and shooting pool. Donnie breaks, the cue ball clacks the tip of the triangle, balls separate. I line up my first shot. "I'm solid." I smack the one-ball into a corner pocket.

Donnie rubs chalk on the tip of his cue stick. "That's a laugh. If you were really solid, you wouldn't want to be a priest."

I'm bent over the table, hoping to graze the three-ball into the side pocket. I hit the three-ball head on, but it ineffectually thumps the green felt bumper and clatters into a nest of balls. "What's that supposed to mean?"

Donnie eyes the table looking for a shot. "You're just a kid. Do you want to turn out like old Father McCoy who huffs and puffs like a red-faced steam engine?"

"What about Uncle Tool? He doesn't huff and puff."

Donnie takes his shot, tries for the ten-ball, and misses.

"Way to go, bigshot."

"Tool doesn't count. He's our uncle."

I rest the base of my stick on the floor and stare at my brother. "Sure, he counts. I want to be a priest like Tool, not like old fat McCoy. I want to hear confessions and forgive sins. I want to coach the parish school baseball team, say Mass, and bless people when they're dying."

Donnie pokes me with his cue stick. "You gonna absolve me of my sins when I go to confession and tell you I got a hard-on thinking about Linda Carmody?"

I brush the chalk mark off my black T-shirt and line up the next shot. "I'll only absolve you if you're truly sorry about that hard-on." This time, I sink the three-ball.

"Nice shot, and I've never been sorry about a woody."

"Then you're going to hell." I survey the table, looking for a shot, bank the seven-ball off the rail and miss the pocket. "When I'm a priest, I'll pray for all the kids like you that are walking around with hard-ons."

"Gee, I'm deeply relieved. Wait till you're a priest walkin' around with your own boner under your long black dress."

"It's called a cassock, but maybe I'll be wearing a uniform. I might want to be a military chaplain hearing dying guys' confessions on the battlefield. It's your shot, bird-brain."

Donnie sinks the eight-ball. He just lost the game and is going to hell.

I smile at the memory as I lie on my bed. How naïve, smart-mouthed, and defiant I was as a kid. Unlike now, when I'm filled with doubt.

Donnie barges into the room and interrupts my thoughts. "What are you doing? Hiding out in here?"

"What are *you* doing? I thought you had to work at the deli."

"Traded shifts with somebody. Got stuff I need to get done today. What's the matter with you anyway? Your face is longer than a log of salami."

"I feel lousy. I blindsided Melon and busted his arm."

Donnie is rummaging through the top drawer of the bureau. "You what?"

Donnie abandons whatever he's looking for and sits down on his bed across the room. I tell him about Melon and the canceled track meet.

After I've finished the story, Donnie breaks the silence in the room. "You should have busted both his arms. The little creep had it coming."

"But I'm studying to be a priest."

"You're like the old man. You got a hot temper. What, you think priests don't feel anything? They get pissed off like you and me."

I hate to admit it, but maybe he's right. I am like my father. "Sometimes I even get pissed off at God."

"See, just like Pop." Donnie's on his feet, searching another drawer. "The old man's pissed because of Anne. Why are you pissed at God?"

"Same thing. You know. He took my sister."

Donnie bumps the drawer shut and stands over me. "God never took Anne. Her what's-his-name asshole boyfriend got her killed. He was driving too fast."

"So you're pretty mad too?"

"Course I am, Sherlock. I'm real pissed off my sister's dead."

"How come you never talk about it? How come nobody in this damn family ever talks about Anne?"

"Because we don't want to think about it and get all wacky like the old man. Look, I gotta go do stuff. Enough of this talk. Try to be more like Ma. She cooks, gardens, goes to church. She stays out of trouble."

Donnie slams out of the room. I pull the bedspread off the pillow and nuzzle in for a nap, but sleep eludes me. Donnie says I got Pop's temper. That's why I shoved Melon. Crazy Melon.

I reflect on the stupid happenings of New Year's Eve. We could have all gone to jail for underage drinking, or worse yet for getting in an accident while under the influence. Maybe I *should* have busted both his arms. I doze off thinking my anger was justified, and Melon was the cause.

I sleep soundly until early afternoon. When I wake up and go downstairs, Ma is stirring thick soup with a big wooden spoon using the back of her free hand to brush at strands of hair matted against her moist forehead. Face parched, sagging cheeks, eyes heavy and distressed. Her brow an accordion of wrinkles as she stirs minestrone. Was the heat too high? Would vegetables scorch and stick inside the pot?

She turns the gas flame down to simmer and places a silver lid over the pot, apparently satisfied that in this moment the soup is fine. She wipes her hands on her blue apron, enters the dining room, and sits across from me at the table. "Did you have a good sleep, Raymond?"

"Yeah, Ma." I feel irritated when she mothers me, so I change the subject. "How come you never make biscotti anymore?" I love the smell of her soup, and I used to love the taste of it when I was a kid, but lately my taste buds must have changed or something. The soup tastes a little slimy, like she hasn't siphoned off enough fat.

"I will make biscotti, but tell me, Raymond, why is it you don't like to pray the Rosary with me anymore?"

I prayed the Rosary with her when I was a kid. I wanted to kneel beside her, feel the brush of her sleeve against my arm, feel her close beside me. I wanted to meditate with Mom on the mysteries of the Rosary, but now I'm seventeen, the Rosary feels monotonous. Even the Virgin must get tired of all those repetitious "Hail Mary's" buzzing around her ears.

Also, I don't think Jesus wants us to be thinking so much on His Crown of Thorns or the whipping He got along the Via Dolorosa.

Maybe He'd just have us love one another. Except for Melon. I can't even bring myself to like him.

I do love my ma, which brings up a problem. I don't want to love her too much. Saying the Rosary with her feels like touching a banana slug; it makes me queasy. "I'm on vacation, Ma. I'm just too tired for the Rosary.

"Raymond, we used to feel so close with our devotions."

A banana slug leaves another silver trail. "Geez, Ma, I'm in the seminary, for Pete's sake. I do enough devotions." A guilt snake rises up and darts its black-arrow tongue. "How about I pray the Rosary with you one night a week?"

"So, you'll spare me one night a week?" I detect fire in her eyes, a twinge of sarcasm in her voice. "Is your vocation beginning to wane?"

Wane? My mind races. What kind of a word is "wane"? Ma does more praying in a day than all the guys at St. Jerome's. Suddenly I can't wait for vacation to be over. Listening to Ma makes my skin itch. "My vocation is fine, Ma. I'll be going back to the seminary next week. I'll pray the Rosary with you whenever I can."

Ma gets up from the table and returns with a bowl of soup and sets it in front of me. "The soup is for dinner, but I'm going to give you an extra bowl now. I'm so thankful we had this little talk."

My stomach feels queasy, but I get the soup down. Noodles, bits of beef, and carrots slide down my throat. I butter a piece of chewy French bread she's put in front of me. I swallow a wad, hoping it will sop up some of the greasy soup in my gut.

"Raymond, I'm reading about St. Agnes. She chose beheading rather than give up her virginity."

I feel my stomach turn. I think of Alice. Our bodies molded together in a slow dance. "Geez, Ma, why do you tell me this stuff?"

"You're studying to be a pillar of the church. Don't you want to know its history? Aren't you interested in what I've been reading?"

"Don't believe everything you read, Ma."

Her color rises, her voice a pitch higher. "Don't you believe in the lives of the saints?"

"Some of it, but some of it seems too far-fetched, all the torture and burnings on the spit."

She's standing beside my chair, her finger wagging over my soup bowl. "The road to hell is paved with stones of doubt, Raymond, and hell is forever."

My stomach growls. "Hell" is one word that makes me sweat. Hell is a big subject at St. Jerome's. Sometimes I dream of the Devil with his horns and pitchfork. He smiles at me and licks his lips. His tail flicks like the tongue of the snake. In the background, the red and yellow flames of eternity.

I get up from the table and hurry my empty bowl to the kitchen sink. "Books were written by people, Ma. That author was probably born two hundred years after St. Agnes got beheaded. Thanks for the soup. I'm going back upstairs."

I try to pass through to the dining room, but she traps me in a hug. "I miss you when you're away at school, Raymond. Your father and I are not close, but at least I know you're heeding God's call."

I pull away and take the stairs two at a time. In my room, I flop on the bed. Heeding God's call. I guess if I were really heeding it, I would phone Melon, ask how he's healing, and apologize, but I can't bring myself to call him. Some stubborn part of me isn't ready to take the blame. I decide to face him back at school regardless of the outcome.

11

I'M GLAD TO FINALLY LEAVE HOME and get back to St. Jerome's, where it's time to face the music. Time to face Melon.

I find him in his room as he unpacks his suitcase and stuffs underwear into a dresser drawer. I knock on the open door. "Sheetsy, I'd ask you in to my abode, but you know the rules." He grins big and walks into the corridor and reaches up and pinches my cheek with his left hand. His right arm, in a cast, rests in a brown sling.

"Look, Melon, I'm—"

"Sheetsy, stop blubbering. You turned me into a wounded soldier, and I need you to sign my cast. Also need you to do any written homework for me due to my inability to write."

"Damn it, Melon, I'm sorry I busted your arm."

"Raymond, Raymond, my good friend St. Raymond. I messed up your track meet. Maybe I had it coming." He gives me a light, smiling punch on my shoulder with his good hand. "Actually, don't worry about the homework." Melon wiggles his fingers out the end of the cast. "I think my little pinkies can hold a pen."

The smile draws me in every time. For all Melon's devious faults, it's hard to hate the guy. I toss my suitcase into my room and don't bother to unpack. It stays packed for two weeks. It's still packed on the night of the great disturbance.

On Tuesday at midnight, I've been awake for hours, with my usual obsessions over Alice, Iron Jack, and the blonde. My thoughts get interrupted by a yell from Melon's room: "Whoa, what the heck! Melon's voice followed by a squeaky female voice: "Melon, we thought this was Raymond's room."

Sweet, sweet Jesus. Alice Derry. I gave her Melon's room number. Then I hear the Cat. "I'll see you in the morning, Mr. Chantelope." I hold my breath. Melon's door closes. The Cat's footsteps pad off into the night. Melon's getting the boot for sure. Maybe he'll implicate me. I get back into bed, pull the covers over my head. Retreat into the safety of darkness.

If I get the boot, I may as well not even go home. My ma will come apart at the seams. My old man will laugh in his scotch. I might have to call Donnie or Tool. Figure out where to hide until Tool can gently break the news to Ma. I toss and turn well until well past midnight.

During study hall the next morning, I try to work a trigonometry problem. Sine, cosine. I can't concentrate. Nothing makes sense. Half hour into study hall, the swinging door at the front of the room flies open, and the Cat makes his appearance. He looks directly at me, and my blood freezes. But he walks down the aisle toward Melon's desk. He taps Melon on the shoulder. "Come with me, son."

The study hall is hushed in a deathly stillness. Seminarians poised with pens and pencils; no one writes. We all stare at the Cat and Melon. Melon stands. Red-faced, with a sheepish grin, he turns, raises his cast, gives a little finger wave, and follows the Cat out of study hall. That's how they do it here. That's how you get the boot. Summoned out of study hall by the Cat. No good-byes. Get the boot, and you cease to exist, gone, disappeared and never to be thought of again.

I hold my breath, knowing the Cat will pounce on me next. I'm sure Melon's going to spill the story of Alice Derry. In a daze, I stare at the study hall door, expect it to swing open any moment. In my addled brain, I think some more about getting the boot. I could hitchhike to

Los Angeles. My old man's brother lives in Anaheim. Maybe I could hide out there. Or maybe I could duck out at Alice's. Her parents never seem to be home. This is her fault. She owes me.

Eventually, the bell sounds for the end of study period. No Cat. I'm still here. Safe in the protected world of St. Jerome's, but the rest of the day, an empty space just off my right shoulder—a vacuum—follows me around like a shadow. No more Melon. Only an emptiness that keeps me off balance, like I'm walking around with one shoe on.

I broke Melon's arm, and now I'm responsible for him getting the boot. I try not to think about it. In fact, I refuse to think about it, but the more I push down the thoughts, the stronger they become. I lied to Alice about the room number. If I hadn't it would be me getting the boot. I'm a lying coward, full of enough anger to hurt a fellow seminarian.

Throughout the day, whispered rumors buzz and circulate like the thrum of honeybees. "Melon and some girls on the corridor."

"Sheets, what do you think happened?" The sun has dropped behind the hills; I walk with Lankin and Georgie Thurmond in the still evening air.

We stop on the small footbridge that crosses the creek between the main campus and the playing fields. I lean against the wooden bridge rail and study a trickle of water as it threads its way through the rocks. "I don't know, Lankin. I don't know what happened."

After evening prayers, the student body floats across the courtyard in collective shadow. The Grand Silence. Without Melon, the silence is more profound, and I notice a homesickness like I experienced the first year in this place. No Melon to distract me with his wisecracks and silly grin. No Melon to lift my mood the way he did that first year.

I regress into a gut-wrenching homesickness. I long for the strength in my father's callused hands. I want to see his fingers folded into a tight fist of anger. I want to hear him swear and pound the dinner table. In my room, I kick off my shoes and send them skittering under the bed. I drop to the floor and do push-ups, and with every dip of my chest, I seethe with blood pumping in my arms. I'm raging. Alice Derry. Melon gets the boot. Iron Jack lies. Lucas Foyt dies.

Push-ups don't help much, but I continue to do them every night, and each night I add ten more repetitions. I'm up to five sets of ten repetitions before the day I storm into Iron Jack's room all keyed up and angry. I pound on his door during the time between study hall and breakfast, when we are supposed to clean our rooms and make beds.

Iron Jack shouts, "Come in before you break down the door." Jack's standing in the middle of the room, wearing black pants and coat, and his Roman collar. He's holding a flyswatter and stares up. "Mr. Sheets, good morning." He must have good peripheral vision to know it's me, because I feel like he's talking to the ceiling.

"Father, I'm responsible for Melon getting kicked out of school, and I want to know about New Year's Eve."

"Be right with you, Mr. Sheets. Right now, I'm a mighty hunter stalking a fly." He smacks the swatter high up on the bookcase, and the little black fly somersaults to the carpet. Iron Jack retrieves the remains with a piece of paper and tosses the paper and the fly into the wastebasket, then drops into a swivel chair behind his desk. "Please sit down."

"I don't want to sit down, Father. I want to know about the blonde on New Year's Eve."

"Mr. Sheets, are you threatening me? Look at your hands."

I stare down at my clenched fists held waist high. "No, I'm not threatening you; I'm just mad."

"The chair, Mr. Sheets. Take some deep breaths."

I slump into the soft high-backed chair, try to calm myself. Iron Jack leans forward, his elbows on the desk. "I will be getting married later this summer, and the woman you refer to as 'the blonde' has a name. It's Kathleen Harris, and she practices nursing at the VA hospital in Palo Alto."

"But what about your promise to God?"

"It was a heroic promise—perhaps too heroic. Mr. Sheets, I've learned heroes take journeys; the purpose of these journeys is to find out what we are made of, who we really are. Eventually, these journeys lead us home."

"So your *home* is Kathleen Harris and not God?"

"I detect understandable sarcasm. I have not abandoned God or my promise to God. After many, many long months of red tape and letters of permission from Rome, I have been accepted as a candidate for the priesthood in the Episcopal Church. The Episcopal Church allows priests to marry, so I will still be doing God's work."

"So you're giving up your Catholic faith?"

"Faith is in the heart, Mr. Sheets. It's what you believe in your gut. Faith doesn't need some religious name tag. Now what is it you wanted to say about Mr. Chantelope, or Melon as you call him?"

I unravel the story of Alice Derry, how she asked for my room number and I gave her Melon's. I feel Iron Jack as he studies me. Every once in a while, he gives a tiny nod of reassurance. I tell him about the dream of Alice and the crescent wrench, how she says, "I can fix you, Raymond Sheets."

"Ah, symbolism," Iron Jack says, "Remember symbolism. Maybe she can show you the way to thread love and gentle softness into your heart."

"What do you mean by 'thread,' Father?"

"Disregard the word, Mr. Sheets. Substitute 'infuse' if you wish. I'm only thinking out loud. Explore the dream on your own. Think of symbolism and possibilities. How about we look at Melon?"

"Melon's a knucklehead, Father. He makes me laugh, but he brings me trouble."

"Let's concentrate on the laughter, Mr. Sheets. I believe there's a trickster, a joker, a knucklehead named Melon in all of us. Sometimes we need to call on that knucklehead to get us out of taking ourselves too seriously."

"You think I need to act like Melon?"

"Once in a while, in medias res, yes, we all need to act like Melon. Not a constant Melon though. Too much of it is where the trouble comes in. Balance, Mr. Sheets, everything in balance."

"Balance." The word moves softly across the room. "I'm out of balance, Father."

"Mr. Sheets?"

"My sister. My sister's dead, Father. What kind of God takes away my sister?" Tears begin to flood my eyes. With clenched fists, I catch my breath. "Damn it, what kind of God is that?"

Jack remains silent. I brush at the tears with the back of my hand.

"I knew about your sister. I thought it strange we never discussed her death in detail."

"I tried to push it away. We're not supposed to dwell on what happens back home. My sister's death is part of my home life. Even at home, we never talked about it. It's like she just disappeared."

"Mr. Sheets, your sister's death is a part of you. Don't suppress those feelings about your sister, or about Lucas Foyt for that matter. You have a right to those feelings, and don't let anybody tell you different."

"I'm mad at God, Father." The tears stream. "I'm mad at God, and I can't stand to cry."

"Tears release tension. It's a passing storm. Sit where you are until the storm stops, Mr. Sheets."

"Damn it, Father, I never cry." My fists are clenched, and the tears subside. "I want to punch God."

"Be angry at God. I think God might welcome a little fistfight."

"I thought anger's a sin."

"Anger is a feeling, not a sin. What does your God look like?"

"He's not just my God, He's everybody's God." The tears have stopped; my breath calms.

"Well then, what does everybody's God look like?"

"I don't know…He just looks like God…sits on His throne in the sky…long beard and a big stick in His hand. Why are you asking me this?"

"What if God is not a person, Mr. Sheets; what if God is all spirit? What if another name for God is love?"

"I don't understand you, Father. Your questions make me dizzy."

"The love you feel for your sister—maybe this love is God."

"Father, you sound like a heretic. Maybe you've been taking in too much of this Jung guy."

"Believe me, I'm no heretic. I'm only raising questions, looking at possibilities. And, yes, I do find Jung helpful."

"I don't feel right, questioning God."

"Perhaps God begs to be questioned. If God is a man, maybe He's sick and tired of being thought of as a bearded angry old guy with a stick."

"I don't know…"

"It's a journey, Mr. Sheets. Question everything. Answers will come. Sometimes it takes years. The important thing is to keep listening. Keep searching."

After the last bell of evening, in the darkness of my room, for the first time in weeks, my thoughts become as clear as the lights in the valley far below. My sister. Alice Derry. The tapered, long-flowing beauty of women. The spirit of God. I breathe easy into sleep.

The spring days of classroom and sports unfurl, and the nights of silence move quickly in these last few weeks of school. On the third Thursday in May, Uncle Tool comes to visit St. Jerome's.

He eats lunch in the refectory, sits up at the priests' table. A visitor always means the rule of silence lifts. The lunch chatter is loud today, as if the student body already tastes the excitement of three months of freedom and the heat of summer vacation.

After lunch, I wait for Uncle Tool to make his exit from the refectory. Tool places one hand on my shoulder as we walk the brick hallway that runs along the stucco arches of the porticoes. We walk together out the door and down the steps where sunlight swaths the cedar trees.

As we walk down the long drive, we talk about my mother and father and home. We approach the berry patch where the tangled bushes now sprout white-petal blooms. We stop to look at swarms of golden-brown honeybees lifting yellow specks of pollen from the flowers. I'm remembering Alice and the touch of a berry on my tongue when Tool stuns me.

"I'm leaving the priesthood and taking a job as a social worker in Seattle."

"You're what?"

"I'm quitting, Raymond. Your brother agreed to take over payments on my car. The car's in great shape. It'll be a good deal for Donnie."

I stare at the bees in silence. I can hear the sizzle of their wings. "Why are you quitting? Aren't you supposed to be a priest forever?"

"Look, this isn't easy. It was a big decision." Tool has his hands on his hips. I study his face above the Roman collar. His hair slicked back like a rock star.

"Is it a woman?"

Tool smiles. "Sort of. Not a particular woman, just women in general. Like you, I went into the seminary after eighth grade. As you know, the seminary's a pretty protective place. After twelve years, I'm a priest out in the world, and here's all these women prettier than angels."

"So it's the celibacy thing?"

"Partly, but the other part is that women make up half of humanity, and the church treats them like second-class citizens." We retrace our steps up the drive toward the school.

"What do you mean by that?"

"This is tough, Raymond. You're my nephew in a seminary, and I'm knocking the church."

"Tool, Father Castaic is my confessor, and he told me to question everything. So I'm asking how do you think the church mistreats women?"

"Did you ever see a woman on the altar serving Mass? Women can't be priests. The church is stuck back in the dark ages. What do you think Castaic would say about that?"

"I don't know what he'd say. We call him Iron Jack, and he's leaving the church too."

"What?"

I'm thinking, *What is with these priests who can't keep a commitment?* My anger rises. I feel betrayed. "I said he's leaving the church. He's gonna become an Episcopal priest."

"When did you find this out?"

"About three weeks ago." I spit this out in exasperation.

"Sorry to hit you with my news on top of it."

We near the buildings, and guys are gathered around Tool's blue Ford. Two guys push on the rear bumper, bouncing the car up and down. "Hey, Father, the shocks on this heap are a little spongy!"

Tool smiles and shouts, "Hey, you break it, you buy it!"

One of the guys calls out, "Can't afford it, Father, we're taking the vow of poverty!"

Tool gives the guys a dismissive wave and turns to me. We stand at the base of the main steps. I don't know if Tool knows it or not, but the guys from San Francisco refer to him as Uncle Hot Rod. "I hope I haven't discouraged you. You look a little disheartened."

"Yeah, no big deal. Iron Jack says I got to keep searching. Keep asking questions. What's my mom say about you quitting?"

"Your mom's a pretty serious lady. Took it kind of hard, but she'll manage, I'm sure." Tool extends his hand, and we shake.

"My dad's probably laughing in his scotch."

Tool laughs loudly and says, "I don't doubt it." He looks over at the Ford, sees the guys have wandered off. "Iron Jack sounds like quite a guy."

"He's okay. Kind of talks in riddles."

"Riddles need answers. Keep searching, Raymond. This car belongs to Donnie as of next week. I'll see you soon."

The blue Ford disappears down the main drive. With Melon gone, Tool leaving, and Iron Jack about to disappear, my chest heaves with loneliness.

In the heated days of spring, I run barefoot and angry. New shoots of grass bend under the fury of my footfall. Anger displaces loneliness. I feel I could run forever.

On the last day of the school year, the Cat approaches me as I walk through the porticoes toward the refectory. "Mr. Sheets, please report to Father Barrington's office after breakfast."

This can't be good. The Cat drops the orders on me and struts away, his white socks flashing beneath the hem of his cassock. I'm stunned. The hairs on the back of my neck bristle. Nobody gets summoned to Father Chuck's office on the last day before summer vacation unless they're getting the boot.

The boot. The refectory vibrates with din of silverware and loud voices anticipating the start of three months of freedom. I feel sullen and withdrawn. I stare at my tablemates as if they were strangers.

"Sheets, can I have your bacon? You hardly touched it." I fork the crisp strips over to Georgie Thurmond. "I was just joking. You sick or something?"

"The Cat told me to report to Chuck's office after breakfast."

Georgie lays down his fork, eyes me like I'm suddenly radioactive. "The boot? What did you do?"

"Nothing that I know of."

After the morning meal, I cross the quad, enter the building through the door near the bell tower, and push the button that summons the rickety elevator with the black accordion steel door. The elevator shudders and rattles and smells of old wood and machine oil as the antiquated cables and pulleys cart me up to the second floor of the administration wing.

In the silent corridor, I knock on the door of the vice president's office. Seconds tick away before Chuck opens the door. "Come in, Mr. Sheets."

He ushers me into an anteroom. Father Van Camp, the president of the seminary, sits in a high-backed chair. "Sit down, Mr. Sheets." Father Van Camp rests his porky hands in his lap. Chuck plants himself down in a third chair.

We call Father Van Camp "Beansy." Except for meals, we seldom see Beansy around the campus. To me, he has always seemed like a short, pudgy, ineffectual mystery with vacant brown eyes behind his gold-rimmed glasses.

Beansy supposedly runs the place, but Chuck provides the muscle. I mean rugged oak-tree muscle. A stern man with stiff, curly hair the color of gnarly gray bark and a rip-rap voice like the growling churn of a cement mixer.

I catch myself gritting my teeth under the stare of these two men in their black cassocks and brittle white Roman collars. Chuck has his right leg crossed over his left knee. A crucified Jesus with His chin to His chest and His crown of thorns looks lonely on the tinted-yellow walls.

Beansy breaks the silence. "Mr. Sheets, we've summoned you because we've discovered some hindrances to your vocation."

"Hindrances, Father?"

"You've broken some rules, Mr. Sheets," Chuck snaps.

"As you know, we randomly censor incoming and outgoing mail," Beansy chimes in. "Did you or did you not mention a young lady in a letter to your brother?"

"Yes, Father, I might have mentioned a girl, but what rule did I break?"

Both men ignore my question. I notice a tight-lipped, surly grimace on Chuck's steely face. "Rumor has it that earlier in the academic year, you were seen riding on the back of a motor machine, and a young lady was at the controls."

"The machine was a BSA motorcycle, Father." I feel my anger rising. "The name of the girl is Alice Derry." My eyes well up with rage. "Why don't you just tell me I'm getting the boot?" I stand up and lean into Chuck's face. "Damn it, just say it, and I'll be out of here!"

Beansy leaps to his feet while Chuck holds my glare. I feel my father's righteous anger. Beansy has a hand on my arm. "Calm down, son, that's enough. We do feel that you belong back out in the world. Perhaps you're not priest material. We've tried to contact your parents but have not been able to reach them. Tell them to call me with any questions."

"You're right! It is enough! And leave my parents out of this. I'll tell them when I'm good and ready." I head out the door, slamming it behind me.

12

Back in my room, I pack my suitcase. I hear the roar of glass-pack mufflers through the open window. I look out and see my brother, Donnie, amusing some of my fellow students as he revs the tailpipes on the two-tone blue Ford that used to belong to Tool.

Within minutes, Donnie stands in the doorway of my room. With his slick hair, jeans, and olive-colored Hawaiian shirt with white palm trees, he looks like a casual film star. I sit on my suitcase and try to press it closed.

"Didn't know you owned so many clothes, little brother. We gonna take the bureau?"

I snap the hasps shut and stand. "Nah. Leave it for some guy next year. We don't need it at home, and I won't be back."

"Get off it. You're Ma's ticket to heaven. You'll be back."

I take a long look out my window at the familiar cedar trees, and beyond the trees to the haze that hovers over the houses and the air station far across the valley. "I'm done with it, Donnie. I'm nobody's ticket, especially not Ma." I can't bring myself to tell Donnie I got the boot.

Donnie picks up my suitcase. "You'll lose the bet to the old man."

Out in the corridor, closing doors, voices, the echoes of footsteps. "He'll let me work it off digging ditches."

Donnie puts his free hand on my shoulder. "I'd rather stay another year than dig ditches."

"No booze, no girls, big brother. You wouldn't last a day here."

"Booze, okay, but girls, that's a tough one. Maybe the ditches aren't so bad."

We walk down the flight of stairs, and I tell Donnie to go ahead to the car because I've got to stop and see someone.

I knock on Iron Jack's door. "Enter."

I turn the handle and push the door. Inside, Iron Jack is wearing glasses as he sharpens a pencil with a penknife. "Mr. Sheets, the end of another year."

I put out my hand. "I won't be back, Father, as I'm sure you know, so I wanted to say good-bye. Besides, I know you won't be back either."

"If it's any consolation, I was the only one at the faculty meeting who voted not to expel you."

"I appreciate that, Father."

Jack looks me in the eye as we shake hands. "The journey is about balance, becoming who you were meant to be. Watch for pitfalls and jokers, Mr. Sheets."

"Thanks, Father, I will." The guy and his damn riddles. I turn quickly and close the door. I've never been comfortable with good-byes.

Out on the drive, I shake hands with classmates. So far, St. Jerome's rumor mill hasn't spread the news that I got the boot. I settle in the passenger side of the Ford, and Donnie turns on the ignition to the car's throaty roar. The Coasters croon "Charlie Brown" on the radio. We pass the berry patch where my life started to change. "Need to make a stop, Donnie. Down the street, the house with the roses."

Donnie waits in the car while I go up the entry walk and knock. Alice answers the door. She wears white Ben Davis carpenter overalls. The canvas fabric is cut deep along the sides, and I see the top of Alice's bare leg. I have the feeling she has nothing on underneath. "Raymond Sheets!" She drapes her arms over my shoulders and pulls me into the house.

I reach back and close the door. "Look, Alice, we've got to talk."

She let's go of me and pulls back, closes her eyes. "I know. I know. I got Melon kicked out. It's my fault, but he came by to see me and told me it's okay."

The curtains are drawn. The house all shadows. "He came by? When?"

"About two weeks ago. He had a camera and said he was going to sneak up to the school and take some pictures of the grounds."

Alice tugs at the brass button that holds up the suspender of her overalls. "I told him I was sorry, but he just smiled and said, 'No big deal; it was meant to be.'"

I tell Alice I won't be back in the fall. Right now, I'm through with the seminary.

"That's good, Raymond Sheets, because I want to show you something." Alice pops loose both shoulder straps of the Ben Davis overalls. She drops the front flap. I stare at her breasts. They're smaller than I imagined. "Do you like them?" She asks so matter-of-factly, like she was asking if I like jelly beans or chocolate cake.

"Of course I like them, Alice, but aren't you afraid your mom or dad's gonna walk in?"

She ignores my question. "Want to see more of me?"

Outside, Donnie blasts the horn. "Look, Alice, I have to leave, and—"

"Melon saw all of me. He took some pictures."

"He what? He took some pictures of you naked?" Donnie hits the horn again. I open the front door and yell, "In a minute! Just give me a minute!"

I close the door and turn toward Alice. She steps out of the Ben Davis pant legs. "Shit, Alice, get your clothes on." She stands with her hands on her hips wearing nothing but a downy V-patch of pubic hair. "You should never let Melon take pictures of you. Get your damn clothes on."

"He said he was going to use them to do sketches from. It's just the human body, Raymond Sheets. Lots of people go naked on the beach in Hawaii. Hug me, Raymond Sheets, I don't know why you're—"

"Sketches?" She's tight against me. My arms envelope her back. I talk into her hair. "You believe that, Alice? Melon means trouble. Melon's a—"

Someone knocks at the front door. We both jump. Alice breaks away, picks up the overalls, and hustles to the back of the house. I open the door a little and use my body to block the entry.

Donnie puts his hand on the door. "Come on, Ray, I got to get back to the city."

"Just a couple more minutes—"

Before I finish the sentence, Alice is back tugging at the door. "Hi, I'm Alice." I'm relieved she has her overalls on.

"Alice, this is my brother, Donnie."

"Your brother? You guys don't look anything alike. That your car?"

"Mostly the bank's. Used to belong to my uncle. Now I make payments." Donnie's inquiring eyes shift back and forth between me and Alice in her low-cut overalls.

I step out the door and onto the tiny porch. "Have to go, Alice. Donnie's got to get back to the city."

She's framed by the doorway and looks innocent in her white Ben Davises.

The roses flanking the entry walk are in full bloom. A spring breeze kicks up, and petals fall. I reach for her. She finds my lips. Finds my tongue. "Do I taste better than berries, Raymond Sheets?"

"Much better, even better than litmus paper." I nuzzle into her ear. "And I lied, I do dream."

"I know you do." We unwrap ourselves from one another. "Litmus paper?"

I smile and tell her it's nothing. "Keep working on your tan. I'll be back." I walk toward the car.

"I'll make sure I'm tan all over, Raymond Sheets."

In the car, Donnie turns the key and guns the engine. Alice has her hand raised, and I wave to her as the tires spit gravel and screech as they grab pavement. "So, what's the story, little brother?"

"What story?"

The radio thumps out a bass beat. Donnie turns it off and closes the windows. He leans forward and stares at me. "A little piece in overalls has the hots for you and you say, 'What story?'"

So, I tell my brother everything. The berry patch. New Year's Eve, Lucas Foyt. I tell him about Melon and Iron Jack. I tell him about my doubts and fears, and it feels good to unload. I hesitate telling him about Alice and the overalls. I've talked for over a half an hour, and Donnie hasn't said a word until we cross the causeway that skirts the edge of the bay.

"That's the new stadium. That's Candlestick Park."

I've bared my soul, and my brother's talking about a ballpark. "Donnie, you been listening to me?"

"Haven't missed a word. Just trying to lighten it up a little. So, how was the good-bye?"

"I'll mostly miss the bells."

"The bells? I'm talking about leaving the hussy, not the school."

"She had nothing on underneath the overalls, and she dropped them in front of me."

Donnie hoots and hollers, stamps his foot; one fist thumps against the headliner. "All my youth," he yells, "I been trying to get into panties, and my goofy brother, the seminarian, has this chick drop trou right in front of him, and he misses the goddamned bells!"

I bat my brother's arm down from the headliner. "Knock it off, Donnie!"

"Sorry, Ray, sorry, sorry, sorry, but this is outrageous!" Donnie quiets down. "So, what is it you miss about the bells?"

"I miss not having to think. The bells telling me what to do next."

Traffic slows around Silver Avenue. "Welcome to the world, little brother. We're orphans, and you got to learn to be autonomous."

"Orphans? We got a mother and a father."

"I got news for you. Your father's concerned about W. M. Sheets Mechanical, and your mother's too wrapped up in religion. She's got her head in the clouds, and you're about to break her heart."

"I'm not responsible for her heart."

We inch down Franklin Street into the bowels of the city. "Now you're talking, little brother. You're only responsible for yourself." Donnie shakes his head and smiles, and his smile reminds me of Iron Jack's *trickster, joker, knucklehead.*

"Damn, a chick strips right in front of my little brother, and all he misses are the bells."

I smile. "Donnie, where'd you learn a word like 'autonomous'?"

Donnie pounds my shoulder. "I've evolved. I belong to an exclusive literary society."

I reach over and lay on the horn. "And you're also full of shit."

The traffic moves in a rhythm between stoplights, and two orphan knuckleheads motor along Oak Street, shouting and laughing, looking for home.

Home. St. Francis Wood. Some of the most upscale houses in San Francisco. Donnie parks the Ford in the driveway. Leathery green leaves of tall rhododendrons in multicolored bloom in front of the house. Pinks, whites, and reds.

Prime real estate. W. M. Sheets Mechanical, second generation, must be doing all right. My grandfather started the business with "a pickup truck and a shovel," as he used to say. My father propelled it into the large commercial corporation that exists today.

The radiant flowers add to the magnificence of the house. Still behind the wheel, Donnie has his door open. "I wouldn't mention anything about quitting the seminary. Ma's already a bit touchy with her brother ducking out of the priesthood."

I continue my façade, refusing to let on I got the boot. "Tool caught me off guard with that one. Says it's mostly about women. Think he has a girlfriend?"

A light breeze nudges the rhododendrons and cools the inside of the car. Donnie slams the door shut. "Tool's full Italian. Most Italian guys wake up in the morning and can't zip up their pants till noon. I'm only half Italian, and I got my own problems."

"Yeah, I bet you're a stallion. Seriously, do you think there's a woman?"

"How the heck would I know? Do I look like an encyclopedia? I do know my little brother, the squeaky-clean seminarian, has been doing a little diddling on his own. Now outta my car, I got some important business to attend to."

I stand on the driveway and lean in the open door. Donnie has the glass-packs rumbling. "Wait a minute till I get my suitcase."

"Hurry up and grab your baggage, and remember, not a word about quitting."

"What, is she gonna self-destruct if I tell her? I will keep it from the old man though. If he finds out, he'll be hounding me for his hundred dollars."

Donnie revs the engine. "Like he needs it." He backs out into the street as I lug my suitcase to the front door.

Inside, heavy curtains block the light outside. The house lies in shadows like a shrouded basilica during Lent. "Ma, I'm home."

She comes down the hallway. I set my suitcase on the deep marble shine of the entryway. She hugs me too tight; her breasts flatten against me, and I want to pull away.

"Raymond, I'm so glad you're here." She unfastens herself and steps back. "Uncle Tool is leaving the priesthood." She wears a blue apron covered with a floral design of tiny darker-blue flowers. She looks haggard and unkempt, like she hasn't slept in a while.

"I know, Ma. he came down to see me."

"He came to see you? He didn't try to influence you, did he? He didn't try to talk you out of your vocation?"

"Easy, Ma, I have my own mind. Besides, Tool's not like that." For the first time, I notice strands of gray in my mother's hair.

"It's North Beach. The nightclubs. He hasn't been himself lately. Maybe if he got reassigned to another parish, away from all those beatniks and topless bars, he'd come to his senses."

Ma follows me down the hall to the kitchen. "Maybe he *has* come to his senses." I lift the lid off a deep saucepan simmering on the stove. Tomato bubbles gurgle up slow like little explosions on Mars. "Ma, this smells great." I dip the tip of a large stirring spoon and sample the sauce. My tongue comes alive to the savory taste of garlic, tomato, and a hint of zinfandel. "Woo, home cooking! What say we slice some French bread and soak up a little of this sauce?"

"Raymond, what do you mean 'maybe he has come to his senses'? And that sauce is for your father's dinner. You leave it be. I want to hear everything your uncle told you."

"Only thing he said was, 'I'm quitting, and the car goes to Donnie.' Maybe he figured out being a priest wasn't for him." I rush onward, my words spilling out even before I can think. "I don't even know if it's for me. And why is it always 'my father's dinner'? Aren't the rest of us going to eat?"

I head back to the entry and pick up my suitcase.

Her voice echoes after me: "Raymond, your father works hard for us, and what do you mean you don't know if it's for you?" She marches up to me and latches onto the arm holding the suitcase.

"Just what I said, I may be quitting the seminary. And just because he works hard doesn't make him some grand pooh-bah who rules over the spaghetti sauce."

"Raymond, you're going to be a priest. You're my hope. Don't let me down with talk like that."

I pull her away from her hand. The suitcase makes a metallic clack as I defiantly smack it down on the foyer marble. "Ma, I got to make my own decisions!"

She suddenly looks old and pathetic as she wrings her hands and stares at the floor. "You're all I've got, Raymond. The only one I can talk to." She looks up at me, pleading.

"What do you mean? You've got Dad to talk to."

"Since your sister died, he sits in his chair with his scotch and stares at the TV. Maybe if I was on television, your father would listen to me."

I pick up the suitcase and march toward the stairs. "I know, Ma. Anne was his favorite, but she's gone, and Pop has to get over it. We all do. I miss my sister too."

I'm halfway up the stairs when she calls out at a hysterical pitch, "First my brother, and now my son abandons me."

"I won't abandon you," I yell over my shoulder. "We'll talk about this later."

In the upstairs hallway, I open the door to Annie's room. Twelve sets of lifeless eyes, smaller than rosary beads, stare at me from behind the glass door of a case on the wall. Her miniature doll collection.

Sunlight spills through a window and bathes a section of hardwood floor. A black-and-white poster of a ballerina on tiptoe above a white headboard. Tufted pink bedspread, flawlessly smooth. An alarming silence roams the room like a bully. I back out and close the door.

A telephone extension rests in a niche along the heavily troweled white stucco walls of the hallway. The hall seems narrow and tight, after the expansive corridors of St. Jerome's. On a whim, I set down the suitcase and dial Melon's home number. He picks up on second ring. "City zoo, Mr. Fox."

Melon. Always the clown. I scale my voice low in my throat: "And this is Charlie Barrington, begging you to return to St. Jerome's. Giving you the boot was a big mistake. Please come back."

"Sheetsy, buddy! For once in your life, you sound a little jovial. How's my favorite seminarian? You know, you could get the boot for just talking to me. I'm no longer supposed to exist."

"I'm no longer a seminarian. I got the boot too."

"St. Raymond got the boot? I'm stunned. What happened?"

"They censored one of my letters to Donnie about Alice. Word got around I was on the back of her motorcycle."

"I never said a word."

"I know you didn't. You know how rumors go."

"You tell your ma? She's already shook up about Uncle Tool."

"How'd you know about that?"

"Hey, the Melon keeps his ear to the ground. Besides, your hot rod brother gave me a ride to school one morning."

"Where you going to school?"

"St. Ignatius. My old man is an alum, and he pulled some strings. They don't quite know what to do with me, coming this late in the semester. Enough about me. Sounds like little Jesus might need some serious counseling from doctor Melon. Come on by later, and we'll watch *Roller Derby*. Ann Calvello, Joanie Weston. Skating maniacs for the *Bay Bombers*, good Catholic girls with big knockers."

"Speaking of knockers, you took some pictures of Alice."

"Word gets around when Melon's on the prowl."

"Nobody's going to develop pictures of a naked girl. You need to give me the film."

"Welcome to the twentieth century, Sir Galahad. There is no film, they're *Polaroids*. And when did you become the little minx's moral protector? For a nominal fee, I'll let you have a peep."

"Melon, you're an asshole. I'll be over after dinner." I hang up the phone before he makes another wisecrack.

I enter the room I share with Donnie, which is a few steps down the hall. I toss my suitcase onto the bed. Looming over it is a large black-and-white poster of Roger Bannister breaking the four-minute mile.

Three framed pictures of the blue-and-white Ford hang on the wall above the bed on Donnie's side of the room. Three different shots of the car: front, rear, and sideview. The sideview shows Tool behind the wheel, thick black hair, sunglasses, white T-shirt, and tan arm waving at the camera. The picture is signed in black ink in the lower right corner. "Take good care of my baby. Uncle Tool."

I am cramming my clothes into the top drawer of my bureau when I hear my father downstairs. His voice fills the house like the deep-throated organ pipes in the chapel at St. Jerome's. "Do I smell my favorite pasta sauce?" he blares way too happily. He either drank too much, or Sheets Mechanical was low bidder on some big job.

My second guess is on the money. Besides, my old man was never a happy drunk. "Elana, break out the champagne," I hear him bellow as I run downstairs. "We won bids for all the mechanical work on both the new intermediate school and the new high school going up in South San Francisco."

In the kitchen, he wraps his arms around my mother's waist. My six-foot-four father has my mother lifted up toward the ceiling. My mom shrieks, "Walter, put me down. I'm happy for you, but I'm not in the mood for craziness."

My father loses his smile, sets my mother down. She sure knows how to dampen a mood. For once, it's good to see my dad not cussing "God, the Asshole," who got my sister killed.

"Pop, congratulations."

My father turns, and his face lights up again. His eyes glisten like he drank one or two scotches before he left the office. "Look who's home." He takes my hand. "A little soft, sonny boy. Monday, you go to work. We got to get some calluses on those hands." Then the strangest thing, he lets go of my hand and wraps his arms around me and actually kisses the top of my head. He's usually reluctant to even give me the time of day. His kiss nearly brings me to tears.

Donnie arrives in time for dinner, and the mood at the table resonates festivity. We raise our glasses of Zinfandel, we toast the team of estimators at Sheets Mechanical, we try to elevate my mother's mood by toasting her as reigning queen of spaghetti sauces, and we toast everything short of God and America. With the exception of Mom's sad eyes, we're one happy family. Then all hell breaks loose.

It starts slowly when my father answers a phone call on the third ring. He goes into the kitchen, just off the dining room. "Well, if it isn't the spoiled priest…kind of ran out on your commitments." My father's loud, happy voice rapidly turns to sarcasm. "Yeah, well, now that you finally got some smarts, maybe I can put my seminarian son on the phone and you can talk him into getting his head screwed on right…" My mother lays down her fork and grips the edge of the table. "Walter, stop!"

"Elana, it's your guitar-plinking communist brother calling from Seattle." He drags the extension cord into the dining room and hands the phone to my mother, who immediately stands and scuttles back into the kitchen.

My father lowers into his chair and twirls his pasta with his fork.

"Pop, it's not Mom's fault her brother is a communist." Donnie smiles. "Why don't you ease up a bit?"

"Watch it, pretty boy. Your mother's beside herself because her brother left the priesthood; her nerves are on edge, and I got to live with the woman."

"Donnie's only trying to lighten it up, Pop. If she's got bad nerves, treat her gentle."

My father's jowls are prominent on either side of his scowling mouth. His eyes blaze. "Whoa, little man, you don't even live here most of the time. Come Monday morning, I want you at our job site on Bryant Street at seven o'clock sharp. We're going to toughen up those lily-white hands."

Mother finishes the phone call. As she stands behind her chair, the fingers of her right hand gently touch her lips. She's frail. Deep wrinkle marks under her eyes. Her face, ashen. I want to step in and rescue her, but I remain glued to the chair. "Walter, Raymond has to attend Mass every morning while he's home. He can't get to work by seven."

My old man slams his hand on the table. "Don't start with me, Elana. You push this kid too hard to be a priest. Never mind Mass. You're so wrapped up in church and your holy Jesus books. You have no idea what it takes for me to put food on this table," he bellows. "You and your Mass! The God you worship at your Mass took my daughter from me. Your God is an asshole!"

Donnie slides his chair back from the table, braces for trouble. "Pop, we all lost Anne. Mom lost a daughter too…"

My mother screams, "Raymond, answer me! Do I push you—?"

Before she can finish the sentence, Mom slumps to the floor. Donnie catches her before she hits. I jump up from the table, unsure of what to do. Mom's left arm shakes. She tries to get words out of her slack open mouth, but the words slide out as gibberish. Donnie has landed on his knees with Mom's head cradled in the crook of his arm. He yells, "Ma! Ma! What's the matter?" Donnie flashes me a look of urgency, snaps his head toward the kitchen. "Dial the operator; we need help!"

My voice quivers into the phone as I give the address and ask for an ambulance. I hear my father's moan in the dining room: "Elana, hang on. Don't you dare leave me. I'm sorry. I'm sorry."

I enter the room and lock eyes with Donnie, then look down at Ma. The lids of her open eyes flicker like she's trying to understand. I remember the eyes of our spaniel puppy named Prancy after she got hit by a car. Her eyes flickered just before she died.

My dad takes over down on the floor, one beefy hand under Ma's head. Donnie draws back, stunned. Within minutes, the street outside becomes a blaze of flashing red lights.

First in, the fire department. Helmets and bulky black coats fill the dining room. Next, ambulance attendants. A collapsible gurney snaps up. A clear plastic respirator mask covers Mom's face as attendants wheel her out the door. My old man walks beside her down the front stairs. All this going on, and I'm bent over with my hands on my upper legs like I can't get my breath. I have crazy thoughts like, *Who's going to clean up the dinner dishes?*

I want to yell at a gray-haired couple walking a black Labrador. They stop to watch as the ambulance and fire engines disappear in the distance. I want to reassure them she's going to be all right.

Donnie hustles me to the car.

"We didn't lock the front door." I feel like my words aren't connected to my brain.

Donnie wheels the Ford out of the driveway. "Who the hell cares?"

I press my feet into the floorboard. "God's not the asshole, it's him." Evening fog slips east from the ocean and caresses the eucalyptus trees as we catch up to the ambulance that carries our parents toward the University Medical Center.

13

THE SKYLINERS CROON "SINCE I DON'T Have You" on the radio. The impact of the song hammers me. I'm stirred by a strong sense of guilt that I told Ma I might be quitting the seminary. I tried to get her to leave me alone, and now I want her back. Donnie quickly snaps off the sound as if the words are toxic. "What do you think happened to her?"

"I've got no idea." My eyes are glued to the back of the ambulance as I try to shake off the guilt. We accelerate on Laguna Honda Boulevard as we pass the reservoir.

Donnie looks at me. "Think she'll die?"

"Die! Heck no, she won't die." I've been trying to avoid that thought ever since the medics carted her out. "Don't say 'die.' If she dies, it'll be my fault."

"What the hell are you talking about?"

"I told her I was thinking about leaving the seminary."

Donnie grips the wheel, leans forward, and stares at me. "Have you lost your mind?" He is close to losing his temper. "I thought we talked about that?"

"She had to know sooner or later, damn it! Tool and the old man are as guilty as I am! And what about Anne? Her death had an impact. And besides that, I got kicked out!"

"Okay, take a deep breath." Donnie's back to driving, weaving through traffic. "She's not gonna die, and the old man can be a real jerk—and you got what?"

"Kicked out! The boot! Finito! It's done. Finished. I was holding off telling anybody, but there it is."

"What happened?"

Why I got the boot will seem ridiculous to Donnie. I know he won't believe me. "They censor mail. Spotted a letter to you about Alice. Then someone saw me riding on the back of her motorcycle, and word got around."

"You got the boot over a letter and a motorcycle? That's bullshit. There must be more to it."

"Nope. And don't breathe a word of this. Especially not to Ma."

"I won't, but maybe it will be easier for her to take when she realizes even the priests think her holy little prodigy is not meant for the priesthood."

I hear sarcasm in Donnie's words. I snap at him, "What do you mean?"

"She believes everything the priests say. For her, priests can do no wrong. If a priest says her son Raymond is not fit to be clergy, then it must be so."

We turn right on Judah and slow for traffic where Judah runs into Parnassus. The ambulance sirens ahead, leaves us stuck in traffic. Donnie keeps spouting his theories. "The old man might be right about her being stuck on religion. I mean, she walks around with her head in the clouds. Priests quit. Kids die. Maybe she needs to face reality. Get her feet on the ground."

"Maybe you're right," I tell Donnie. But in reality, I don't think Ma will ever get her feet on the ground.

The ambulance pulls into a huge garage that fronts a big lettered sign that glows red: "Emergency." Donnie slows; we watch the attendants unload our mother, wheel her past automatic glass doors. The old man walks beside the gurney.

UC Medical Center, high on a hill, overlooks Golden Gate Park. I wonder at light beacons flashing in the distance, possibly from the towers on the Golden Gate Bridge. Donnie looks for parking as we circle the block.

We park on Third Avenue near Irving and hike the hill to the Med Center. The receptionist in emergency sits behind a glass enclosure. Donnie bends down to a speaker in the glass. "We're here to see Mrs. Elana Sheets, wheeled in a couple of minutes ago."

"And what is your relationship to the patient?" The girl's jet-black hair cascades and shines. More guilt. My ma's in bad shape, yet I'm deeply attracted to this girl. She looks fit with tight curves.

"We're her sons."

"Please take a seat. I'll check on her status." The girl disappears behind reflections on the glass, and we settle into worn brown chairs with thin chrome armrests. The three rows of chairs around us looking like they came from a 1940s soda fountain.

Two chairs to our left, an olive-skinned woman in a black coat with lots of lint on it tightly holds an infant in a blue blanket. The baby wails, its tiny pink fists knotted up in a frenzy. The mother gives us an apologetic look.

Donnie nods to her. "Sounds like the little fella's in pain."

The woman tucks in her chin, grips the infant a little tighter. A door opens. A nurse with a green surgical cap calls out, "Mrs. Gambezzi!"

The woman with the infant stands and hustles toward the nurse. The woman wears Dutch sandals that clatter against the floor.

The foxy receptionist returns to the glass enclosure. She talks through the voice box to a heavyset Hispanic woman with a five-or six-year-old boy clutching her denim skirt. The kid hides his face in the folds of the skirt and coughs in a deep liquid rasp.

Behind them stands a brawny construction-worker-type. He wears khaki shorts and leans on crutches. The dirty cast on his right leg is covered with red and blue inked signatures.

Donnie sprawls in the chair, legs stretched, hands on stomach, fingers intertwined like he's waiting for a bus. "Busy place. That kid belongs in a TB ward, by the way."

After a few minutes that pass like hours, the surgical cap nurse stands in front of us. Green baggy scrubs, silver stethoscope, clipboard in hand. Her nametag reads "Martha Hanley, RN." Lots of freckles. She glances at the clipboard and eyes Donnie. "Mr. Sheets?"

Donnie straightens up in his chair. "We're both named Sheets."

We follow her out of the waiting area and into the emergency ward. Lots of beds and cubicles separated by white shower curtains strung from runners on the ceiling. She leads us to a gray metal desk. "Dr. Gans will be with you shortly."

I sink into a swivel chair. Donnie half-sits on the desk.

Soon enough, the doctor appears. Tall and wide, Gans is a linebacker in scrubs. Brush-bristle black hair. Flattened nose. "Your mother has had a fairly serious stroke. We have her stabilized, and she's on her way up to ICU. Your father is with her."

Donnie stands, arms folded. "She going to make it?"

"Treatment for a stroke is critical in the first couple of hours. She got here in time, and while she's in serious condition, she should pull out of it. Meanwhile, your father asked me to tell you to hang out in the waiting room, and he'll catch up with you in a while."

I sit in the chair, dwarfed by Gans, who reminds me of Iron Jack towering over me. "Can we see her?"

"Not a good idea right now. We're waiting to get some test results back, and the folks in ICU will probably give her some mild sedatives. You can look in on her a bit later."

Donnie slouches in a waiting room chair while I step out into the cool night air. I use a pay phone outside the glass doors. Melon picks up quickly. "Sheetsy, where the heck are ya? You're missing *Roller Derby*."

"I'm up at UC. My mom had a stroke."

Melon voices real concern. "Geez, Sheetsy, she going to make it?"

"It's serious, but she should make it. I'll catch *Roller Derby* another time."

"Keep me posted."

"I will, and thanks for once not being a smartass."

"My pleasure, little Jesus. Lemme know if you need anything."

Donnie stretches out with his arms folded against his Hawaiian shirt, trying to keep warm. I fold into a chair next to him. It's nine o'clock, and I am tired from the long day that started with the morning wake-up bell at St. Jerome's.

Morning Mass in the chapel, ages ago. My mind turns to Alice Derry and her overalls. Melon and his camera, my mother on a gurney. Meanwhile, sad and disheveled people straggle into emergency and stop at the glass enclosure. The lobby grows busier as the night wears on.

I pick up a month-old *Time* magazine from an adjacent chair. Arnold Palmer is pictured on the cover. He swings a club in a sand trap. Inside, the magazine features photos and stories of nonviolent civil rights protests throughout the South.

By ten o'clock, I nod off, the magazine splayed across my lap. At half past ten, I wake to see our father lumber across the waiting room, the heavy footfall of a large-boned man who could stand to lose some weight. "Let's go home, guys."

Donnie springs from his chair. "What do you mean, 'go home'? How's she doing? Can't we see her?"

"She's sound asleep. Nothing to see. We'll check on her in the morning. Doc says she's gonna make it."

Donnie shoots me a questioning look and shrugs. "Pop, the car's down on Irving Street. I can drive it up the hill."

The old man massages his eyes with thumb and forefinger. "Naw, let's walk. Fresh air might feel good."

We walk at a rapid pace. I wonder if it's too fast for the old man. He often huffs and puffs when he walks, but I reassure myself. This is, after all, a steep downhill. Waves of mist dim the streetlights. "One of these days, your mother and I are going to retire in the desert. This dampness makes my joints ache."

Retirement in the desert. I feel better thinking that at least my pop figures she's going to live.

A silent ride home until we turn into the driveway. I'm in the back seat. My father turns to me. "You go to church like your mother says, sonny boy. Get to work as soon as you can."

"Look, Pop, I might…never mind. Whatever you say, Pop."

The old man looks low on oxygen as he trudges up the stairs, a monumental effort to summit the front porch. Donnie pulls a canvas car cover out of the trunk of the Ford. "I'm almost more worried about him."

I hold one end of the cover and pull it down over the front bumper. "Me too. His breathing sounds labored."

In the house, the old man rests in a brown recliner in the living room. I help Donnie clean the mess from dinner. Spaghetti dishes. Salad bowls. Silverware. I have rinsed red sauce off the last dish when the old man calls out: "How about somebody pouring me a drink."

I dry my hands, pour two fingers of Cutty Sark in a water glass, and bring it to him.

"That's an awful big glass, sonny boy." He wears a smirk like he's laughing at some inner joke.

"Got it, Pop." I carry the bottle from the kitchen and add a healthy dose of scotch to his glass.

By the time Donnie and I finish the cleanup and stow away the china, the old man is asleep, his mouth open and his head tilted against the back rest. The empty water glass sits on the floor beside the chair. Donnie finds a heavy blanket from a linen closet. The centerpiece of the blanket sports a large textured image of a gray elephant. Above the elephant's head, a halo of little red hearts. Donnie covers the old man, who by now expels a soft wheezing snore, the noise gentle and regular like the hiss of surf across the sand.

Upstairs in our room, once I'm in bed, I start talking into the darkness. "You think she's gonna be okay?"

"I think so, but maybe we should have gone in to see her just in case," he grumbles.

"I gotta feeling she'll be fine." I say this to reassure myself, but I feel anxious thinking about Ma. Instead, I try concentrating on the receptionist at the hospital. The way her long, dark hair cascaded over her shoulder. Her sharp profile. The way her breasts pushed at her sweater. "Donnie, when did you first start thinking about sex?"

"The day I was born. What the hell kind of question is that, at a time like this?"

"Just wondering. You ever been laid?"

"Just wondering what? Your mom has a stroke, and you're wondering if I been lucky enough to score? I don't kiss and tell. That kind of information is confidential. Besides, you been in priest school. What the heck do you know about sex?"

"I thought about it in third grade."

"Now this ought to be good. You saying you got laid in third grade?"

"Course not. That's when I started thinking about it. Parkside Elementary, before we moved into this ritzy neighborhood and went to Catholic school."

Donnie chuckles. "That's right, in Catholic school, sex doesn't exist. What's your point?"

"No point. Just a memory. Miss Laura Donovan was my third-grade teacher, and she loved California history. One day, she showed us a movie about the Gold Rush, and a voice recording accompanied the movie."

"I remember Donovan." Donnie yawns, words dragging. "She was a fox. So, what about the movie?"

"It was kind of funny. During the narrative, gold itself became personified. Gold would say something like, 'Behold, I am El Dorado, the bewildered one.' During one of those segments, in the dim light of the movie, Ed Tomasello, who sat next to me at a two-student desk, poked me in the ribs. I looked over, and he had his pants unzipped and his penis out. Right when gold declared, 'Behold…the bewildered one,' Ed Tomasello laughed and shook his penis back and forth."

Donnie snaps at me. "Don't say 'penis.' Never say 'penis.' It sounds dumb and uncool. Say 'pecker,' 'dong,' 'dick,' or even 'tally-whacker.' You'd be laughed right off the street if you said 'penis.' What's with this talk? Your mother's in the hospital, for Pete's sake."

"Tally-whacker! What kind of a word is that?" The question tumbles out of my mouth before I can run it by my brain. I hope it doesn't make my brother think I'm real dumb. "What's the big deal? I'm just saying it to you. Besides, I don't want to think about Ma. I just want to talk."

"Especially don't say it to me. It's clinical and very uncool. And what's that got to do with learning about sex? You go queer or something when you saw what's-his-name's dick?"

"Course I didn't go queer. Another time, Theodore Whistler, who sat across the aisle, had his elbow on the desk and scrunched his forearm against his bicep and laughed as he formed a hairless vagina."

"'Vagina!'" Donnie nearly shouts. "You sound like you should be wearing a white coat and working in a lab! Say 'snatch,' 'pussy,' or even 'poon-tang!' I see I have to catch up your education between third grade and now. Enough of this, your saintly mother's very ill."

"She's going to get better, I know she will." It feels like a relief talking to my brother, unlike the solitary nights alone in my room at the seminary. "Right now, I want to tell you about my childhood. Funny you should mention 'lab,' because on that same day, Theodore Whistler asked me if I wanted to join a private fucking institute that met at his house on Saturday morning."

"I've heard enough. Go to sleep." Donnie's riled.

It's been a long stress-filled day. I suddenly feel like the clown or joker Iron Jack talked about.

Like Melon. "Wait, there's more." I'm taking pleasure in getting Donnie worked up. "All I had to do to join the institute was pay Theodore Whistler a quarter, and I was in. Unfortunately, I didn't have a nickel to my name, so I declined. Besides, I was only half sure about the word 'fucking' and I had no idea what an institute was."

"I remember Whistler. His old man was a psychiatrist. That's probably where the kid learned the word. Enough bullshit. I need my sleep."

"Wait, one day in class, Miss Donovan was reading us a story about two boys playing with matches. She read: 'If two matches rubbed together, they could light.' The class started to snicker about things rubbing together, and most of the snickers I figured were from the institute."

Donnie starts laughing. "Stop it, you're killing me…"

"Miss Donovan said, 'Boys and girls, why are you laughing?' I could see she was disturbed."

"Disturbed…" Donnie howls and pounds his pillow. "I think I'm going to piss my shorts…"

In a deadpan voice, I say, "I was in love with her at the time. I had this fantasy about rescuing her from a fire."

I can't see my brother in the darkness of our room, but he laughs hard enough that I imagine tears streaming his face.

"Little brother, where do you get this stuff?"

"It just came to me."

I've allowed myself to be a trickster and a clown, and I smile into my pillow.

The room quiets. "Donnie, you think Ma's going to be all right?"

"She'll be fine. I wish we had gone in to see her though."

"Yeah, me too." In deep silence, my jumbled thoughts dart to Ma carted out to the ambulance. To Melon and the Polaroids. To Alice Derry naked, her overalls crumpled at her feet. I fall asleep wondering what she looked like in third grade.

Sleep. Dreams. My old man polishes the driver's door on a fire engine with a rag that looks like a baby's diaper. I want to talk to him, but he points to Melon, who drags a large canvas fire hose. Melon unravels the hose behind him as he walks toward piers along the waterfront. "We have to hurry, Raymond Sheets, Cutty Sark is burning."

Saturday morning. Donnie wakes me. He lifts the edge of my mattress and shakes it up and down. "Wake up and pee, the world's on fire."

I cradle the pillow with my arms and mumble, "I don't care, let it burn." Then I remember Ma and the hospital. "I was actually dreaming about something burning. What time is it?"

"Eight o'clock." Donnie's dressed and tosses the bedspread over his rumpled sheets and blanket. No Ma to have him neaten up his bed. "We're taking the old man to Zim's for breakfast. Then over to the hospital. What was burning in your dream?"

I swing my feet to the floor. "The Cutty Sark ship on the scotch bottle was burning. By the way, you'd never last in the sem, making your bed like that."

Donnie ignores the dream reference. "Hey, the way my pants bulge down around the fly, they wouldn't want me anyway." He leans into a small round mirror on the dresser and gives his slick black hair the final once-over with a comb.

Downstairs, the old man looks rumpled in yesterday's clothes as he gulps a glass of water in the kitchen. "About time, Choirboy." He sets the glass on the counter and ruffles my hair. "Sleep well?"

"Yeah, Pop, slept good. Looks like you spent the night in the chair."

"You're right, Choirboy. I'm gonna run up to my room and change." He massages his right temple with the heel of his hand. "Meet you guys in the car in fifteen minutes."

On the driveway, I help Donnie uncover the Ford, and he stashes the tan tarp in the trunk. "The old man's in a good mood for a change. Maybe Ma ought to have a stroke more often."

"Geez, Donnie, don't say shit like that."

I climb into the back seat. Donnie sits behind the wheel. "I just mean after all that happened last night, the guy's acting sentimental, ruffles your hair and asks how you slept. Usually he wants to punch your lights out."

"Maybe the stroke's making him sense his own vulnerability."

"Vulnerability. The guy's about as vulnerable as a concrete wall. Don't go all psychosomatic on me. Where you learn words like that?" Donnie talks over his shoulder like a cab driver.

"Same place you learned the word 'psychosomatic' dipshit. What I mean is maybe he's sensing him and Ma don't have too much time left on this earth."

"The guy's such a mean bastard, he'll probably outlive the two of us. Cool it, Mr. Vulnerable's coming."

Pop wears his brown McGregor windbreaker. I'm amazed by his size, the breadth of his shoulders as he settles into the front seat. "I called over to UC. Nurse says your mother's in and out of sleep. A good time for a visit might be after nine thirty."

Donnie wheels out of the driveway. We're silent as the car bumps over the streetcar tracks along Ocean Avenue. We turn north on Nineteenth. Saturday morning traffic is light, and Donnie makes an illegal left turn onto Taraval. The old man growls, "The cop station is just down the street. You're lucky you didn't get pinched making a turn like that. Besides that, it's dangerous."

Donnie parallel parks along Taraval, just up the street from Atlas Heating, where Melon borrowed the Studebaker. "Don't worry, Pop. I drive with my eyes open."

"You better, wise guy. I don't wanna be sued because my kid ran over some pedestrian."

Inside, Zim's is nearly empty. A teenager in blue pants and a white shirt that says "Chevron" sits in a booth and checks the menu. A myopic older guy at the counter reads the morning paper, the newsprint nearly plastered to his thick rimless glasses.

Zim's has booths along two walls and a counter lined with sugar and salt containers and silver cream dispensers. A young waitress with black bangs and page boy hair hands each of us menus and napkin-wrapped silverware. Nametag on her white blouse reads "Denise Maxx," and she's slim-waisted, busty, and cute. "Can I get you guys coffee"—she looks at Donnie—"and don't I know you?"

"Yeah, City College, last semester. Taylor's biology class. I'll take my coffee black, and where do you spend Saturday nights?"

My old man has a tight-lipped grin as if to say, "That's my boy." He raises one finger to Denise Maxx and mouths, "Black."

I tell her I want cream and sugar just as she turns back to Donnie and says, "Sorry, I have a boyfriend. He's in the Marines."

Denise gets cups and pours our coffee. My old man plants his elbows on the counter, holds the cup to his lips with two beefy hands.

Donnie leans forward and smiles like a clown. "Hey, I didn't ask you to marry me. I just meant we go out and have some laughs. He's in the Marines, he'll never know the difference. Besides, what kind of a guy would leave you for the Marines?"

Denise's porcelain cheeks turn rosy. Her blue eyes say no nonsense. She retrieves a pad and pencil from her waist apron and is poised to take our order.

The old man orders eggs straight up, gives Denise a smile. "I'd stay away from Romeo. You'd be better off with Raymond here." The old man nudges me in the ribs and chuckles.

I feel myself blush to the roots of my blond hair as I order French toast. Donnie still studies the menu. "Thanks, Pop," he banters, "you just ruined my Saturday night."

"Your Saturday night never had a chance with me." Denise, with pencil and order pad still at the ready, turns to Pop. "Thanks for the warning. Soon as he tells me what he wants for breakfast, I'll stay clear of him."

"Good idea." Pop leans over the counter and enjoys the fun.

"Okay, Romeo, what are you gonna order? And it's nice of you to go out to breakfast with your father."

"Yeah, I'm a nice guy. I'll have a stack of hot cakes. This is my brother, Ray. We're going to visit my mom in the hospital."

Denise tears a sheet off the pad and places our order on the high stainless counter that separates the restaurant from the kitchen. She turns back to Donnie. "Nothing serious, I hope."

"She had a stroke, but she should be okay."

Denise turns toward Pop. "Oh, I'm so sorry…"

The old man's smile disappears, and he gives her a short little nod of thanks. Zim's starts to wake up as more customers drift in. Denise, all business, pours coffee and takes orders.

Somebody must have popped some money into one of the silver little jukeboxes at one of the booths, for Richie Valens starts to croon "La Bamba." The old guy with the thick glasses mumbles, "It's too early in the morning for that kind of noise."

After a few minutes, Denise places the cakes, toast, and eggs in front of us and hurriedly refills our coffee. Quietly, she speaks to Donnie: "Most Saturday nights I'm at Mel's on Geary with some of my girlfriends."

Donnie pours syrup over his cakes. "Yeah? Maybe I'll see you there sometime."

We leave a generous tip, and Denise gives us a little finger-flutter wave as we go out the door. I give Donnie a light punch on the shoulder. "Marine boyfriend's gonna hear about you and bust you up good."

"Hey, I'm a second-string linebacker on the JC football team. He'll know better than to mess with me."

We settle into the car, and Donnie makes a U-turn in the middle of Taraval. We're stopped at the signal at Nineteenth when the old man slowly shakes his head. "I can't believe the two of you came from the same parents."

Donnie revs the engine. The glass pack mufflers roar. "What do you mean, Pop?"

"You chase every skirt that flutters in front of you, and Choirboy in the back seat studies to be a priest."

"Choirboy can't help it. His nuts are only the size of BBs."

I reach over the seat and twist Donnie's ear. "Shut up and drive, hotshot. I might just phone Denise's boyfriend and tell him to bring a platoon of Marines to work you over."

"My asshole's puckering and my shorts are in a knot, little brother."

"On second thought, I might save the Marines the trouble and work you over myself."

Strange how the old man's smiling big. It's like he never really noticed us before, and he just now discovered he has two sons and they're equipped with a sense of humor.

Donnie weaves the Ford through fast-flowing traffic along Nineteenth and turns onto Irving Street. We fall into a somber silence as Donnie guns the car up the hill from Irving to Parnassus and stops in front of the main entrance to the hospital. Pop gets out of the car. "ICU's on the fourth floor. I'll meet you guys there."

By the time Donnie and I park the car and make our way up to the elevator, Pop comes out of ICU. The heavy door gives a whoosh as it closes behind him. "You'll have to go in one at a time. Hit the buzzer on the right side of the door, and someone will let you in." He glances at each of us and looks away like he can't hold our gaze. "She don't look so good."

Donnie hits the buzzer. Disappears into ICU.

Pop walks to the end of the corridor, his hands in the pockets of his khaki pants. He stares out a large window. I walk up beside him and look down on the eucalyptus, pines, and cypress that spread their branches over Golden Gate Park.

We stand in silence. I stare down at the trees, but I'm thinking of other trees. The oaks in the hills beyond the fields of St. Jerome's. Trees. Rooted. Flexible. Able to ride out storms.

Pop breaks the silence: "The merry-go-round. Right down there in the park. We used to take you kids there once in a while on Sundays."

"I remember, Pop."

"Your sister…she loved that merry-go-round."

I'd never seen the old man cry until now. He pulls his right hand out of his pocket and grabs my shoulder. He wraps his palm and powerful fingers around my flesh and digs into my collarbone. He stifles a sob. "She don't look so good, Choirboy. She don't look good at all."

I'm speechless. Unsure of what to say or do. I focus on the trees. Think of the merry-go-round. Remember a Sunday from long ago. After the merry-go-round, a picnic on Sharon Meadow. My sister doing cartwheels on the grass.

I don't know how long we stand there. My pop wipes a tear out of the corner of his eye with his thumb; I want to make a swift retreat. It's hard to know what to do when you see your old man cry.

A tap on my shoulder interrupts my thoughts. I turn to Donnie, find his face ashen, lips compressed to a tight line. I raise my thumb and motion to the old man's back. I shake my head slowly, hoping Donnie gets the signal that the old man's in a world of hurt.

I walk to the ICU door and press the button. A nurse in green scrubs lets me in to a room of shadows punctuated by a green-lit screen that scintillates little pyramid lines of yellow light. For some reason, I flash on triangles in geometry class. Then I see Ma's closed eyes.

The left side of her face sags like her skin won't hold up the left side of her mouth. Hair gray and wiry, complexion sallow and eerie in the strange light of this room. "Hey, Ma, it's me, Raymond." I lean close to her ear.

The only response is the subdued hum of machines and an occasional tweak from the lit-up screen. I take her hand in mine and squeeze a little. I notice the tubing to her nose. Her hand feels cold and frail. "Ma, you stay strong. Me and Donnie and Pop, we're pulling for you."

I lay down her hand and quickly turn away. My eyes well up, and I want to run out of the hospital and down the hill to the park. I want to run fast, until I'm bent over and breathless among the sheltering shadows of the trees.

We're quiet in the elevator ride down to the street entrance. Pop breaks the stillness when we get to the car and directs Donnie to drive across town to Sheets Mechanical's main office and corporation yard near Army Street.

Pop's got his formidable arm stretched across the back rest of the seat. He looks toward Donnie but talks to me. "We'll go pick up a vehicle for you, so you can make it to church and then go to work."

"Look, Pop, about church, I don't have to—"

"Yeah, you do have to…you do like your mother says and get to daily Mass."

The drive across the city takes about twenty minutes. I dissolve into silence. The old man's moods can be unpredictable. I'm not about to argue with him when he's depressed.

Sheets Mechanical takes up half a city block. Donnie stops at a side entrance to the equipment yard, and the old man gets out and unchains a gate. We wheel in among the orderly stacks of pipe, pallets of fittings, and trucks of all sizes.

As the old man goes into the back door of a two-story building, Donnie and I get out of the car. "When you gonna tell him, little brother? Some time you gotta let him know you're not going back to the seminary."

"Shit. I know I got to tell him, but not right now. One minute he talks like I'm a candy-ass for wanting to be a priest, and now he's practically insisting I stay in the sem. Little does he know, they don't want me back."

The old man comes out and tosses me a key. He points to a small white pickup truck. "Take number 104. It's yours for the summer."

Number 104 is a '59 Ford Falcon with "Sheets Mechanical" painted in small lettering on each of the doors. "Thanks, Pop. Is it okay if I stop by Melon's on the way home?"

"You stop by wherever you need to, but don't forget about your mother. She's going to need us to be with her at the hospital."

"I'll visit her tonight, Pop."

"You better, and I'm telling you, no screwing around in that vehicle. If I hear of you driving like your salami-head brother, you'll be walking to work."

The old man has reverted to his usual surly self. I climb in the Falcon and don't bother to answer.

It's been months since I've been behind the wheel of any vehicle, and I nervously navigate the little truck through city traffic. It is nearly noon when I park in Melon's driveway.

Melon's in front of the house hand-watering the little patch of lawn that comes with every home in the Sunset District. He shoots a spray of water at the Falcon. "Lysander, my son, I see Daddy fixed you up with some wheels. How's your mom?"

I'm hesitant to answer Melon's question about my ma. I don't want to talk about her with anyone that's not family. I keep my answers brief. "Saw her this morning. She didn't look good, and she was in some kind of deep sleep."

Melon shuts off the hose at the house spigot. "They probably dosed her up with medicine to knock her out. Come on in the garage and have a brew."

I follow Melon into the shadows of the tight little garage. We scuttle around the rear fins of a black '57 Plymouth that looks in showroom condition. "Anybody ever drive this thing?"

"That's my old man's pride and joy. He pays me to wax it once a month whether it needs it or not." Melon opens a cooler in the corner of the garage. "Have a beer, Sheetsy." Melon hands me a Hamms.

"I thought your father was on the wagon?"

Melon sits on the cooler looking like a content little Buddha. "He is on the wagon. This is my private stash. If you told me you were coming, I would have had these on ice."

I lean against the Plymouth and take a sip of the beer. "So, let's see the pictures."

"Sheetsy, Sheetsy, relax and enjoy the suds. Your mom had a stroke, and you want to look at pictures of a naked girl?"

"C'mon, Melon, quit horsing around. Where's the Polaroids?"

"First things, first, Lysander, my son, tell me about your mom."

Reluctantly, I give Melon the story of the last few hours. Fire department. Ambulance. Hospital…"She's still in ICU, but the outcome looks good."

Melon takes a long pull on his beer and then stares down at his feet like he just realized he has shoes on. Without commenting on Ma's stroke, he looks at me with a smile. "Finish the brew and I'll show you your girlfriend as you've never seen her before."

I casually tip my head back and drain the can. "I have seen her."

Melon's voice raises an octave. "You seen her naked? Sheetsy, you little devil, were you peeking in her bedroom window?"

"Course not, idiot, and never mind how I saw her."

Melon opens the cooler, and we toss the beer cans in. Then he squeezes my arm. "I don't know why you want to see the pictures when you seen her in the flesh."

"Cut the crap, Melon. Show me the pictures."

My head feels a little fuzzy from the beer as Melon leads me through the garage and into a basement rumpus room. "We got to be quiet when we get upstairs; my ma's sleeping."

We fumble up a dark, narrow staircase and through a door into a sunlit hallway. Melon puts his finger to his lips and whispers, "Be real quiet."

The hallway carpet is beige and needs a vacuum. The house smells a little musty. Melon leads me into his bedroom, which looks like half sleeping quarters and half art studio.

An easel is set up and holds a large pencil drawing of a girl sitting on a motorcycle. She sits sidesaddle with her bare back showing. She's looking over her left shoulder. Melon is a real artist, for the face is undeniably Alice. "Melon, you drew this?"

"Course I did. It's not exactly Rembrandt, but I'd call it a pretty good likeness of your little girlfriend." Melon lounges back in a swivel chair with his feet up on a cream-colored bedspread.

"Amazing. You got any more drawings?"

"A few starts that didn't pan out. I tossed them." He swings his feet from the bed and opens a desk drawer. "Here're the Polaroids."

He hands me a small stack of photos. I spread them out on the bed. Eight pictures of Alice. Two on the bike. One in the backyard on a chaise lounge. She looks up and smiles, a large straw hat covering her midsection.

Two of the pictures show Alice behind a garden bush that only reveals her head, legs, and bare feet. Two pictures in the house of Alice as she looks up with a pen in her hand like the photographer's interrupting a writing session. She looks up from shadows that tint her neck, collarbones, and the top of her breasts.

In the last picture, an arm sticks out of a slightly open front door, the back of the hand extended, elongated fingers of the right hand seeming to show off a ring.

"What's with this last one?"

"I dunno. Parting shot. She wanted to highlight the ring."

"I never noticed the ring."

"Course not, Sheets. You were blinded by love, but the Melon's detached. Nothing gets by the Melon. I got the eye of an artist."

"Melon, you're so full of shit. Where's the rest of the pictures?"

Melon tears open a little tinfoil packet from out of his wallet. "That's all there is."

"You mean to tell me you never took pictures of her full-on naked?"

Melon blows up a white plastic balloon. He pinches off the neck just before it looks like it's going to burst. "Sheetsy, I'm an artist, not a pervert, but I can tell you what a good piece of ass feels like. Know what this is?"

"Looks like a balloon."

"It's a condom, my son." Melon wears the soft smile that gets me crazy. "I always carry a couple when I'm around naked women."

I feel my anger rise. "What are you saying, Melon? You saying you had sex with Alice?"

Melon lets the condom go. It flutters in the air and lands deflated at the foot of the easel. "Sheetsy, Sheetsy, I never kiss and tell."

I lunge and hammer him to the wall. His glasses fly off. In the process, his foot catches on the leg of the easel, sends it crashing to the floor. I yank him down and hold him to the floor with my left hand. My right hand is drawn back to deliver a punch. That's when I notice someone in the doorway. She's barefoot and wears a slip. I get up off the floor. It's Melon's mother.

"Phillip, what's going on in here?" Her speech is drawn and tired. Her hair matted, stringy. Dark circles under her eyes.

Melon's on his feet. "Nothing, Ma. Me and Raymond were just horsing around. Sorry to wake you."

She stares at me like she's trying to focus and figure out who I am. "Yeah, sorry, Mrs. Chantelope."

Melon's mother looks confused, shakes her head in disgust, and disappears into the hallway.

"Holy crap, Sheets, I was only kidding you." Melon's picking up the easel from the floor. "I never touched your little girlfriend."

I spit out a whisper: "Melon, if you didn't touch her, your joking gets too damn much sometimes."

"Raymond, Raymond. Easy." Melon takes the picture off the easel. "Here's a little peace offering." He rolls up Alice and the motorcycle and hands me the drawing. Melon puts his glasses on again and stares at me with innocent eyes that make me question my brash accusations. "She's your girl, buddy. Course I wouldn't touch her. Now her girlfriend Melinda, hum-baby, that's a different story."

"You got the hots for Melinda?"

"Hey, she'd do in a pinch. How about we watch a little *Roller Derby*?"

"Naw, better check in at home."

"Yeah, yeah, your ma." Melon leads me to the front door. "Good luck with that."

Once we step outside on a landing down a few steps from the porch, I ask him, "Melon, what about your ma? Everything okay there?"

He looks at the little patch of lawn that borders the driveway. Jams his hands deep in his pockets. "Pills. Pills and wine. I don't know what's going to happen." His sadness passes like soft wings of a dark bird. In another second, Melon's back to his old self as he reaches into his back pocket and retrieves his wallet. "Here, Sheetsy, you'll probably use this before I ever will." He hands me the foiled packet of a condom.

"What about Melinda Garret?"

Melon takes a stance like a pudgy little boxer and fakes a slow-motion punch toward my nose. "When the time is right, the Melon will be armed and ready. You go straight home, Lysander, my son. Just because you carry protection doesn't mean you can jump the first little girlie you see."

"Bless me, Father, I would never…"

Melon's all grins. "See ya, Sheetsy."

∾

The weeks of June warm up in our little sun-belt of St. Francis Wood, while in the outer Sunset, toward the beach, when the wind is right, the lonely bleat of foghorns sounds a warning to ships coming in from the sea.

Mr. Sako in his blue ball cap moves a small ladder throughout the yard as he patiently deadheads the spent flowers of rhododendrons. What the plants lack in flowers is made up by the lime-green burgeon of tender new leaves. I try deadheading beside him. He tells me, "Snap only the spent flower, not the leaves."

Mr. Sako wears a plaid cotton shirt, and red suspenders hold up his blue jeans. He moves the ladder carefully from shrub to shrub as if my mother's rhododendrons were the most important plants in the world. "Notice your fingers, notice the flowers. Pay attention, Raymond."

I try to focus, sun on my shoulders. I scrutinize the snap of each dead flower stem as I break away the spent blooms. Mr. Sako exudes a calming silence. My mind wanders to St. Jerome's. I feel comfortable with this man. "Mr. Sako, I got kicked out of school."

Mr. Sako climbs one more rung on the ladder, reaches for a withered flower. "How so?"

I look up and shade my eyes with my hand. Mr. Sako teeters like a hazy vision in the sunlight. "It's a very strict school. They told me I broke too many rules."

"Perhaps they never heard of the 'middle way'?"

"The middle way?"

Mr. Sako descends the ladder. A white smile ignites his leathery face. "Too strict, never good. Answer usually in the middle."

Mr. Sako moves the ladder as I ponder the middle way and continue to deadhead the flowers. "I feel like a bad person for breaking the rules."

"You a good person. Just need a little work like all of us."

I drop a handful of dead blooms into a five-gallon bucket. "I'm afraid to tell my mother I got kicked out."

"When the time is right, she will know, but perhaps now is not the time."

My mother is home now. After five days in ICU and another week on a nursing floor, she was moved to a rehab facility for nearly four weeks. Pop held a board meeting while Ma was in rehab. The board consisted of Donnie and me. "I'm hiring Mr. Sako's wife as a caregiver. She'll cook, clean, keep track of Ma's medicines and appointments."

Pop had a construction crew do a rush job on the big downstairs rec room. The pool table was pushed up against one end wall. Sheets Mechanical remodeled the rec room into a one-bedroom apartment for the Sakos. They rented out their furnished home in the Richmond District, so we now have a live-in caregiver and a gardener. When Pop puts his mind to it, things get done.

Ma smiles more now. Her smile is only on one side of her mouth, with the left side of her face stiff and droopy. But her half smile somehow seems peaceful, like she learned some kind of wisdom in the struggle up from the darkness of her stroke. It's Monday, and I look in on her before I head out to face the day. "Morning, R-R-Raymond." The words tumble out forced and distorted. A little spittle trails from the corner of her mouth.

I lean over the bed and kiss her on the forehead, which is cold as window glass. "Morning, Ma. How you doing?"

"Gud. Mrs. Sako likes baysmnt?"

"It's a nice little apartment, Ma, wall-to-wall carpet. Small little kitchen, but she mostly cooks upstairs and eats with us."

Ma raises her good hand and slowly brushes it across her forehead. "M-M-Mr. Sako?"

"He doesn't say much, but I think he likes his new home. Gotta go, Ma."

"You t-t-to church?"

"Yeah, Ma, going to Mass." I wave to her and leave the room. I feel guilty about my bold-faced lie.

Nobody but Donnie and Melon know I'm not going back to St. Jerome's, and even they don't know that most mornings I have eggs and coffee at Zim's instead of going to Mass before work.

I park the little truck against the curb along Taraval. The sidewalk shines with the damp from last night's fog. Inside, Denise Maxx waves me to an empty seat at the counter. "How come your brother never comes in with you?"

"Different hours. He works at a deli over in North Beach. I think you scared him off with your Marine boyfriend."

"Yeah, I'll bet he scares real easy." She hustles around the end of the counter with a coffeepot. "I'll be with you in a sec."

I look over my shoulder; she pours coffee at a booth. The hem of her yellow dress hikes up above her calf as she bends into the table.

She's back and grabs an order off the kitchen pass-through counter. "Remind your brother, Mel's on Geary. Most Saturday nights."

"What about the Halls of Montezuma?"

She scribbles down my order of eggs and coffee. "Hey, like your brother said, 'Let's just have a little fun.' Besides, I don't want to be your sister-in-law after the way I've seen you mop up egg yolk with your toast."

"Sorry, I guess I eat Italian-style. You should see my brother eat." I spit the words out, feeling a little angry at Donnie's success with girls.

She must sense my resentment. She picks up two hot plates off the counter, quickly turns toward me. In her porcelain face framed by black hair appears a blue-eyed wink. "You're actually kind of cute." Then she wades into the morning breakfast clatter.

She thinks I'm cute, not Italian, drop-dead, good-looking handsome like my brother. Her words feel like a lopsided compliment. A kind of compliment you might give a little kid. Nevertheless, driving to work, I smile as I weave through traffic. The day seems brighter, more cheerful. What the heck, I'm glad she thought enough of me to say anything at all.

Work is mostly driving the truck, keeping job trailers supplied with fittings. Sometimes the old man has me in the office tallying up hours on employee time cards. I spent the hardest day with a shovel cleaning out a ditch behind Tony Serrano, who ran a trenching machine.

"Hey, you ever whack off in priest school?" he asks me. We're eating lunch sitting in the doorway of a Sheet's Mechanical trailer that is big as a moving van.

"What kind of a question is that?"

Serrano's skin shines with olive oil and grit from dust. Hair black like Donnie's, and a smear of mayonnaise trickles down his chin. "Just wondering. Isn't that what priests do?"

"I don't know. Maybe some of 'em. You're wearing part of your sandwich on your chin."

He wipes the back of his hand across grizzled stubble, then reaches down and grabs his crotch and gives it a shake or two. "You become a priest, you ain't never gonna lay any pipe. You know what I mean?"

I feel like grabbing the condom out of my wallet and casually blowing it up Melon-style. Make this idiot think I've laid a lot of pipe, priest school or not. "Yeah, well, I'm probably quitting anyway."

"Good move. I figure God invented pussy to be enjoyed."

Serrano's ten years older than me. I feel glad I don't have to work with him every day. It kind of makes me laugh how he's an older rough cut of Donnie. Both of them Italian with the same thing on their minds.

$\sim$

"Hey, little brother, let's say we go by Mel's and I'll show you the ropes."
It's Saturday night, the end of the same week that Denise Maxx called
me cute. I never told Donnie I talk with her most weekday mornings.

I haven't been to Mel's since New Year's Eve with Melon and
Terminal in the Studebaker. "Sounds good. Guess I ought to feel hon-
ored learning from an expert."

"Nothin' but the best, little man."

We're driving north on Nineteenth, radio's off, and Donnie
launches into a big-brother lecture. "The first thing you got to do is
grow your hair out. A blond crewcut just isn't cool. Nobody scores with
hair looking like yours."

We turn east on Geary. "How about Alice dropping her overalls?"
I don't like bringing Alice into the conversation, but I feel a strong
need to defend my haircut.

"That was an anomaly…"

I laugh out loud. "Anomaly! One year of college and you talk like
some professor…"

A metallic blue '56 Chevy pulls alongside us and blasts its tailpipes.
Donnie looks over and smiles at the slicked-back guy behind the wheel.
Both cars punch out, and we're suddenly doing sixty miles per hour
down Geary Street. "Whoa, Donnie, slow down!"

Donnie backs off the gas and lets the Chevy go. "You're right, better we
go to his funeral than have him come to ours. Now about your haircut…"

We rumble into Mel's parking lot, lights reflecting off custom paint
jobs of shimmering hot rods. Donnie pulls in next to a fluorescent-or-
ange Chevy. Guy with sweeping hair, trying to look like Elvis. Blond
girl cuddled up next to him on the seat. Any closer, she'd be in his lap.
They both munch burgers.

I watch the blonde in the Chevy when Donnie blurts: "Whoops,
there she is."

"There who is?"

"In the booth inside Mel's. The waitress chick from Zim's."

I spot her through the windshield. She's sitting in a booth with three other girls. She has a straw to her lips. Those same lips that pronounced me "cute." I'm suddenly jealous of my good-looking brother. Donnie starts the car and backs out of the parking place.

"What are you doing? Are we leaving?"

Donnie parks the Ford in a darker back area of the parking lot. "I need you to do me a favor."

"What kind of favor?"

"I need you to get in the back seat and lie down on the floor. I'm going to throw the car cover over you."

"Have you gone crazy?"

"Look, just do it. I'm gonna talk her into the car, and I don't want her to see my little brother tagging along."

"Tagging along where?"

Donnie pops the trunk open and gets the car cover out. "To wherever, now get down on the floor."

"Wait a second, I don't want to be in the car while you're getting laid."

"Don't worry about it. You might learn something."

"Sounds sick to me. Besides, I'm not getting on the floor while you're in Mel's drinking a shake. I'll sit in the back. If I see you come out with her, I'll duck and cover up. I think your chances are slim to none. If you don't talk her in the car, you owe me a couple of burgers and something to drink."

I roll the car cover into a ball and climb into the back seat. Donnie's bent down at the sideview mirror, smoothing his hair with his fingers. "Don't count on those burgers. There's not a girl on the planet who wouldn't want to jump in the car with this Italian."

"Yeah, yeah, just make sure you don't eat like an Italian."

Donnie straightens up. "What's that supposed to mean?"

"Nothing. Just go…"

I watch my brother strut the parking lot like he owns Mel's. He stops at a maroon '54 Ford with a spot of rust-colored primer on the rear trunk lid, leans down, and talks to somebody through the open window. He's up and laughing with a big guffaw as he weaves his way between cars and enters the restaurant.

I feel alone, with the balled-up canvas car cover on the seat beside me. Jealousy hits me again. I think about finding a phone booth, calling the Marines. Getting Denise's boyfriend and his whole platoon to teach my brother some manners.

In the neon light of the restaurant, I see Donnie. His fingers rest lightly on the edge of the table where Denise and three girls in the booth stare up at him. I can't quite make out their expressions. I imagine they think dreamy Adonis has just dropped out of heaven. I'd like to fill them in. He's my grease-ball brother who mops up spaghetti sauce with French bread.

In less than five minutes, Denise stands up and walks out with Donnie. I get a side view of her breasts in a tight blue sweater just before I slump down to the floor and cover myself with the tarp.

I hold my breath when I hear the door open. "Nice car. Yours?" Denise's musical voice. Tender like a love song.

"All mine. Bought it off my uncle."

I'm on my side. My head rests on the inside of my right bicep. Don't know how long I can lie in this position. The car door closes, and the other door opens and closes. Donnie's behind the wheel.

"How come your uncle sold it?"

"Got a job transfer to Seattle. Rains a lot there. Didn't want to see his pride and joy turn to rust."

Donnie starts the engine. Turns on the radio. Fats Domino croons: "I'm gonna be a wheel someday." My shoulder becomes uncomfortable.

"Thought we might cruise Geary then head out to the Circle."

"Why the Circle?"

The car's in motion. My arm and shoulder are killing me.

"You know…just sit and talk. Listen to some music. When's your boyfriend get out of the Marines?"

"Another two years. He left for Okinawa three weeks ago."

"Pretty far away. You must miss him."

"Sometimes I do. Sometimes I'm mad at him."

"Don't blame you for that. I was thinking Marines, but then I got offered a football scholarship to UC Davis. Division-two school, but it fits right in with my plans to major in premed."

"You want to be a doctor?"

My body shifts around on the floor with the left and right turns and changes in speed. I get a cramp in my left calf, bite my lip, and try not to make a sound. Donnie's voice continues: "Yeah, I've always been interested in the human body." Fats is well into the song: "I'm gonna be a wheel someday…I'm gonna be somebody…"

The cramp lets up. Donnie eases off the gas, the glass pack mufflers do a throaty roar, and I use the noise to quietly shift my arm and turn partially on my back, hoping Donnie doesn't decide to move the seat back.

Denise says, "I think that's wonderful, you want to go into medicine."

I want to pounce out of my hiding place and shout, "Medicine! This idiot passes out at the sight of blood. He's trying to get you out to the Circle at Lake Merced to work his medicine on your body!"

The Twilighters move into the first bars of "Sea of Love." Stop-and-go traffic along Nineteenth Avenue. Right turn onto Sloat

Boulevard. I feel like a blind man as I track the journey. Big sweeping turn onto Sunset before we roll to a stop. Donnie's voice: "Well, here we are. I always feel pretty peaceful near the lake. My dad used to take my brother and me trout fishing here when we were little."

"That's so neat. I liked your dad when I met him, and your brother's so cute."

Donnie shuts down the engine but keeps the radio on. She really does think I'm cute. I'm all ears.

"Yeah, my brother's a great kid. He's a little shy."

"I guess I shouldn't tease him about mopping up his eggs..."

"What are you talking about?"

"You know, he's in Zim's every day for breakfast, and he uses his toast to mop up the egg yolk."

"My little brother is in Zim's every day?"

Denise is blowing my cover. "Come with me...to the sea...the sea of love..." The Twilighters in the background while Denise reveals how I spend my mornings. I feel like a bigger bullshitter than Donnie.

"Yeah, he said you'd probably like to be there with him, but that you had a different work schedule."

"Of course I'd like to be there. Forgot he said he eats there. You tease him all you want; he can take it."

"So what kind of doctor do you want to be?"

"I'm not sure at this point...probably emergency room...why don't you slide over a little closer and we can talk about it."

My left calf cramps again; my jaw clenches against the pain.

"I think I better stay where I am."

"What's the matter, the Marine? Okinawa's seven thousand miles away."

Paul Anka launches into "Lonely Boy." My leg cramp comes on strong; I become afraid my face is going to get stuck in a pained expression forever.

"Not just him…I hardly know you."

"I'm no mystery. Just a regular guy who wants to go into medicine, but right now I kinda feel like the guy in this song."

"What, you're lonely?"

"A little. Just broke up with my girlfriend. I really thought she was the one. Then there's my mom being sick. I used to confide in her a lot."

The leg pain is excruciating. I sweat under the car cover. My low-down brother is using our mother's stroke as a reason to get laid. The car cover smells like mildew.

"Who was your girlfriend?"

"Nadine. Nadine Ottoboni. You wouldn't know her. She's from San Bruno. It was mostly her parents. They had her convinced I'd never amount to anything."

I'm nearly in tears with the pain. I'm just about to call out when the pain lets up. Nadine Ottoboni is my old man's secretary. She has to be in her forties.

"I'm a little lonely too." Denise's voice is nearly a whisper. "I'm sorry about your mom."

I feel Denise shift her body across the front seat. I want to pop up and grab her by the shoulders. Tell her my brother is full of shit. The car goes silent except for the radio. "I'm just a lonely boy…lonely and blue…"

Silent except for Paul Anka singing away his sorrows. Then I hear a car engine and the crunch of tires on pavement. Sounds like some-body pulled up behind us. Car doors open. The radio in the other car is tuned to the same station. Paul is belting out, "All I need is someone to love…" That's when Donnie's blue Ford begins to bounce up and down violently.

Denise lets out a scream. I hear laughter and hoots outside the car. Donnie has his door open. "Hey, you assholes, knock it off." More laughter. Car doors slam. The other car screeches rubber as it pulls away.

Donnie's back in the Ford. Denise whimpers. Paul's finished his song. The radio announcer tells us it's Saturday night and we're tuned to KYA.

"Easy. Easy. Just some kids bouncing up and down on the bumper. Pulling a prank."

"Please take me home." Denise sounds like she may be crying.

"Sure. Stay close to me, it's okay. Just some kids horsing around."

The radio's off. Denise's voice sounds like she can't quite get her breath. "I want to go home now."

Donnie keys the engine. The muffler gives a throaty moan. "Where do you live?"

"Five minutes away on Lakeview."

I hear the snap of the emergency brake release. Donnie punches into reverse, swings the car around, and peels out of the parking lot.

"You're mad, aren't you?" Denise sounds like a little girl, not the wisecracking waitress from Zim's.

"Darn right I'm mad. I'd like to get my hands on those punks."

"I'm sorry. I got scared…then there's my boyfriend…"

From under the car cover, the rumbling mufflers vibrate the back of my head. My teeth and gums ache. Damn smell of mildew. Tomorrow morning, I'm definitely calling the Marines. My brother is a jerk.

"Look, it's okay. I'm not mad at you. Your boyfriend should never have left someone as pretty as you. Here's Lakeview; which house is yours?"

"Fourth house on the right."

The Ford stops. I'm still glued to the backseat floorboards, and I can't believe what I hear next: "Let me hold you for a while, just rest against me till you calm down…"

"I am calm, and my dad may be looking out the front window."

I hear Denise slide across the seat. The car door opens and slams. Donnie's yelling, "Hey, Denise, wait…"

From under the car cover, I can't hold my tongue. "No vagina tonight, hotshot, and you owe me big time for this one."

Donnie pulls away from the curb in front of Denise's house. "I told you, don't ever say 'vagina' in my presence. Say 'pussy, Choirboy."

Finally, I'm up off the floor and yelling at my brother: "After the bullshit you slung tonight, I'll call it anything I want to."

From the back seat, I start singing: "Nothing could be fina than to be in your vagina in the morning…"

"Shut up, asshole." Donnie's talking over his shoulder.

"After the bullshit I heard you sling at that poor girl, who's the asshole here? No vagina, no vagina, no vagina tonight!"

Donnie jams on the brakes in the middle of Ocean Avenue, reaches over the seat, and grabs me by the shirtfront. "Knock it off, Raymond."

"Easy, big brother, I been stuck like a mole in a hole under that stinking car cover. Now I'm just having a little fun." A car pulls up behind us. Somebody's laying on the horn. Donnie turns and puts the Ford in gear. Tailpipes rumble. We're silent for the rest of the ride.

It's after midnight when we get home. The lights are on in the house. Mrs. Sako meets us inside the front door. Her mouth is a tight line, eyes downcast.

Mrs. Sako grabs my right arm with both of her hands. Tears brim in her eyes. "I'm so sorry, boys; your mother passed away tonight."

14

I CATCH A GLIMPSE OF POP AT the dining room table. His head is down, and he appears to be clutching a glass of scotch. I feel my knees about to buckle; as I pull away from Mrs. Sako, I do a dizzy shuffle into the dining room. I steady myself, left hand against the table edge, right hand on Pop's shoulder. I catch myself digging my fingers into the flesh behind his collarbone. "Geez, Pop, what happened?"

Donnie abruptly thuds into a chair across from Pop. Tears stream down Pop's face. He has a hard grasp on the scotch glass. "She was the love of my life. I went in the room. She looked so peaceful. So beautiful." Pop starts to sob. "They carried her out in a bag. They took her away."

I hunch over, feel a mix of jolting sadness and disbelief. All I can think to do is massage Pop's shoulders. I'm crying now. I fight the salty streams running off my face and onto the back of Pop's shirt. Donnie's elbows are planted on the table, his face in his hands. Mr. and Mrs. Sako stand beneath the arched entry to the kitchen. He has his arm tight across her shoulders.

Mrs. Sako pulls away from her husband and puts her hand on Pop's bald head. "Come, Mr. Sheets. I'll help you to your chair."

Donnie comes around the table. The three of us hoist Pop up. He's limp as a child. He allows us to guide him to his recliner in the living room. Donnie gets the blanket with the smiling elephant. We cover Pop up. Mr. Sako brings a washcloth, and Mrs. Sako gently bathes Pop's face.

Donnie heads for the stairs. Unsure of what to do, I follow him. Inside our room, we face each other, and Donnie grabs me. He has a hard grip on both of my biceps. He shakes his head slowly back and forth. "I used her as an excuse to get laid."

"I killed her, Donnie. I told her I was quitting. I killed her, and now I can't make it right. I'll never be able to make it right."

Hearing that again, Donnie lets go of my arms, sits on the edge of his bed. He says, "Stop it! Goddamn it, stop! She killed herself. She was wound up tighter than a bedspring. You didn't kill anybody. She did it to herself."

After the tears stop, I lie down on the bed and face the wall. I listen to Donnie undress, getting ready for bed. He turns off the light. The room so still. In the silence, I feel like a kid again. A young kid, afraid of the dark. "Donnie."

From across the room, my older brother's voice: "Yeah."

"How come I never got hair on my chest like you and Pop?"

"What kind of question is that at a time like this?" Donnie almost shouts, then catches himself. "You don't have hair because you're strong and tough. Hair don't grow on iron. Now try and get some sleep. We gotta help Pop get through this. We gotta help each other."

I keep still for what seems like an hour. I hear Donnie breathe, regular and easy. I get up and leave the room. I pad down the hall in stocking feet and enter my sister's room. I am angry at her for leaving us, yet in her room, I have the comforting sense that a part of her is here. She's going to help us get through this sad and complicated dance. I drop onto her bed and cry into my sister's pillow until I can't cry anymore. *Hair don't grow on iron.* I pull myself together. The tears have relieved my sadness. I feel a new sense of resolve. I've got to help my pop.

I pull the covers from my sister's bed and pick up her pillow. I drag the bedding down the stairs and spread it out on the floor near Pop's feet. His mouth is open, and his eyes are closed. He's splayed across the chair, his face creased and pale. I look in the dining room. Mr. and Mrs. Sako apparently can't sleep. They sit hunched over steaming cups of tea. They both look in my direction and then slowly turn away.

I curl up on the carpet and pull the covers over me, staying close as I can to my pop. In case he needs me.

The three days after my mom's death pass quickly. I don't know if time always speeds up when someone dies. There seems to be so much to do. When my sister died, Mom and Pop made all the calls, made the arrangements. I just don't remember the clock moving so fast. This time, it's up to Donnie and me. Pop hasn't shaved since Mom died, and he's well into his Cutty Sark.

Donnie phones the Sheets side of the family. I call Mom's Italian relatives. When I reach Uncle Tool, he exhales a long, strident, "Jeeeesus."

That's not exactly the response I wanted to hear.

"Raymond, what do you want me to do?"

"I don't know, Tool. I guess just get down here as soon as you can."

Pop mumbles in the recliner: "She's at Duggan's in Daly City. You pick out the casket. And we want flowers, lots of flowers. Don't worry about the cost. She deserves the best. And the flowers…" Pop's sobbing now. "God, how she loves flowers."

Little by little, we get through it. Mrs. Sako contacts a caterer and lays out Pop's dark suit. She even helps him shave. Mr. Sako spreads fresh mulch around Mom's rhododendrons. The yard smells like a sweet pine forest. Tuesday night, the rosary. The church on Wednesday morning.

The church is where I see Alice. She's in a pew about midway up the aisle and standing next to Melon. They turn toward the casket as we wheel it by. I catch Melon's scrunched-up face that seems to say, "Hang in there, champ." Alice looks like a porcelain figurine in a long blue coat.

The church is also where I begin to choke up. The smell of incense, the candles. I have to bite my lip when old Father McCoy's deep voice intones: "'May the angels lead thee into Paradise.'"

Holy Cross Cemetery. The mortician has us arranged by height. Donnie has the right front corner. Big Al Blazes, my pop's best friend from high school, carries the left front corner. Pop and Al used to play high school ball together.

Uncle Tool and I carry the middle of the coffin, followed by Mom's shorter cousins, Vince and Angelo. We gently unload the coffin from the back of the hearse and carry it across a sloping lawn. Mom in her coffin feels heavy. My white-gloved hand holds tight to the polished handle, and I worry I might lose my footing on the damp turf. If I lose my footing, it'll send me, Ma's coffin, and five other guys tumbling down the slope.

The slope levels out near the grave site. Fog is drifting off to the east, and in the glare of the sun, I see women dab at their eyes. Pop's relatives, mostly in sport coats and open collars, intermingle through a crowd of Italians in dark suits. I can't look at the open grave. Or, off to the side, the mound of fresh earth covered by a canvas tarp.

We place the coffin on a purple-skirted metal stand. Free of the weight, I turn and look at my pop. He's leaning forward, head bowed, and his beefy hands rest on the foot of the coffin.

I break away from the pallbearers and place my gloved hand up high on my Pop's back. I feel him shudder, and I look away to the edge of the crowd of mourners. Alice and Melon stand near a pure white concrete angel. Also standing near the angel, I'm startled to see, is Iron Jack. How did he know? He must read the obits. I feel comforted by his presence.

The hard part is walking away after the graveside service. We are leaving my mom all alone. It's gut-wrenching, and all I can do is mumble to myself: "I'll be back, Mom. I'll be back to visit."

Donnie and I walk my pop toward a limo that will take us home. Pop is inconsolable as we seat him in the back seat of the long black car. The limo driver holds the door open, and I'm about to get in when I feel a hand on my shoulder. I turn and look up into the face of Iron Jack. "I'm sorry for your loss, Raymond. I'm an assistant rector over at Grace Cathedral these days. My door is always open to you."

Jack wears a tweed sport coat and a white clerical collar. I'm stunned he called me "Raymond" and not "Mr. Sheets." I try to make sustained eye contact and force a smile. "Thanks, Jack." Then I slip into the limo. Jack gives a wave and a small, sympathetic grin as the car pulls away toward home.

The house is filled with a rush of caterers in white aprons moving familiar egg sandwiches cut into triangles from the kitchen to the dining room table. Donnie and I get Pop settled in his easy chair. Donnie pours Pop a scotch and sets the glass on a little end table.

Pop has his elbows propped on the soft arms of the chair. His face rests against the edges of his hands, the tips of his fingers together like a steep roof over his nose. His eyes seem lifeless. Donnie looks at me and shrugs.

I mouth the words, "Maybe coffee."

Donnie heads toward the kitchen while I man the front door with Uncle Tool. I feel numb. I shake hands and receive hugs from people who look familiar, but I can't place all their names. Big Al Blazes comes up the front steps with Vince and Angelo. "Thanks for your help, guys. The lawn was a little treacherous."

Angelo looks like an olive-skinned Mafioso in his black suit. "Yeah, I was afraid we was all gonna go down." He grips my shoulder. "Sorry about your ma; she was a good person."

Tool makes small talk with the line of people. I feel secure with him beside me. I hear him respond when Angelo hugs him and says, "The skirts get to you, Tool?"

Tool chuckles, "More like the legs."

I start to tear up as Angelo files into the house. Vince pats me on the cheek with the flat of his hand and quickly averts his eyes.

Big Al doesn't seem to notice my misery. "I remember the day they first met, Raymond. She was a looker, your ma." Al's voice pounds like he's telling the whole world. "We were playing Galileo High School at Funston Park in the marina. Your pop was catcher. She kept hanging around the backstop. Couldn't take her eyes off him."

I wipe at my eye with one finger and whisper to Al, "Maybe you can go talk to the catcher. He's not doing so good."

Al lowers his voice. "Got it covered. Real bad time for him now."

Al lumbers away, and the people keep coming. Cousin Lois, Aunt Ida, and Uncle Frank, relatives I don't usually see except at weddings and funerals. When the people coming in the door thin out to nothing, I feel like I need to be alone for a minute. I leave Tool to man the door for any latecomers, then I make my way through the crowded house and duck into the kitchen. I scoop up three little egg sandwiches and dart through the pantry and out the back door.

Alice and Melon are sitting on the rear steps. They both turn when the back door opens. Melon has an open bottle of beer in his hand. "Hey, buddy, how you making it?"

I sit down a little higher up on the steps. "I don't know. Kind of numb right now."

Alice stands and turns toward me. "Wasn't sure if I should come, but Melon insisted. We talk on the phone almost every week."

"It's okay. I'm glad you're here. You want an egg sandwich?"

Alice takes the triangle of bread and nibbles like a shy little chipmunk.

"How about a beer, Sheetsy?" Melon offers. "I brought a six-pack."

"He better not have a beer," Alice says. "Alcohol can make you feel depressed. I know that's how it affects my mom."

"Yeah, I better not." I can't believe Melon brought a six-pack to my mom's funeral. "So, you talk on the phone every week?"

"I keep Alice up-to-date on what's going on in the big city."

"He told me about your mom's stroke....I'm sorry she died, Raymond."

It hits me then. Right in the middle of chewing an egg sandwich, tears stream down my face. Alice moves up the steps and sits beside me. She wraps her arm around my shoulders and leans her head into my chest. "You're allowed to cry when your mom dies. Go ahead and let it out."

Melon stands, beer in hand. "He's got to mingle. Come on, Sheetsy, in the house, there's people that need you."

Alice stomps her foot on the step. "No, Melon, let him grieve. He's not feeling good. If he needs to cry, let him!"

"Just trying to snap him out of it."

Alice is adamant. "He needs to pass through it, not snap out of it!"

I sense the tension between my two friends, and I pull away. Alice releases me, and I wipe at my eyes with the back of my hand. The three of us return inside the house. Beer in hand, Melon wanders off into the crowd. Alice stays close to me in the kitchen. Donnie corners us.

"Hello again, you're Alice from the house with the roses."

"And you're Donnie of the blue car. Sorry about your mom."

"Yeah, thanks." Donnie's doing a good job of covering up his sadness. He's moving about the kitchen taking care of drinks. With just a slight tremor in his voice, he answers Alice. "It was a shocker."

He pours scotch over ice, then a little shot of water from the sink faucet. He must have learned the moves from working in the deli.

"Gotta run this out to Big Al. I think he's trying to keep up with Pop. Why don't you go over and sit with Aunt Nanette? She's by herself on the couch in the living room."

I take my lead from Donnie and try and stop thinking about myself as Alice and I thread between people. Vince is in the foyer telling a dirty joke to Jerry Vinson and Ed Lauer, two of Pop's crew from Sheets Mechanical. "So, she bends over and lifts her skirt…" Vince stops as I walk by. Jerry and Ed wipe the smiles off their faces. Vince flat-hands my cheek again, and he winks at Alice.

We pass Pop in his chair. Melon, down on one knee, holds his beer and looks at Pop. Big Al stands over the two of them. They're all smiling, even Pop. Still gets me how Melon can talk to my pop better than I can.

The couch is a floral print of blues and pinks, and red roses. Aunt Nanette is blind, with white hair. She wears dark glasses even indoors because she says she doesn't feel comfortable with people looking at her eyes. I take her hand. "Aunt Nanette, it's Raymond."

"Of course it is, dear, I'd know your touch anywhere." Aunt Nanette has this continuous smile like she's about to engage in the most wonderful conversation of her life. "And who is with you, Raymond?"

It floors me how she can feel someone else's presence. "My friend, Alice."

"Alice. I had a friend named Alice when I was young. Let me touch your hand, dear."

Alice glances at me and smiles, holds out her hand to Nanette, who says, "What a lovely little hand, and I feel a ring."

"My father brought it to me from Thailand." Alice bends forward and talks loudly into Nanette's ear. "It's a black sapphire, with a little cluster of blue sapphires around it. It feels good when I wear it. It's like my father is always with me. The big sapphire reminds me of my father's eyes."

"What a wonderful gift. My father was also a world traveler, and you don't have to shout, dear. My hearing is quite good. It's just my eyes that are a bother. Sit down here next to me and tell me about yourself."

Alice settles in next to Nanette, and I slide tight against Alice until our legs touch from the knees up. "My father's in the Navy. We live in Mountain View right near Raymond's school."

At the mention of that, I nudge my elbow into Alice's ribs. She questions me with her eyes, and I shake my head.

Nanette replies, "Oh dear, Raymond's school. I once ran my hands over his face. He's such a good-looking boy. Good-looking boys should never become priests.

"I was raised Catholic, but my father was a Protestant who never went to church. He once said to my mother: 'Oh, poop on the Pope.'"

Alice laughs. "What did your mother say?"

"She raised a big kitchen knife she was slicing onions with, waved it at my father while shouting, 'Heresy, sacrilege,' or something like that. I was little, and my eyesight was good. Thinking back on it now seems most amusing."

Alice looks at me with the Devil in her smile. She takes hold of Nanette's hand. "Raymond may not be going back to that school."

Nanette answers like I'm nowhere in the room, "Dear me, I hope he never does. Such a good-looking boy."

"I'm still here with you on the couch, Aunt Nanette."

"Of course you are. I'm just poking a little fun at your nice friend. You two move along now. I'm sure you have better things to do than talk with an old lady, and Raymond, your mother will be proud of you no matter what you do."

Alice and I stand, and with a spurt of affection, Alice leans down and puts her hand on Nanette's shoulder. "I like you, Aunt Nanette."

"I like you, too, dear. You take care of Raymond."

Alice takes my hand, and we cross the room. Melon is standing now, and he is jabbering away to Big Al about *Roller Derby*. Melon and Big Al look like bosom buddies. My pop has a forced grin like he's trying to listen but his heart's not in it. In spite of his size, he looks shrunken in the easy chair.

Alice lets go of my hand, taps Melon on the shoulder. "You okay to drive?"

Melon turns, sweeps his arm in a grand gesture, smiles like he's holding court with the two old guys. "I'm more than okay. A couple of beers never affect the Melon. Ray, why don't you introduce Alice to your dad and Big Al?"

Before I can open my mouth, Alice turns toward Big Al. "Nice to meet you, I'm Alice Derry." Then with more grace than I expected, she leans down to my pop; she gently places her hand on his forearm. "I'm sorry your wife died." My father tightens his lips and gives an almost imperceptible nod and puts his hand over Alice's.

I'm amazed this girl with the motorcycle who poses for naked pictures can bring out so much tenderness in my pop. I feel a lightness in my chest. Maybe it's love.

We break away from the house, and I walk Alice and Melon toward his dad's '57 Plymouth parked a block away. At the foot of our driveway, I take Alice's hand, feel the ring, and run my thumb over the stones. Moving my arm up across her shoulders, I draw her in close. "Thanks for talking to my pop."

She leans her head into my chest as Melon pipes up. "It's gonna take time, Sheetsy. Your old man's gonna be fine."

Alice pulls away and doubles up her fists. "Stop it, Melon. Just stop!"

Melon shrugs and hurries to the car. Alice takes my hand, and we continue walking. "He just doesn't get it."

I manage a tiny sad smile. "He's a clown," I whisper. "He thinks he's trying to help."

At the car, Alice gives me a bear hug, her breasts pushing against me. She holds on for the longest time. "Sorry about your mom." With my chin resting on her head, my eyes are wet. I hug her tightly. The body contact feels magnetic. I don't want to let go.

Melon calls, "Sorry to be the one to break up the moment, but I got to get this girl home before my old man knows his black beauty's missing."

Alice talks into my chest. "Melon…I swear…"

I try to block out Melon by feeling the animal warmth of Alice as I nuzzle her hair. "Easy. Easy. Don't forget you have to ride home with him."

Melon unlocks the car. Alice and I release each other, and I take her hand and hold it in front of me. "Never noticed the ring before."

"I've had it for over two years. It fits me now, and I feel older when I wear it." The center stone of the ring shines deep black like the wax on the Plymouth.

Alice pulls away and slides into the car. Melon starts the engine and turns the wheels from the curb. Alice's window lowers. "Call me, Raymond Sheets."

I cry as the car pulls out and disappears around a corner. I feel a shiver of loneliness in the late afternoon shadows of cypress and eucalyptus. Ma is dead. I walk toward the house shaking my head in disbelief. The eucalyptus trees are still growing. The house looks the same. I imagine people everywhere are going about their business as usual, opening their mail, pushing shopping carts down the aisle of the market. Hard to believe. The world keeps going, and my mother is no longer in it.

My legs feel tired and heavy as I mount the front stairs and enter the house. Pop is silent and drunk in his chair. Donnie and Tool try to act as hosts for the party. I try my best to smile and help out, but I feel withdrawn in a house full of guests with no one to talk to.

The days after Mom's funeral seem long and tedious. Mr. and Mrs. Sako stay on, fix our meals, take care of us. My pop drinks a lot, and Donnie and I keep our distance.

Nighttime's the worst. I pull the covers over my head. The sheets are wrinkled and unruly under the blankets because Ma no longer makes the bed. I kick my ankle free from the twisted sheets. I fall in and out of a restless, sweaty sleep. My words haunt me like a constant whine of pesky mosquitoes. "I'm thinking about quitting the seminary, Ma." I can't get those words out of my head.

I startle awake, cover my ears with my hands to silence the words. My heart races. Goddamn it, the way she looked at me. Bony fingers raised to her gaping mouth as if to stifle a scream, skeletal shoulders hunched, pleading gray eyes. She had aged years in just a few months, body worn to a shadow. Why did I even tell her?

My breathing comes fast and shallow. Anxiety trembles in my chest. "Damn, Ma, why did I have to become your ticket to heaven?" I'm pissed at the sack of guilt she left me with. I begin to pound the edge of the mattress with my fist. I hoist myself up on one arm and smack the pillow hard. I utter a hiss through my clenched and grinding teeth, "Goddamn it, Goddamn it, Ma."

"Jesus, what's going on?" My brother's question probes the darkness. He's out of bed and on his feet. "You having a bad dream?" He stands over me. "What the hell are you doing?"

I rip at the blankets, swing my feet to the floor, and sit on the edge of the bed. My chest heaves. The night air feels cold on my bare legs. "I killed Ma."

"You killed Ma?" Donnie remains standing in the darkness. "What the hell are you talking about?"

"I told her I might not want to be a priest, and she died."

"Come on, I told you, that's bullshit. Maybe I killed her. Maybe the old man killed her with his drinking and bellowing. He messed with her more than anybody. Maybe Annie's death killed her. Then there's our fucking Uncle Tool, the ex-priest. Calm down, for Christ's sake. I think we all killed her, or maybe her own weak thinking killed her. How about the church killed her? She took it all way too serious."

My eyes water; my breathing slows. I shudder in the cold night air. "You mean you think about this stuff?"

"We live in a nuthouse. Course I think about it. Now calm down and go to sleep."

I slide beneath the blankets. Take some breaths. Push Ma out of my mind. I think of my sister, but that makes my eyes well up. I remember the way her mouth slid into a grin as she taught me to dance. "Move like you're in warm liquid. Loosen up, you're stiff as a scarecrow."

We were wildly dancing to "Rock around the Clock." Willowy Anne with long chestnut hair was leading, spinning me around the basement. "One, two, three o'clock, rock…" In that brief second of hesitation in the lyrics, I remember Anne's laughter, her smile. Where did she learn such happiness? Not in this house. She didn't learn to smile from our mother.

Ma wore dreariness like dark, wrinkled clothes. Downcast eyes and sagging mouth, worry lines. Ma was cheerless, yet I miss her. Or maybe I miss the way I used to be with her as a kid. As a kid, I sat next to her on the sofa while she read to me *The Lives of the Saints;* our arms touched. She felt warm.

She would wake me at six in the morning, pull out my math book to help me with homework. She was determined I wouldn't fail math.

I miss her in other ways. The way she bandaged my cuts, packed my school lunches. The way she pecked around the house like a nervous bird.

When Anne died, I lost Ma to the house. All she did was vacuum and dust the furniture. Pop raged at all of us. Donnie hung out more and more with his gang of friends. Pop sniped at me. Ma was the only one who stood up for me.

When I was fifteen, I yelled at Pop after Anne died. "You're not the only one who's sad here!" I stood up for Ma. I was going to be a priest. A grown-up, spiritual, manly man of God. Ma's ticket to heaven.

Then I pulled the rug out from under her. Told her I might quit the seminary.

Quiet tears streak my face. Across the room, Donnie snores while I cry for Ma and my sister.

I cry, and my breathing settles. Ma's death starts to recede to an ashen stain.

Hell, death, a vengeful God. Ma had fragile nerves. Maybe the church did kill her, or maybe it was the way she was wired, hand-wringing, sad eyes that hardly smiled. I feel sad she couldn't get her feet on the ground. Her head stuck in the clouds, her vision distorted. Screw it, Donnie's right. She may have killed herself.

15

I GUESS POP THINKS I GO TO Mass every morning before work. I still
go to Zim's most mornings when I'm sure Denise is working. I feel
odd when it comes to Denise Maxx, knowing what I know about her
and Donnie in the car. I don't have the nerve to tell her I was in the
back seat the whole time. "You're a nice guy," she tells me. "Too bad
your brother's a creep."

"Why do you say that? You hardly know the guy." I'm sitting at the
counter, mopping egg yolk with toast and feigning innocence.

"We parked at the Circle one night. He said he wanted to become
a doctor. I feel he told me a bunch of lies." Denise hurries off with a
glass coffee urn. She returns and slaps an order sheet on the metal
pass-through bar to the kitchen.

I chew on the salt taste of bacon. "A doctor? The guy nearly passes out at the sight of blood. He hasn't been the same since Ma died.
We've all been a little out of whack since then."

Denise wipes down the blue counter. "I'm sorry about your mother, but he told me the lies *before* she died."

"What other lies did he tell you?"

Denise looks over her shoulder toward the kitchen. "I can't talk
now. Starting to get busy." I feel a thrill at her subtle invitation. Denise
wants to talk to me. "I'm through with work and school after four, if
you'd like to meet me somewhere."

I wipe my mouth with a paper napkin, trying not to look surprised by Denise's candid words. She smiles, rakes my face with her eyes. Life suddenly feels exciting and a bit dangerous. A definite distraction from thinking about how much I miss Ma. "Sure, I'll meet you wherever you want. I should be free of work after six."

"How about seven? Lake Merced. The Circle. I'll be driving a '54 baby-blue Ford."

I jump up from the counter, leaving a too-generous tip. "See you at the Circle."

My pulse jackhammers as I walk out of Zim's. Unbelievable, Denise is a looker, and she wants to meet me at the Circle. I feel nearly drunk with anticipation as I sail through the day and drive to job sites delivering parts for Sheets Mechanical.

At 7:00 p.m., I pull into the asphalt parking area at Lake Merced and park next to Denise's blue Ford. She smiles when she sees me and motions with her hand that she wants me to get in her car.

I hesitate for a tiny second, wondering what she wants with me. I shut down the engine and get out of the little pickup. A coastal fog-laden breeze slides off the lake, making the interior of Denise's car feel warm and inviting. Low sunlight slivers between distant cypress and eucalyptus trees. A rusted old green Chevy is the only other parked car in the Circle.

Denise reclines into the corner of the car where the edge of the seat meets the doorframe. She stretches her legs in black pedal-pushers across the floor mats. "Thanks for coming, Raymond."

I don't know how to act in the presence of this blue-eyed girl neatly packaged in a soft lavender sweater. "So, you want to talk about my brother?"

"He's not going to UC Davis on a football scholarship, is he?" Her tone, matter of fact, more like a flat statement than a question.

I play the middle ground, not wanting to directly admit to my brother's bullshit. "Not that I know of."

"I broke up with the Marine. Sent him a letter saying I didn't want to wait around for him anymore." Denise has her hands on her outstretched lap. Slowly rubs the fingers of her left hand with her right thumb. "You have a girlfriend, Raymond?"

I briefly think of Alice, but I can't let her get in the way of Denise. Anyway, Alice is not really my girlfriend, yet I feel a little deceptive when I answer. "No, I been in the seminary."

Denise tilts her head quizzically. "What's a seminary?"

I'm surprised by her question. "It's a Catholic school where they train guys to be priests."

"Wow!" Denise barks in disbelief, swings her legs under the steering wheel, and sits up. "You're going to be a priest?"

"*Was* going to be a priest. They kicked me out." In the excited intimacy of the moment, I don't mind confessing to this girl.

"Why, what did you do?"

I think about explaining Alice and the motorcycle, but it would only sound lame. "The faculty didn't like my attitude. They were real jerks about it. They said I was too worldly."

"Worldly? Were these people like monks or something?" She shifts her body, leans toward me. I feel a tingle in my lower abdomen when she places her hand on my knee. Whoever thought talk about St. Jerome's would turn on a girl?

"Sort of. They were pretty strict."

"I never knew anybody who lived like that. Was the seminary like a monastery? Did you wear hair shirts?"

I laugh, feeling momentarily superior about my inner knowledge of St. Jerome's. "Kind of like a monastery, but no hair shirts."

"Are you real religious?" A cautious question, like she's asking if I might have a contagious disease or an inoperable cancer.

"I'm not sure what I am, but I like hearing different people's beliefs. Iron Jack thinks God is love."

"Who's Iron Jack?"

I give Denise a brief rundown on my former spiritual advisor. "You ever think about God?"

"Not much." She looks away through the windshield toward the trees where dusk begins to smudge the evening sky. "Once when I was a kid on vacation in the mountains, I looked up at the Milky Way. Mom said it was God's carpet. Later, I joined the teen fellowship group at the Presbyterian church, but mostly to check out the guys."

"Sounds like more fun than the seminary."

"I guess, a little more fun, but I'm more grown-up now. I sometimes like more serious talk. I miss our morning conversations."

"Yeah, I don't go to Zim's on the days I know you're not working."

"Are you just saying that to be polite? Do you really like me?"

"Course I like you. You're pretty and fun to talk to." I tell her the truth, but at the same time, I feel deceptive like I'm becoming my brother.

"Have you ever been with a girl?"

"I danced with this girl named Alice on New Year's Eve."

"No, I mean have you ever, you know, made out?"

I feel my face flush. "Not exactly." I'm embarrassed by my lack of sophistication.

She must notice my discomfort. "Don't worry, I can teach you things if you want. How old are you?"

My heart tom-toms in my chest. "Eighteen."

"I'm two years older than you. My boyfriend and I were pretty serious, but we never went all the way. Still, I can show you things."

I feel feverish. A red truck parks next to us. Two older guys in jeans and heavy jackets get out and retrieve fishing poles from the truck bed. One guy has a wicker creel hanging by a strap on his shoulder. They hustle down the embankment toward the lake. "Like what?"

"Like where to touch me. I take sex ed in college, which is mostly diagrams of where the uterus is and stuff. I've also seen some Italian movies. I took a foreign film class, and I know what inflames me."

"Inflames you?"

"What stirs me up. What makes my body tingle."

I feel a blood rush in my groin. "Sounds like I should take those classes."

"You don't have to. You have me. Mr. Lynch, my sex ed teacher, says it's normal for young people to experiment."

Denise says the word "experiment" like she's talking about a beaker full of liquid in chemistry class. But when she puts her hand on mine, I'm miles away from any chemistry lab. "Do you feel close to me? We can start now if you want."

My breath is panting in my throat. "What about the fishermen?"

She lets go of my hand. "You're right. This place creeps me out anyway, ever since I was here with your brother."

The intensity recedes, and I try to fan the flames. "We could go to my house. My brother went to Tahoe with some guys, and my pop works late, and he never comes into my room."

Denise perks up. "Where do you live?"

"St. Francis Wood."

"You live in St. Francis Wood and you have your own room?" All of a sudden, my pop's house and the neighborhood we live in takes on new importance. Denise seems intoxicated with excitement.

I try to sound indifferent. Once again, my brother's imposter attitude is starting to rub off on me. "Not exactly my own room. I share a room with Donnie."

"Ugh! Don't even mention your brother's name."

"Not another word about my brother. You want to follow me home?"

I drive slowly so I don't lose Denise in traffic. I think about being hidden in the back seat of Donnie's car. I feel creepy and deceitful, like I really *am* becoming my brother. When I get home, I park in the driveway. Denise tucks her car behind my truck. She hops out of the Ford. "Wow, quite a house. The front yard looks like a miniature park."

I lead her up the front steps. "My mom's rhodies. She loved those plants. They only bloom for about three weeks, but it's quite a display."

I open the door to the cold, stern, polished marble of the foyer. "I'm home!" The house echoes emptiness. Mr. and Mrs. Sako must be downstairs in their apartment.

Denise stands under the arched entry to the dining room. "Pretty fancy chandelier, and I love the neat texture of the walls. Seems a little dark in here, though."

"Yeah, Ma keeps this place shadowy like the inside of some Gothic cathedral." I catch myself using the present tense. Ma died, and I sense her looking down on me and this strange girl who is about to give me some lessons. Conflicting thoughts fly through my head. I miss Ma, but right now, I'm glad she's not here. I shake the thoughts and bound up the stairs. "Come on, it's lighter in my room."

My eager pulse throbs as Denise briefly scans the walls, then lands with a bounce on my brother's bed. She lies on her back like she owns the room. "Who's the guy in the pictures?"

"That's my Uncle Tool. He used to be a priest."

"He's like you, too good-looking to be a priest. Why did he quit?"

"I don't know. Probably a woman. You think I'm good-looking?"

"Wouldn't be here if I didn't. Come and lie down with me."

I approach the bed and kick off my shoes. Denise scoots over, making room for me on top of the comforter. I feel tight and anxious as she lightly runs her hand across my forehead. I don't dare tell her this is Donnie's bed. "How did two brothers who are so different come from the same parents?"

My tongue feels thick as a sausage when I answer. "I dunno, that's the same question my old man asks."

She's up on one elbow. Her face inches from mine. "I like you, Raymond, and I want you to touch me."

"T-touch you where?" I stammer.

She turns on the mattress so her face is pressed to the pillow. "Lift the back of my sweater."

She hoists her body ever so slightly as I slide the bottom edge of her sweater up to her shoulders. I feel awkward and at a loss for words. "Your skin is warm," I babble.

"Touch my spine with your fingers, Raymond. Touch my spine lightly and unfasten my bra."

I pull at the elastic of her bra and tug at the mystery of the metal clasp. I trace the tiny divots and bumps of her spine with my fingertips.

"That's it," she murmurs into the pillow. "Rub my back with your hands."

I can't figure how I can use both hands on her back without sitting up. From the depths of the pillow, she reads my mind. "Get on your knees and straddle me, Raymond. I saw this in a movie. Rub me hard and slow with both of your hands."

I feel my dick harden as I straddle the soft hump of her backside. Denise mews happy sounds while I move my hands up and down her back. Then she arches slightly and pulls her sweater up over her blond head. "Kiss the back of my neck, Raymond."

I place my hands on either side of her shoulders and lean my lips into her neck. With one hand, she reaches and lifts her hair. "Kiss me where my hair reaches my neck. Kiss me, Raymond, kiss me, and I'll show you how to touch me."

My heart revs like a race car. I bury my head in her hair and nibble at the scent of her lemony skin. I'm pressing into her when the door to the room bursts open. "What the hell is going on here?"

I quickly look up and hop off the bed to face my furious brother. Donnie pushes me backward, and I fall across a screaming Denise. "What the hell is this? What are you doing on my bed? What the hell are you doing with her on my goddamned bed?"

Denise is pinned to the bed by the weight of my body. She's squirming and shouting. "I was teaching him how to love me. Your brother's sweet and not a blowhard and a liar like you."

Donnie grasps me by the shoulders and yanks me to my feet. "What do you mean I'm a liar? What have you been telling her, little brother?"

The room feels close, oppressive. For the first time in my life, I feel hatred for my brother. I want to smash him, rip Uncle Tool's smiling picture off the wall, scream at my mother for leaving. I rush Donnie, grab him by the shirtfront. "I didn't tell her anything!" My father's fury rises in me. "I didn't tell her a goddamned thing!" My bellowing voice is gorged with adrenalin, and I shove my brother. Donnie plants his feet, silences me with a hard fist to my face. The pain is fierce and startling. I back off and press my palm to my left eye.

Denise shrieks, "Leave him alone!" She has her sweater on, clutches her twisted bra in her hands. "You're not going to be a doctor. You were just trying to get into my pants!"

"Maybe I will be a doctor, and it looks like my brother knows way more about getting into your pants than I ever thought of! Get her out of here, Ray! The two of you get the hell out of here!"

I grip Denise's arm and drag her out the door. "Screw you, Donnie!"

The hallway reverberates with my shout as I push open the door to my sister's room and pull Denise inside. She pulls away from me and sits crying on the edge of my sister's bed. The untethered bra looks pathetic in her hands.

Beady eyes from my sister's doll case give a collective stare. I want to rip the case from the wall. "He is a liar," I seethe. "He's also an ass-hole, all that bullshit about breaking up with his girlfriend."

Denise sniffles and inhales a stuttering breath. "That's the only part I believed. He said her name was Nadine."

"He used the name of my old man's secretary, Nadine Ottoboni. She's in her forties."

"He told you about the Circle?" Denise is on her feet, her eyes wide with rage. "He told you all about me? You knew about the lies?"

I momentarily close my eyes. I'm sick and tired of secrets. I take a breath, begin to spit out the truth. "I was there, Denise, I was on the floor in the back seat. I was under the car cover."

Her fists pummel my chest. "You're creepier than he is!" She backs up and begins swatting at my face with her bra. I feel a prickly sting under my throbbing left eye, still sore from my brother's fist.

I grab her wrists. "Damn it, I didn't want to be there…"

Denise twists free of my grasp and lands an explosive kick to my right shin. "The creep brothers! You're both sick!" She continues to scream and wail all the way down the stairs. "I hate you, Raymond Sheets!" Her words echo in the foyer before she slams the front door.

I clench and unclench my fists, feeling smaller than the miniature dolls eyeing me from the wall case.

I march back to my bedroom where Donnie packs a gray over-night bag resting on his bed. "I thought you were going to Tahoe."

"I am going to Tahoe." He yanks open a dresser drawer, slaps some underwear into the bag. "I haven't fuckin' left yet. You're a be-hind-my-back little shit, brother. I don't know how the hell you got her up here."

My eye pumps with pain. I stand across the room, talk at Donnie's back as he zippers shut his bag. "She wanted to come up here…"

Donnie has the bag by the handle, swings it hard as he turns toward me. "I don't wanna hear it! Don't say another word about it!" We stand inches apart. My brother's brown eyes snarl a warning. I have my hands on my hips, feet nailed to the floor as I hold my ground.

"Sure, let's not talk about it! Let's be silent! Let's not ever talk about Denise, or Ma's death, or Ann's death! Let's walk around like the old man, all torn up inside and silent as a goddamned drunken zombie!"

"Screw you, Ray!" Donnie bolts out the bedroom door and down the stairs.

"Go on to Tahoe!" I stand at the top of the stairs. "Go to Tahoe, bullshit some waitress and get yourself laid, but don't ever talk…" My voice trails off as the front door slams on me for the second time today.

My chest heaves and contracts like a bellows as I angrily descend the stairs. Mr. and Mrs. Sako bustle about the kitchen. Mr. Sako places two cups from my mother's china set on the sideboard, and Mrs. Sako pours hot water. "Would you like some tea, Raymond? It may help to soothe you. It seems you and your brother have had a disagreement?"

I sit with them at the dining room table but decline the tea. "Sorry you had to hear us fighting."

Mrs. Sako smiles. "Brothers fight. It's most natural. Easy to happen when everybody misses your mother. Perhaps a cold cloth on your eye?"

"Thanks, Mrs. Sako; my eye will be okay, but you're right, we all miss her, and nobody wants to talk about it. My brother runs away to Tahoe; my father drinks. It's like we're supposed to forget about her. And my sister's dead too. Her room is a shrine, her bed all made up like she might be coming home any day now."

Mr. Sako wraps his dark rough hands around the teacup. "Compassion, Raymond." His brown eyes flicker like agates under the dining room chandelier. "Be kind to yourself and kind to your brother. Nothing stays the same. Life very complicated."

"Must be complicated." The tone of my voice becomes softer in the presence of this wise man. "So complicated everybody wants to ignore it. My mother ran off to church. My father runs to the bottle."

"Go slowly, Raymond, like the flowers in your mother's garden. Flower buds open slowly."

Mr. Sako means well, but "flower buds open slowly" sounds like something I read in a fortune cookie when my mom and pop used to take us up to the Chinese restaurant when I was a kid. Our family was complete back then, and Annie and Ma were alive. Life was not complicated.

I leave the table and go to my room, thinking how quickly things change from the excitement of feeling a girl's back to the sting of her bra swatting my face.

16

With Zim's and Denise no longer an option, lots of mornings I go down to the beach across from Playland, sit on the seawall, and stare at the waves. I think of Ma. The house is empty without her in the kitchen cooking, voicing her concerns about Tool, and making worried small talk while stirring spaghetti sauce.

Occasionally, I phone Alice from a booth near the Playland arcade. She answers, then calls me back so I don't have to keep plunking change into the phone. Our conversations vary from where I'll be going to school in September to her mother's drinking problem. I tell her my old man's trying to drown himself in scotch, and one morning I tell her about Donnie and Denise and Lake Merced.

Alice snickers. "You stayed under the tarp the whole time? That's creepy."

"That's exactly what Denise said."

"What? She found out?"

"It's a long story. Denise and I were getting kind of cozy, and then I told her about the tarp. She kicked me in the shins and went screaming out of the house."

"You two-timing me, Raymond? Just kidding. Actually, I kind of got the hots for Melinda's older brother, but he's twenty-three, so I don't have much of a chance."

My voice is punctuated with jealousy. "He's probably a dipshit anyway." I sound harsh and catch myself. "Nice to have you as a friend, Alice."

"Same."

Some days, she asks with real concern, "How are you feeling?"

"Okay," I answer, and sometimes I am okay. Other times, I feel a gut-wrenching loss. During some of the calls, we just breathe together in the silence of the phone lines. Alice seems to have lost some of her rebellious attitude, and her voice and the sea both soothe me.

One evening during the last week of August, I find myself alone with my pop in his office. I have purposely stayed late and pretend to transcribe the hours on employee time cards. I know it's time to tell him I'm not going back to St. Jerome's. He's hunched over a slanted table studying a set of blueprints. A glass of scotch rests on a narrow shelf above the table.

"Pop, I'm going to owe you some money."

With his elbows on the table, he turns his head toward me. "Why would you owe me money, Choirboy?"

I feel my heart race. "The hundred dollars. I'm not going back to the seminary."

"Your mother wouldn't like that."

"I know, Pop, that's my point. I think I was studying to be a priest because she wanted me to."

My father is standing over me now. Pointing his finger, he says loudly, "Don't you ever refer to her as 'she.' You refer to her as 'my mother.' You show some respect, you understand me?"

I push away from the desk and stand up to face him, "Sorry, Pop—"

"You better be sorry. Your mother's a good woman. Goddamn it, she's a good woman…"

He sweeps his arm across the desk, sends the time cards cascading to the floor. As he returns to the blueprint table, I resist the urge to run away. "Sorry, Pop, but you're not the only one that misses her. Donnie misses her, and damn it, I miss her too. It's painful to all of us, not just you. You're pissed off at God, and I understand that, but don't take it out on me. I'm hurting just like you!"

With his elbows on the table and his face in his hands, he says, "I know, Choirboy, I know you are...now head on home. Mrs. Sako's probably got a nice dinner cooked."

"You can't drink it away, Pop. The scotch is going to kill you."

He looks at me and slowly nods his head. Tears spill over his cheeks. He blinks his eyes and starts to say something, then stops. He can't get the words out. I retrieve the time cards from the floor and lay them on the desk.

"Where you gonna finish school, Choirboy?"

"I was thinking St. Ignatius if I can still get in."

"We'll make sure you do." He reaches for his scotch. "Go home, Choirboy. Just go home."

I leave my old man with his booze, hoping he doesn't get in an accident on the way home. I don't know who to talk to about his drinking problem, but I need to do something before he kills or injures himself or somebody else.

Summer begins to wind down. I do mostly office work for Sheets Mechanical except for Tuesdays and Thursdays, when I drive the Falcon to supply houses and pick up parts to be delivered to various jobsites. On delivery days, I sometimes take my lunch hour at the beach across from Playland.

I enjoy Playland at noon in summer. The air is filled with sounds. Kids screaming from the plunge and thunder of the roller coaster, the music of the carousel, and the cackling racket of the

189

orange-haired Laffing Sal, the automated mannequin that can be heard all over the park.

The beach becomes one of my favorite stomping grounds. After lunch on the seawall, I run on the firm, dark sand near the surf line and let the cold salt water cascade over my feet and ankles.

Playland, smelling of taffy and cotton candy, and the pungent air of the beach soothe the lonesome feelings after my mother's death. Running seems to ground me.

The main connection between my old life and what lies ahead is Melon. On the first Saturday in September, I give him a call to see if he wants to run on the beach. "Sheetsy, you know my body is adverse to physical exercise, but I'll gladly go down there and eye the dollies. It's going to be a beautiful day outside, and the girlies will be flocking there like flies. Let's pick up Georgie on the way."

"I don't know about Georgie. He's due back at the sem tomorrow."

"That's why we got to give him a send-off. A little good-bye celebration for the squint-eyed little sucker."

Melon has the garage door open when I pull up in front of his house. He tosses his cooler in the back of the truck, and we drive the avenues toward Georgie's. "What's in the cooler?"

"Lots of ice, my friend. Lots of ice and a few thirst-quenching libations from 'the land of sky-blue waters.'"

"When the heck you gonna learn, Melon? We almost got in a bunch of trouble with beer on New Year's Eve."

"We've matured, old buddy. New Year's was centuries ago. Just trust old Melon."

Georgie's mother answers our knock at the front door. "Good morning, Mrs. Thurmond. Is George available to take a ride to the beach with Raymond and me?" Melon's ability as an actor never ceases to amaze me.

Mrs. Thurmond reminds me of a quiet little bird. I get a feeling she's going to pat her sunken chest with the palm of her hand and say, "Oh, dear me," but instead she calls back into the house: "Georgie, someone's here to see you."

Georgie appears and pushes his dark-rimmed glasses higher up on his owl eyes. "Hi, guys." Both he and his mother are small and skinny. The two of them standing side by side don't fill the doorway.

"Good morning, old buddy. It's a wonderful day out here. Raymond and I thought you might like to get a little sunshine. We're headed out to the beach."

"I don't know, guys. I got a lot to do."

"Oh, go on, Georgie. A little fresh air with your classmates might do you good." Mrs. Thurmond is all chirpy smiles. "He's been so morose lately."

"Okay, I guess…"

The three of us clamber down the steps as Mrs. Thurmond peeps, "Have fun, boys," and closes the door behind us.

Out at the truck, Melon mumbles, "Ride in the back, Four Eyes. It's a little tight up here with Raymond and me. And don't touch the cooler."

The truck gives a little bounce as Georgie settles back near the tailgate. I start the engine. "Go easy on Georgie, Melon. He's a friendly little guy."

"Course he is. Old Terminal's the best. I'm trying to loosen him up. You heard his mother, he's been a little morose lately."

"Yeah, and she doesn't seem to know that you're not one of his classmates anymore. Doesn't have the slightest inkling that Georgie's polite, pudgy little classmate got booted out of the seminary."

"Skatin' on thin ice, Sheetsy. Even Georgie doesn't know *you're* not one of his classmates."

Bantering with Melon is uplifting on this sunlit Saturday. "I think he does know, but I'll tell him anyway. And keep him away from the beer. He doesn't seem to have a tolerance."

"Sheets, I'm gonna start calling you Agnes. Or maybe St. Agnes. You sound like an old woman."

The parking lot at the beach is wedged between lanes of north- and south-flowing traffic along what's known as the Great Highway. I often wonder how many people have been hit as they run across lanes of fast-moving cars. I inch the Falcon between the lines of a parking space. "I'm warning you, Melon. No funny stuff with Georgie."

"Don't worry, Agnes, he's in good hands."

The screams on the roller coaster and the tilt-a-whirl seem louder today. Bigger crowds having their last summer fling before school. Georgie hops out of the back of the truck, and Melon picks up his cooler, and we make our way across the stream of cars and down a set of the concrete steps that punctuate the seawall at intervals. The surf is mild yet loud enough to drown out the sound of Laffing Sal and the screams from carnival rides.

The ocean side of the seawall is constructed of concrete tiers that march up from the beach. The tiers are seat-height and gritty with sand. Melon sets the cooler down and opens it. "Who's ready for some cold suds?"

Georgie mumbles, "Nothing for me, thanks." He sits on the concrete next to Melon, and I take my shoes off and step out of my jeans.

"What, are you gonna give us a striptease, Sheets?"

"I got my running shorts on, idiot, something your pudgy little fanny wouldn't know anything about."

"Careful, Sheets, that's the second time today you called me pudgy."

Georgie gives an audible snicker.

"Well, well, the little Hoot Owl is alive and well." Melon gives Georgie a light punch on the arm. "I was worried about you, my son. Was afraid I was going to have to knock you out and pour some happy brew down your mouth."

The beach begins to come alive with people who spread towels and pop umbrellas. Melon punctures a beer can and pours into an opaque plastic cup.

The sun has not yet risen high enough to fully heat the sand, which feels pliant and cool beneath my feet. "Melon, give me a cupful of that before some cop from the mounted patrol rides up on his horse and takes it away from you." I chug the beer in four swallows. "Sky-blue waters, good stuff. Seriously, don't get busted."

"I can see a cop coming a long way off. Besides, I'll tell him it's lemonade."

I begin to stretch my left calf muscle with the back of my foot up on one of the concrete tiers. "Sure, lemonade with white foam on it."

"Maybe you can tell him it's a medical experiment, and you're ingesting your own urine." Georgie doubles over with laughter at his own joke.

"Terminus, you morose little clown. Your mama would be proud seeing you laugh like that." Melon takes a sip and smacks his lips. "Go run your ass off, Sheetsy. Me and Red Skelton here are gonna watch for babes and have some laughs."

I push off through the dry sand toward the surf line, where a young woman is bent over two intent little blond girls digging with small shovels and slopping the dark wet sand into blue pails with starfish designs on them. The woman glances my way and smiles.

I run south along the water-packed shore. Flocks of small birds on dainty legs skitter like wind-up toys at my approach. I feel I could run forever along this glistening strand of beach. The surf pounds endlessly, and a low, light haze hangs where the ocean meets the land.

I think of Roger Bannister on the wall poster above my bed. Four-minute mile. I run and feel like a rocket. I leave Melon, Georgie, Playland, St. Jerome's, and even my mother's death far behind.

A fisherman in olive hip waders casts a heavy line into the surf. A second man holds the base of a fishing rod against his hip, nods at me, and smiles like we share some mystery about the pull of the sea.

I pass high dunes that separate the beach from the Great Highway. Tall, reedy shore grasses atop the dunes wave southward in a slight breeze. By the time I reach the parking lot at Sloat Boulevard near the zoo, I'm sweaty, light-headed, and elated. I turn north and retrace my route, edging deeper into the surging foam to feel the raw, cold salt water splash high on my legs.

I've been gone about an hour, and it's near noon when I get back to the seawall. The beach is filling fast with sunbathers and picnickers. Toward the far north, a pod of surfers in wet suits slide over the waves like seals below the high perch of the Cliff House Restaurant. In the background, Seal Rocks, covered with bird droppings, thrust their jagged heads out of the ocean like snowcapped sea mounts. Gray and white gulls screech and circle overhead.

I scan the tiered base of the seawall for Melon and Georgie. Crowds have gathered along the tiers. People eat hot dogs, drink sodas out of red-and-white containers from Playland. Amid the oglers and gawkers, people talk and enjoy the day.

I spot Georgie sitting by himself. He leans back against the concrete, his glasses askew near the end of his nose. Sand sticks to my wet feet and ankles as I sit down beside him. "Where's our buddy with the cooler?"

Georgie pushes his glasses up and stares at me for a couple of seconds. "He took off with some girl."

"What girl?"

"I dunno. I think her name was Lynn. She wandered over to us and said she needed a ride home." Georgie takes off his glasses and rubs his right eye, leaving sand grit on his face.

"Georgie, you been drinking?"

"Maybe a little. Melon said he was you."

"What the heck are you talking about?"

"Melon told the girl his name was Raymond Sheets and he'd give her a ride home in the company truck."

"Damn it, Georgie, you better be joking." I stand and pull on my jeans over the running shorts. I button up and reach in my pocket for the truck keys. My pockets are empty. "Shit, did he take off in my truck?"

"He might have. He gave the girl a beer, and then I saw him reach in your pants pocket. He said he'd meet me over at the arcade in an hour or two. Then he picked up the cooler and they were gone."

"And you didn't try to stop him? What the hell's the matter with you?"

"I dunno. There was this girl, and Melon said he was you, and I guess I got confused."

"How long ago did they leave, and how much have you had to drink?"

"I think they left quite a while ago, and I only had a glass or two."

I pick up my shoes and socks and hustle barefoot up the concrete steps. "Get up here, Georgie, and see if we can find that asshole and my truck." I sit on the wall and dust the sand off my feet with a sock. "Damn it, don't stand there gawking at me. Look around the parking lot!"

"I told you, they left, Raymond. I didn't want to come with you guys in the first place. You can see the truck's gone, so don't be yelling at me!"

I yank at my shoelaces and knot them extra tight. I'm getting madder by the second. Damn Melon. No use taking it out on Georgie. "Let's go to the lousy arcade and wait on him. He better be getting his ass back here soon."

"Yeah, I don't want to be out here late. I got to get back to the school tomorrow."

We jog between slow-moving cars. I yell across the heavy traffic, "I guess you know I'm not going back, Georgie."

Georgie stops in the middle of the far lane past the parking lot. A driver blasts him with a horn.

"Shit, Georgie, get out of the street before you get killed."

The blare of the horn startles him, and he jumps clear of the car. "You did get the boot?"

"Yeah, I'm done with St. Jerome's, and they're sure done with me."

We walk into the arcade, where game bells ring and Laffing Sal echoes her cackle. "Because of that girl?"

We have to yell above the noise. "Yeah, because of her. Also forgot to tell you my mom died."

Georgie walks over to a pinball machine and drops in a coin. "I heard about it and was going to call you. Sorry about your mom. I can't believe you won't be there tomorrow."

I scan the arcade and look for Melon. Georgie goes silently intense as he works the flippers. The silver ball bounces from post to post as bells clang and tan hula girls with painted green skirts light up on the machine. Soon, I hear a thump as Georgie wins a free game. "Where'd you learn to do that?"

"Used to come down here all the time when I was in grammar school. Once I won twenty-three free games." Georgie hits the chrome flipper buttons with his fingers and gently shakes the machine. I look on amazed as Georgie—Terminal, the Hoot Owl—wins another game.

I remember Melon and walk out of the arcade, leave the pinball noise behind. I pace the walkway in front of the amusement park and hear the screams of the thrill riders as I curse Melon in my mind.

An hour goes by. No Melon. I wander back into the arcade. Georgie looks like a fevered addict. The tote board shows he's won fourteen games. If something's happened to my pop's truck, I'm out of luck. I no longer have the option of running back to priest school with the Hoot Owl.

I go back outside. Buy a hot dog, lace it with relish and mustard, and wash it down with a Coke. I buy a second Coke and sit on a bench. Another hour gone. I'm about to buy another drink when I see Melon in the crosswalk at the Great Highway and Fulton. I spring up from the bench and run at him, not sure if I should punch him or feel relieved. "Give me the damn keys, Melon."

Melon holds his hands in front of him, palms facing me like he's about to fend off an angry fist. "Easy, Raymond, I don't exactly have the keys."

I knock his hands sideways with a sweep of my arm. I give him a little shove. "Where's the truck, Melon?"

"The truck is a little stuck in the sand, but don't worry——"

"Don't worry, my ass. My old man's gonna kill me if something's happened to that truck. Give it to me straight, Melon. Tell me what happened before I beat the shit out of you."

"We have a little situation, Raymond, but I'm gonna make it right. There was this girl, Lynn, who needed a ride home, and we parked a little north of the Sloat parking lot to enjoy the scenery, and I must have got too far into the sand, and when it was time to leave the back wheel just kept spinning——"

"The keys, Melon, what about the keys?"

"Well, that's a problem. Lynn lives in a flat out on Forty-Eighth, and she has this brother who's big as a house....I walked her home, and he roughed me up and took the keys. And also my cooler by the way…"

"Some guy took the keys? What the hell are you talking about?"

"Apparently, he thought his little sister was inebriated and it was all my fault, so he picked me up by my shirt and tossed me onto a patch of ice plant, and the keys flew out of my shirt pocket. He said something like, 'And you shouldn't be driving, you pudgy little bastard,' and then he took the keys. Lynn was screaming at her brother for attacking me, and all the time I was trying to be a gentleman and get her home safely…"

"Damn, Melon! Damn! Damn! Damn! And you told her your name was Raymond Sheets?"

"I see you been talking to little Four Eyes…the little bastard…I oughta give him a piece of my mind…"

"Melon, leave Georgie out of this. This is all caused by you and your damn cooler." I've got my right thumb and forefinger clenched around the back of Melon's neck, and I push him along the sidewalk toward the arcade.

Inside, a small crowd has gathered around Georgie's machine. He's racked up twenty-four wins, topping his old record.

Melon's all eyes and yells to be heard above the noise: "What's with the little freak? Look at him, he's got a cheering section!"

"He's a pinball wizard. Let's leave him alone until we figure out how you're going to get my truck back here."

"I don't know, Sheets. Lynn's brother is a pretty big guy."

I grab Melon's shoulders and shove him backward toward the entrance. He bumps into a girl about our age. She's tall with straight brown hair. She gives a little squeal. The guy she's with is even taller. Collar turned up on his jean jacket. He gives us a fierce green-eyed stare. Melon holds both his palms up and shrugs. "Sorry, my friend likes to horse around."

Melon's slightly red-faced as I shove him out to the sidewalk. "You better figure it out, Melon. What's this guy's name?"

"How the hell would I know? He was trying to inflict bodily harm. He didn't seem to want to exchange names."

"What about this Lynn? Does she have a last name?"

"Batts, her last name's Batts. Don't worry about her. It's her brother that's the problem. He's big and mean, and she says he plays football."

"Plays football where?"

"Shit, Raymond, the guy wanted to kill me, not give me a rundown on his gridiron skills. He might play for the damn Baltimore Colts for all I know."

I walk toward the phone booth. "Melon, if we don't get that truck back, I'm going to bust your damn face open."

I close the door to the phone booth and dial Andreozzi's Deli in North Beach. "Can I speak to Donnie Sheets, please?"

"This is Donnie." I feel relieved to hear my brother's voice.

"Donnie, it's Ray. You know a guy who plays football named Batts?"

Donnie's tone is cold. We're still barely speaking after the tussle over Denise. "Yeah, Levi, Levi Batts. Plays defensive tackle for City College. Levi's not his real name though. We just call him that because it's short for Leviathan. What about it?"

"It's a long story, but this Levi has the old man's truck keys."

"Look, I'm working, asshole. What the hell you want me to do about your little problem?"

"Man, I'm in a jam, and it's a big problem." I give Donnie a fast version of Melon, Levi, and the girl.

"Lucky the Leviathan didn't kick Melon's balls up to his brains. Go start digging the truck out of the sand. Get some driftwood under the tire. I'll be at the Sloat parking lot in about an hour and a half."

"Dig it out with what?"

"I don't know. Your hands, idiot, whatever it takes."

I leave the phone booth and return to the arcade. "Melon, we got to get Georgie and start digging the truck out."

"How we gonna get there?"

"Run, walk, call a cab, hitchhike, crawl on our hands and knees. What difference does it make?"

Melon stops walking and holds his hands out like he expects to catch some lemon meringue pie falling from space. "It makes a lot of difference. I'm exhausted from getting beat up by Lynn's brother. Then I had to walk from her house to here."

"Melon, do you understand the seriousness of this? You have no idea how pissed off my father can get. Now, we have to get Georgie and dig the damn truck out."

I nudge him into the arcade when he confesses, "I'm not so sure we can dig it out."

The crowd around Georgie gives a cheer as the machine pops another win. "What do you mean we can't dig it out?"

"It's not just one wheel. I drove the truck quite a ways onto the beach. I think all the wheels are stuck."

I feel my face go red. "You drove on the damn beach? The tide's coming in. How close is the truck to the water? What the hell were you thinking?"

"I don't know. The girl. The beer. I just wanted to have a little fun, and then we got stuck."

I elbow my way through the crowd. "Georgie! We have to go!" I have my hand on Georgie's shoulder, and then I feel a hand on my shoulder.

I turn and look into the face of the tall guy in the jean jacket saying, "Let the little guy alone, he's on a roll."

"Look, pal, I need to get him out of here. Why don't you take over his free games?" Georgie's stopped playing. Pinball lights glitter waiting for the next silver ball to be released. "Come on, Georgie. Let's go."

Georgie looks back and forth from the tall guy to me. I hate to rob him of his moment of glory. Jean jacket saves the day by giving Georgie three bucks. "Here, kid, here's a buck for every ten games you won. Mind if I have a go at it?"

Georgie shrugs as I drag him and Melon out of the arcade. "What's going on?"

I herd the two of them across the highway. "Jackass Melon got the truck stuck in the sand down by the Sloat parking lot. We got to figure out how to get it unstuck."

We stand on the sidewalk next to the seawall. Georgie shakes his head. "Melon, you got shit for brains."

Melon turns on Georgie. "Whoa, little man, I oughta bust your face. You're studying to be a priest and saying words like 'shit.'"

I feel near panic about my pop's truck. "Knock it off! Step to the curb and stick your thumbs out! We're hitchhiking."

Buicks and Chevys pass us by. A wood-paneled station wagon. Some guys in a hotrod black coupe yell some obscenities and give us a horse laugh. Minutes pass. The tide moves in. I don't know whether to walk or stand there with my thumb out. Georgie's got his elbow on his hip, thumb up in the air. Melon gives Georgie a bad time. "Hey, pinball king, get your elbow off your belt and lower your thumb. You look like a homo."

"Come on, Jesus, help me out here," I mutter when two girls in a green '53 Lincoln convertible pull up alongside of us.

"Where you guys going?"

"Who knows?" Melon asks. "Might go all the way to LA. We're knights of the road, out for adventure…quite a nice boat you got here…"

I elbow Melon hard in the ribs. "We need to get down to Sloat."

The girl driving is redheaded, freckled, and curly. "Hop in."

Melon sits up high on the back of the seat between Georgie and me like he's some dignitary in a Fourth of July parade.

"Hey, sit down in the seat before we all get arrested." The redhead is armed with confidence. Her friend with mousy hair blowing in the breeze doesn't even give us a look.

I'm relieved by the ride. If we had walked the distance with Melon and Georgie, it would have been at a snail's pace. The girls get us there in less than five minutes. A blue tow truck has a cable extended out to my Pop's Falcon. A police car stands by with lights flashing. Surf foam laps at the wheels of the truck. The mousy-haired girl has her sunglasses pulled down over the tip of her nose. "Wow, looks like somebody screwed up."

Melon attempts to justify the situation, "I bet it's a stolen truck… some punk kids took it for a joyride…"

I thank the girls, launch myself over the side of the convertible, and run full speed toward the tow-truck driver. He works a winch lever off the back of the truck. "You gonna be able to get it out?" I ask breathlessly.

The driver's a rawboned middle-aged guy with greasy blue overalls. "Maybe I will and maybe I won't. What the hell is it to you?"

"My father owns Sheets Mechanical. That's one of his trucks. It was stolen from Playland parking lot a few hours ago."

"Well, whoever stole it didn't leave the keys. Broke into it with a slim-jim. Hotwired it to get it into neutral. Trying to drag it, but the sand's really got a hold. Winch motor's straining. Tide's coming up pretty fast."

"How about digging out around the wheels?" I'm yelling over the pound of the surf and the whine of the motor.

"Got two shovels behind the cab, but I'm not about to get my feet wet."

The Lincoln's gone. I see Melon and Georgie walking toward me, and I scream like a madman. "Melon, grab a shovel!"

The driver holds up his grimy hand. "Lemme slacken the cable. Gets too tight and snaps, it'll cut you and your fat little buddy in half like you was pork sausage."

Once the cable is sagging, Melon and I run toward the Falcon. With each push of the surf, water fills the void we dig behind the rear tires. Georgie gets down on his knees, hurling wet sand from behind the front tire.

My shoes and socks are soon soaked. At least Melon's shoveling at full speed. "I'll show that old bastard what the Melon can do. Did you hear him call me fat?"

I free the right rear tire and run to help Georgie. "I'll call you something worse than that if we don't get this truck out of here."

Finally, the sand is clear. The driver yells, "Get back!" as he starts the winch motor. The rear end of the Falcon lifts free. The little truck rests on its front wheels and begins to inch backward and away as one last slap of a wavelet reaches out, swirls, and recedes into the sand.

"Sheetsy! We're home free! We did it, old buddy!" Melon is as animated as I've ever seen him.

Georgie wipes his glasses on his shirttail. The three of us, soaked below the knees, slog to the parking lot. "The keys, Melon. We still need to get the keys."

A breeze kicks up, and the sun hangs high before it tips into its arc down toward the west. The cop is out of the patrol car and talking to the tow-truck driver. I feel a chill as I walk toward them. "You belong to this truck?" The cop is young, tall, and muscular.

"Yeah, my dad owns Sheets Mechanical."

"How come it wasn't reported stolen?"

Unexpected question. I pause and think how to answer when Melon pipes up, "We didn't want to report it because my buddy Raymond didn't want to admit to his father that he left the keys in the truck."

"That's right." My lie feels as fluid and natural as Melon's. "My old man can get pretty pissed off, so we decided to look for the truck on our own."

"I'll need to see some identification before we release the truck." The cop towers over all of us.

"And I'll need to see some cash." The tow driver stows the shovels behind the cab. "I need thirty dollars from somebody, or this white hunk of junk goes to the impound yard. Your old man can bail it out on Monday."

I pull my license out of my wallet while Melon makes conversation. "You work out of Taraval station?"

The cop looks at the picture on my license and compares it with my face while answering Melon with another question. "Yeah, what about it?"

"Just so happens my godfather works out of Taraval. Gruff Ramage. You probably heard of him."

The cop hands me back the license. "I know Gruff."

Melon has his tight-lipped smile going. Nods his head slightly like he's about to reveal some great truth. "My father works out of Ingleside station. My name's Phillip Chantelope, and I was just wondering if you could spot us thirty dollars."

"Look, kid, even if I had thirty dollars on me, I wouldn't give it to you. This might be a good lesson for your buddy here to not leave the keys in a vehicle."

"I've got five. Three from the pinball guy and two I had on me." Georgie looks cross-eyed, wet, and disheveled.

I thumb through my wallet as the cop hands me back my license. "I got four bucks and some change in my pocket." I give Melon a cold stare. "What you got, Melon?"

"Sorry, Sheetsy, all's I got is some change."

"I'm out of here, and the truck's going with me." The driver spits a stream of chewing tobacco just as my brother's blue Ford rumbles into the parking lot.

I run at the Ford. Donnie leaps out and walks toward me, his jaw tight, forehead crimped. "What's with the truck and cop car? I thought you had a wheel stuck?"

"Long story. I need twenty bucks to pay the tow guy."

"Do I look like a bank?" We walk toward the tow truck. "It's Saturday night; I need my cash."

"The old man will have me by the nuts and twist 'em off if he has to bail out the truck."

"He ought to have Melon by the nuts."

We're beside the tow truck. The driver spits another brown stream. "What's it gonna be, sonny boy? I got work to do."

Donnie fingers a bill out of his wallet. "Damn it, Melon, you're screwing up my Saturday night…"

Melon's khaki pants are soaked and sand-gritty. "I'll make it up to you, big guy…"

"Yeah, he'll probably pay you with a six pack of Hamms." Georgie shivers and hands the driver five dollars.

Melon's cheeks redden. "Watch it, little priest, or instead of a Roman collar, you're gonna have my fingers around your neck."

Georgie turns away and shakes his head. The cop sits half in and out of the patrol car, talking on the radio. He replaces the mike on the dash and yells at the greasy tow driver, "You all square?"

The driver gets down on his knees and removes the cable from the Falcon. "I'm okay. They paid me."

The cop pulls his legs in. Slams the door and starts the engine. Motors alongside us, the window down. "You guys better get this thing out of here before dark, or it will be towed."

He drives off before we can answer. Water oozes from my tennis shoes as I step toward Melon. "The keys, Melon. The football player. Where's he live?"

"Across the highway. Forty-Eighth near Ulloa, but I tell you, this guy's a beast. Look, I can hotwire the truck."

I rage, "You're not touching a damn thing on that truck! We need the keys!"

Donnie puffs his cheeks, blows out an exasperated breath. "Get in my car. I don't understand how three guys from priest school can get in so much trouble."

The Everly Brothers croon "Cathy's Clown" on the radio as we turn off Sloat and head north on Forty-Eighth. Melon and Georgie are in the back. My temper's ready to snap. "Melon, the address?"

"I don't know. I think it was a green two-story with a patch of ice plant out front. I was lucky to get out of there alive, let alone get the address."

Donnie slides the car to the curb. "This look like the place?"

"Could be…"

I turn around on the seat, get up on my knees, and grab Melon by his shirt. "Damn it, Melon, is this the Goddamned house or not?"

Donnie has his hand on my shoulder. "Whoa, little brother. This is the only place with ice plant. Let's see if you and I can get the keys." Donnie has the door open. "You two punks stay put."

We bound the stairs to the front entrance. Donnie knocks twice, and the door opens to a large crew-cut monster with biceps that strain the sleeves of his T-shirt. "Sheets, what do you want?"

"Need a set of keys, Levi." Donnie's tall, but he's dwarfed by the Leviathan.

"No dice. Your lard-ass brother gave my sister beer." The Leviathan has his beefy hand high on the doorframe, and his scowling face looks like he's about to tear off a chunk of wood and eat it.

Donnie knits his eyebrows, turns to me. "What's he talking about? You give her the beer?"

"Not me—"

"Not this twerp. It was a bald little bastard with baby cheeks and glasses." Levi releases the doorframe and cracks his knuckles. Give him a cape, and he could be Superman. "You must have more than one brother, Sheets."

"I only have one brother, and this is him. Raymond, what the hell is going on?"

"Apparently Melon said he was me."

Donnie throws up his hands in the air. An exasperated Italian. "Why would he do that?"

"How do I know? Because he's Goddamn Melon, I guess."

"The little son of a bitch looked like a melon, and he lied to my sister. You bring him to me, and maybe you get the keys back."

"C'mon, Levi, we're in a jam here. No time to fool around."

"Melon. A Melon for the keys."

Donnie motions toward the stairs. "Go get him. No rough stuff, Levi. You're big enough to kill the little fart."

I run full speed down to the sidewalk. "Melon, out of the car. The big guy wants to talk to you. Georgie, you better come too. We might need all the help we can get."

Melon screams, "No way, Sheets, I got nothing to say to that psycho. No way I'm going up there!"

"He won't give up the keys until he sees you."

"I'm not going to hurt you, little man." The Leviathan has descended to the foot of the stairs with his arms folded. His upper arms are thick as my neck. "I just want to have a word with you about drinking and lying. Maybe we'll share a cigar or two."

I shift my weight from one foot to another, try to squish the water out of my socks as I study Melon. All of a sudden, he's a smiling diplomat. "I'd love to have a smoke with you…I meant no harm to your sister. My apologies…just a little teenage fun."

Levi slaps a hand on top of Melon's head. "Upstairs, Porky. Everybody upstairs. We're going to have a little party. You don't mind if I call you 'Porky,' do you?"

"Porky, Pudgy, call me what you want. It's all in good fun."

Donnie's waiting at the top of the stairs. Levi herds us inside to the kitchen. Between the fluorescent lighting and the white linoleum, the place is bright. Levi struts to another part of the house and reappears with a box of cigars. "My old man's Roi Tans. Me and Porky are going to enjoy a smoke. Anybody else for a stogie?"

Silence except for Georgie. "I might try one. See if it'll warm me up."

"Careful, my young friend." Melon holds court. "Powerful stuff for a little fella."

"Shove it, Melon. I'm two inches taller than you."

"Whatever, good buddy. Don't say I didn't warn you."

Levi lights the cigars with a silver lighter. A coffee table lighter as big as my fist. "My old man calls this his flamethrower. Inhale deep, Porky, you're smoking nothing but the best."

Melon sucks his cheeks in. Draws the smoke like a vacuum machine. Levi smiles with the lit cigar between his lips. The kitchen air turns blue with smoke.

Georgie coughs and sputters, "Whew, these things are pretty strong. My eyes are watering."

Levi purses his lips and blows smoke rings. "Takes a little getting used to." He turns to Melon. "You realize my sister's underage and you gave her beer?"

Melon has the cigar between thumb and forefinger. "My apologies. I'm a little underage myself. I tried to talk her out of it, but she insisted on a sip…"

Levi takes a step toward Melon. "Don't lie to me, shrimp."

"Well, I didn't exactly try to discourage her…"

"That's better, punk. Now I want to see you smoke that thing down to the nub. You better not waste one of my old man's Roi Tans."

Georgie hurriedly puts the Roi Tan in his mouth. Takes a nervous drag, bends over with a cough. Melon looks at Donnie and me with uncertain eyes and a half smile. "Our little buddy's having trouble."

Donnie fans smoke away with the palm of his hand. "Where's your parents, Levi? They don't mind us being here and smoking?"

"My old man built a cabin at Camp Meeker near the Russian River. They're up there almost every weekend." Levi walks to a white refrigerator and opens it. "My ma leaves food for my sister and me. She made a big bowl of tapioca pudding. Sit down, Porky, you like tapioca?"

Melon raises the cigar in a near salute. "Ah, tapioca. I'm a big fan of pudding." He slides into an L-shaped bench that borders a breakfast nook table. "Especially like tapioca."

Levi sets a large salad bowl full of dimpled, skin-tight tapioca in front of Melon. Hands Melon a soup spoon. "Dig in, Porky, it's all yours."

Melon's eyes bulge. His lips turn down at the edges. He looks queasy. "What about my friends? What about your sister? Maybe I should save her some pudding."

"Your friends don't like tapioca. Donnie once told me his whole family finds tapioca disgusting. Isn't that right, Donnie?"

Donnie fans his hand again and looks perturbed. "Levi, what the hell you doing? We need to get the keys from you."

Levi ignores Donnie. With his hands on the table, Levi hovers over Melon and blows cigar smoke. "Don't you ever mention my sister again. For you, she doesn't exist. You got that, Porky?"

Melon spoons away at the pudding. "Whatever you say, buddy…"

"Look, Porky, just because I gave you my favorite pudding doesn't mean I'm your buddy. I call you Porky, you call me Levi. You know why I love tapioca?"

Melon answers with a mouth full of pudding. "Not sure…"

"When I was ten, I was up at Camp Meeker. Banana slugs everywhere. They leave little trails of silver. Little trails remind me of the pimply texture of tapioca. When I was ten, I ate two banana slugs. They're covered with mucus. Slid down my throat just like tapioca…"

Melon spits into the bowl. "Ugh, damn."

Levi takes a pull on the cigar. Looks at Donnie and me. Gives us a big toothy grin as he hisses smoke between his teeth. "Better hurry with that pudding, Porky, and finish your cigar. The Sheets brothers are getting a little edgy. They want the keys, and your other little buddy is turning green. He better not puke in my kitchen."

Georgie hacks out a nasty cough. "I need to use your bathroom."

"Down the hall. Second door on the left. You puke in there, you need to clean it up. And flush that cigar. Hold it, on second thought, I'm feeling generous. Maybe Porky wants a second cigar."

"Shit, Levi, we're teammates. We don't have time for him to finish a second cigar." I feel Donnie's anger rising.

"Yeah, you're right. I was getting a little carried away with my generosity. Flush the cigar. It's the same color as what goes down there anyway."

Melon scrapes the bottom of the tapioca bowl. Left elbow on the table. Nub of brown cigar between his fingers.

"I got one more treat for you, Porky. There's three beers left in your cooler. You down all three in ninety seconds, I give up the keys. You take ninety-one seconds, I put the keys down the garbage disposal."

Melon's hunched over on the bench, looking bloated. Georgie gags in the bathroom. Melon looks up and stares at Donnie and me. His eyes plead for mercy.

"That's enough, Levi, you're gonna kill the guy." Donnie has his hands on his hips, looking like he's going to make a stand.

"You're right. One beer every thirty seconds. I'll give him a minute rest between beers. What do you think, Porky? You thirsty?"

Melon sits up straight. Eyes squint behind his glasses. "Sounds fair enough to me. A few beers never hurt the Melon."

Levi produces three cans of Hamms, punctures them open, and sets them in front of Melon. "Porky, when I say go, you down a can of beer. If you hold your throat open, that stuff will slide down same way banana slugs slid down my throat."

Donnie shakes his head, "Jesus, Levi…"

Levi has his hand in the air, finger pointing up. "One, two, three, go, Porky!"

Melon raises the can, tilts his head back as Levi shouts, "Nineteen seconds, Porky! Sixty seconds, and the next one goes down."

Melon delivers. His eyes water, but he forces a smile. "Bring it on, big guy."

Levi leans down into Melon's face. "Don't you ever call me that again, Porky. I told you to refer to me as Levi. Don't you ever get near my sister again. You see her coming down the street, you cross to the other side. Your minute of rest is over. Down another can. You're two seconds behind already."

Melon's head whips back, launching his eyeglasses up and over his head and onto the kitchen floor. He downs the can in twenty-eight seconds and gives me an eye-bulging look of terror.

I retrieve his glasses. I'm getting more and more worried about the keys. Worried about my old man's anger, and I'm even feeling sorry for Melon. "Hey, why don't you knock it off before somebody gets hurt!"

Levi shoots me a stare. I flash on Bluto in a *Popeye* cartoon. "Maybe it's you that's gonna get hurt. You think you're the Lone Ranger or Robin fuckin' Hood or something?"

I move toward the Leviathan, but Donnie grabs me from behind. I struggle to get free. Levi comes forward until he towers over me. "Sheets, your little brother is a spunky little shit. Because we play on the same football team, I'm gonna ignore the urge to beat him to a pulp. Besides, I admire spunk."

Levi turns back to Melon and says, "I've decided to change the rules. You only get a thirty-second break, and your thirty seconds is up right now."

Melon belches and hammers down the final can in the allotted time. I hand him his glasses. He stares at me like he's not sure who I am. Levi pulls the keys out of his pocket and hands them to Donnie. "Here you go, Sheets."

On cue, Georgie returns from the bathroom. We head toward the door like the kitchen's a cattle gate and we all want out at once. "See you at practice, Sheets. And Porky, you better not be puking up any banana slugs on my front steps."

The street's in deep shadow as the four of us get in Donnie's car. I ask my brother, "Is the whole football team as nutty as that guy?"

"Naw, Levi's the nuttiest." Donnie sounds casual and relaxed, like he's Mr. Cool.

Melon burps in the back seat. "Where was his sister?"

Georgie mumbles, "Probably had her tied up and gagged in a back bedroom. The guy is a maniac."

"Listen to the Roi Tan king. You want to call him a maniac to his face?" Melon's speech begins to slur.

"No, but I'll call you a jerk to your face for getting us into this mess, Porky."

"Don't you ever call me that again, little man." I turn to see them scuffling in the back seat. Melon has Georgie by the front of his shirt.

We make it back in the Sloat parking lot. Georgie yells: "Porky! Porky! Porky!"

Melon lets go of Georgie. "I got to get out of the car!"

Donnie rolls to a stop, opens the door and hustles out, pulls the back of the seat forward. Melon's body is inside, but his head is out in the evening air when he vomits a stream of tapioca and beer. The Saturday sun arcs down, flashes explosive orange behind a thick bank of dark clouds.

The world seems like a complicated place as Georgie and I coax Melon into the back of the truck. Melon lies out flat and mumbles, "The big ape bastard never gave me back my cooler."

As I slam the tailgate shut, Georgie shakes his head and smirks. "You ought to be thankful you're still alive, dipshit."

"No way for a priest to talk…" Melon's voice trails off to a moan.

Melon is silent and smells like barf by time we get him home. We walk him to his bedroom without disturbing his mother. Afterward, I drive Georgie to his house in the avenues. He opens the truck door but stays seated. "Thanks for a memorable day, Raymond. Sorry you got the boot."

Georgie Thurmond. Terminal. He suddenly looks like a very wise owl behind the glasses. "I was going to leave anyway, Georgie."

Georgie pops up and out of the truck. Standing on the sidewalk, he continues to hold on to the door. "Be careful of Melon. He could get you killed."

"I'm gonna miss you, Georgie. Say hi to the guys."

Georgie slams the door and taps twice on the roof of the truck as I start the engine and motor away.

I'm awake when Donnie stumbles into our room a little past midnight. Across the dark void between our beds, he says, "The outside world is not for you. You need to make those bastards let you back into priest school before you get yourself in some real trouble." He flips on a lamp on the nightstand beside his bed. Kicks off his shoes and flops on top of the bedspread, hands behind his neck, head tilted up on the pillow. "When were you supposed to go back?"

"Told you. I can't go back, but if I could, tomorrow would be the day." My mind flies to Georgie, who doesn't have a care in the world. Tomorrow, lucky Georgie's going back to the simplicity of the bells. "It's not like I don't wish I could go back." I continue unloading on Donnie. "Life is complicated. Our sister dies. Melon gets the boot and starts smelling like a brewery. Ma dies. Pop's depressed. Then there's Alice; I like her a lot. Sometimes I can't stop thinking about her."

"Maybe the old man can talk them into letting you go back to your bells where everything is predictable. Duck out on all this bullshit. Alice is a nice little piece, but you become a priest, all kinds of women will throw themselves at you."

"Jesus, Donnie, what are you saying?"

"I'm saying that Roman collar is like a magnet that attracts women. Look at Tool. Hot women lined up for confession when they have nothing to confess. They just wanted to listen to your Adonis uncle whisper to them in the dark."

"Now Tool's in Seattle working. He got rid of the collar. So what's that tell you?"

Donnie stares at the ceiling. "It tells me his hot Italian blood was boiling because of too much action coming his way. It got too intense, so he bailed out."

My brother's a simpleton. To him, everything boils down to sex. I'm full of snarky sarcasm. "It's over for me. Why don't you get a Roman collar? Maybe you'll finally get laid."

"Don't need no collar, Choirboy." Donnie snaps off the light. "By the way, I had enough of the old man and the funeral atmosphere around here. I'm tired of fucking school. I'm sick and tired of people dying and all the grieving bullshit that goes with it. I'm joining the army."

I mumble, "Sure you are…" In the silence of our room, I think I hear my brother sobbing, before I fall into a deep sleep of dreams: Denise Maxx is driving my old man's white Falcon. A sign on the door says "Spaghetti Works." A yawning Bengal tiger lounges in the bed of the truck.

True to his word, Donnie enlists despite my attempts to talk him out of it. "You're joining the army because our mother died?"

"I just got to get out of here." Donnie sits across from me at the dining room table. "I'm tired of the old man's long face. Tired of Mr. and Mrs. Sako tiptoeing around the house."

"Hey, they're trying to help us out." My words have an edge to them. "I got to talk to you about something."

"Yeah, what?"

"About Denise."

"Don't ever mention that bitch to me again, got it? Never again!" I push back from the table. "What happened to you? What happened to my brother? You going to leave me here to deal with the old man by myself? You going to run away to the damn army? That's the same as the old man running away to the bottle! You don't want to talk about Denise? Fine!" I've come around the table and look down at Donnie. "Afraid to admit your little brother might have an edge over you when it comes to women? That you aren't the hotshot you thought you were—"

Donnie's chair falls backward as he jumps to his feet, grabs me by the shoulders, and shoves. We tumble to the floor. Donnie hammers my rib cage with body punches. I grab a handful of his hair and twist it with a fury.

I'm trying to yank his scalp out when I see Mr. Sako bending over us. "Boys! Stop now, please." I let go of my brother's hair. Donnie rolls off me, though murder lingers in his eye.

Mr. Sako rights the overturned chair. "What brings this on?"

Donnie and I slowly hoist ourselves up. Donnie glares at me as I explain, "Donnie's joining the army because our mother died."

Mr. Sako turns to Donnie. "Is this true?"

"I'm joining the army because I need a change. Yes, my mother died; she's gone, but she was never here anyway."

Mr. Sako studies Donnie's face with a quizzical look. "How so?"

"She was always in church or had her head buried in her holy books."

Mr. Sako answers softy, "Yes, perhaps preoccupied at times."

"At times? All the time, Mr. Sako! She couldn't give me the time of day, but she's fawning all over the little prince! Her damn little priest!"

I brush Mr. Sako aside and yell into Donnie's face, "That's a lie!"

Mr. Sako places a hand on my shoulder. "Calmness, Raymond, go slowly. Why so much anger?"

"Yeah, *mama's boy*! Why so much anger?"

"And so much rudeness," Mr. Sako whispers. "No call for such rudeness."

Donnie has had all the Far Eastern wisdom he can stand. "I'm out of here." He turns toward the front door. "Enough of this bullshit."

Once he leaves, Mr. Sako comments, "Very angry brother. I hope he calms down. The middle way, Raymond. Maybe a little bit of truth in what he says though."

"What do you mean, Mr. Sako?"

"Deep breaths, Raymond. Sit, please, let's talk."

I sit next to the old gardener with the weathered face and hands. "Remember middle way," he says, "Perhaps some truths hard to look at. Maybe a little influenced by your mother. Not a bad thing to want Mother's attention."

"I think I helped kill her."

He is shocked. "What are you saying?"

"I told her I was thinking of quitting the seminary. Might have been too much for her."

"You only spoke the truth. Regret proper, not guilt. Guilt like a closet of moth-damaged clothes. It was just your mother's time to go."

"I only half believe you."

"Give it time." Mr. Sako smiles. "Belief will come."

17

ON THE DAY OF DONNIE'S DEPARTURE for Fort Ord, we barely acknowledge each other as I drive him to the Greyhound station at Seventh and Mission. "Change the oil every four thousand miles, put on the car cover every night, and don't let Melon ever drive this car, mama's boy."

The words have lost their sting. "Fuck you, soldier. You know they're gonna shave your hair off."

He steps out of the car at the curb in front of the bus station. "Maybe it will air my brains out."

His final words feel like a concession. I watch my brother until he disappears into the bus station. I drive round the corner from Seventh onto Market into light Sunday morning traffic. Dual tailpipes rumble as I accelerate. I'm carefree and independent, yet lonely. Even lonely for my asshole brother.

Lonely, too, for the company of guys from St. Jerome's. My pop pulled some strings and got me into St. Ignatius for my senior year. I joined the cross-country team but haven't yet become close with the group of guys who have been training and competing together for the last three years.

I feel a void as I turn off Market and head south up the Gough Street on-ramp to the freeway. The radio is on high volume to drown out the silence. The Coasters once again crooning "Charlie Brown."

"Charlie Brown…he's a clown…" And my mind goes to Melon. He was pretty quiet and humble for about a week after the incident with Levi Batts. Then he was back to his old self, slipping me drawings during English class, asking me to stop by his garage to have a beer. I went a couple of times and sat on a cooler and sipped a Hamms while Melon polished his old man's black Plymouth.

We made small talk, always avoiding the subject of my pop's truck. "So, how does it feel to be a free man, Sheets?"

I sluiced a mouthful of beer around like mouthwash and swallowed. "A little confusing. I miss the guys at St. Jerome's."

Melon rubbed the hood of the car, palmed a linen rag over the glossy black surface. "You just need a little nooky, my son. That'll clear up your brain."

A little nooky.

The Coasters bring me back to my driving. "He's gonna get tossed…just you wait and see…why is everybody always pickin' on me?" I pass Paul Avenue and Silver Avenue exits and accelerate on to the Candlestick causeway.

On Highway 101, I feel the pull of the south bay. St. Jerome's. Alice Derry. In a few miles, I pass the spot where Lucas Foyt got upended. Melon, Georgie, and I never talked about that night. Each of us holds an unsettling secret of New Year's Eve. My mood goes even darker. *Guilt. Closet of moth-damaged clothes.* I remember Mr. Sako's words yet somehow feel responsible for two deaths in my life.

The highway skirts the sleepy town of San Carlos, edges the salt-marsh waterways of Redwood City. Soon, I spot the monster hangars of the air station and head west toward St. Jerome's. No, toward Alice Derry.

The full-bloom roses brim the walkway to Alice's front door. Reds. Yellows. A sprinkling of white. I press the black doorbell button and wait a couple of minutes. I welcome the heat of the sun-drenched entry step. The door opens a crack, then opens wide as Alice sees me. "Raymond, what are you doing here?"

I motion toward the street and the car. "Felt like taking a ride. Say, what happened to your eye?"

Alice has a black eye. Her left eye is bloodshot, the skin around it is black and deeply bruised. She runs her hands over the top of her head. Her hair sticks up in frazzled clumps like she just woke up. "You should have called me. I'm a mess. This place is a mess. My mom left last night." Alice is barefoot and wears shorts and a T-shirt.

"Your eye, Alice, who did this to you?"

"Nobody. It was an accident."

"What kind of accident?"

"I don't feel like explaining, Raymond. You live in a big house with nice parents. You'd never understand."

"One of my nice parents is dead, Alice. Did you forget that? My sister's dead too, and my brother joined the army. He left me with my dad who drowns himself in scotch, so don't tell me I'd never understand!"

"Stop yelling at me. I'm so tired of people yelling!"

I suck in my breath. "I'm not yelling."

She slams the door in my face. I knock gently three times. No answer. I knock harder. "C'mon, Alice, open up. Let's talk."

"Go away. I'm a mess, and my eye hurts. I don't want you to see me like this. I'm ugly, Raymond Sheets."

"You're not ugly, Alice, you could be bald as Yul Brynner with two black eyes and I'd still think you're pretty." I shout at the closed door and try the handle at the same time. She has it locked. "I'm going to sit on your porch step, Alice Derry. I will sit here all day and all night if I have to. That's how pretty I think you are."

I sit and face the roses, my back to the door. I hear the bolt unlatch; the door opens. Her voice a whisper: "My dad says you can get hemorrhoids from sitting on cold concrete." She scoots down beside me.

"I'll take my chances. Besides, this concrete's warm from the sun. Now tell me who did this to you?"

"My mom's elbow did it, and it was an accident." She leans into my chest. "Please, don't look at my face."

I place my hands on her shoulders and push her back so I can see her fully. "I want to look at your face. That's the most beautiful black eye on the prettiest face I've ever seen. What happened?"

As she stands and reaches a hand down to pull me up, she turns her head away as if to shield me from looking at her eye. "Let's go in the house."

The house is dark. Blinds drawn tight. "You got any steak? Meat on a black eye is supposed to help."

"Only if it's real cold meat. My dad says it's not the meat but the cold that helps."

"Your dad seems to know a lot about concrete and black eyes."

We walk into the kitchen. Dishes are piled in the sink. An empty can of baked beans rests on the white tiled counter. "Yeah, my dad's a real source of wisdom. He knows everything except how to deal with a drunk."

I slide into an upholstered bench behind a Formica table. Breadcrumbs and used silverware litter the surface. "Who's the drunk?"

Seeing the mess, Alice collects the silverware and wipes the table with a damp dishrag. "My mom. My mom's a drunk. Last night, she screams my name from the back bedroom. I open the door and she's naked, and my dad's snapping a wet bath towel at her.

"I yell, 'What is going on in here?' My dad drops the towel when he sees me, and my mom picks up a gold letter opener from her dressing table and runs at my dad. I get between them and get an elbow in the eye. They scuffle, and that's when I go for the gun."

"What gun?"

Alice starts to run water in the sink. "The gun my dad keeps in his nightstand."

"You shot your parents?"

Steam from the sink water rises as Alice scrubs a plate. "I'm not crazy, Raymond. I didn't shoot anyone. I just pulled back the hammer and fired a bullet into the floor to quiet them down."

Alice rinses the plate then comments, "This house is a mess. I can't stand it anymore."

I spot a green dish towel draped through the handle on the refrigerator. Alice scrubs furiously now. I stand and dry the dishes as she sets them on the tile. "What happened after you shot the floor, and where did you learn about guns?"

"They backed away from each other and stared at me. My dad reached out his hand: 'Give me the gun, Alice.'

"I told him I wouldn't give up the gun unless they stopped fighting. My mom, drunk as she was, threw the letter opener on the bed. I think I might have scared her sober. My dad still had his hand out. 'Alice, the gun,' he said. It's a five-shot Smith and Wesson. I flipped the cylinder open and took out four bullets before I gave it to him."

I open drawers, looking for where the silverware goes. "Why'd you empty it?"

"Dumb question, Raymond. He was angry. You think I'm going to give him a loaded pistol? The silverware goes in the second drawer on the right."

"You're lucky you didn't shoot yourself in the foot."

"My dad taught me how to use that gun." I notice a hint of sarcasm and irony in her voice. "My fingers aren't strong enough to pull the trigger unless I pull the hammer back first. With that gun, I know what I'm doing." She pauses, raising a wet hand to her temple. "But right now, my head hurts."

I hang the towel on the refrigerator handle, open the freezer, and take out a package of frozen peas. "Put this on your eye. Go lie down on the couch." It feels strange; with my older brother gone, I'm taking charge. "Any aspirin around here?"

"In the medicine cabinet in the bathroom."

The bathroom is littered with towels, washcloths, tubes of toothpaste, a bottle of Wildroot hair lotion. I find the white-and-yellow bottle of Bayer and deliver two pills and a glass of water to Alice. "Where'd your mom go?"

Alice gulps down the water. "Who knows? Probably some motel."

"Your dad, he run away too?"

"My dad never ran away from anything. He went to work last night. He's probably still drinking at the NCO club after he got off his shift this morning."

I lift Alice's legs and sit on the couch, resting her calves on my lap. "He a drunk too?"

Alice slowly rubs the frozen pea package across her forehead. "He's happy when he drinks. Laughs and jokes a lot. He loves to fast dance with the ladies at the club. His favorite song is Marty Robbins singing 'El Paso.'" Alice swings her feet to the floor, and I have this weird thought, I could have massaged her feet, helped her to relax. "You think you could help me clean this house?"

"Stay on the couch. Just tell me what you want done."

With one hand holding the peas to her eye, Alice picks up an ashtray off the coffee table. "That's all right. I can't lie around anymore. Open the blinds, and get out the vacuum from the hall closet. I'll put stuff away."

Alice moves from room to room like a tornado. I follow her around and vacuum coils of hair from the bathroom floor, dust babies from under beds. I see the hole in the floor where the bullet penetrated wood. The edges of the hardwood are splintered. I look for any trace of the bullet, but all I see is a shattered hole about the size of one of my fingers. I'm amazed by her. I can't believe she fired the gun.

As Alice sprays Windex on the living room windows, dust motes descend around her in the sunlight. I run the vacuum over a throw rug when I feel someone tap me on the shoulder.

I turn and look into the red face of Alice's father. He grins as wide as a dinner plate. "I appreciate you cleaning my billets, sailor, but who the heck are you?"

I shut down the vacuum. "I'm Raymond Sheets, sir."

Alice's father takes my hand and pumps my arm. "No need to call me 'sir,' Raymond Sheets. My name's Lee."

"You met Raymond on New Year's Eve, Dad."

Lee sways on his feet, stares perplexed at Alice. "Who gave you that shiner, little girl?" He turns on me, his smile gone. "You hurt my daughter, sailor?"

Alice grabs her father's arm. "I got the black eye last night, Dad. I got hit with Mom's elbow. Now you better get to bed." She leads him toward the bedroom.

Lee calls to me as Alice coaxes him down the hallway. "Don't ever marry a drunk, Raymond Sheets."

Lee's soon asleep, and the October sun begins to tint the clouds in the western sky with a hint of orange as Alice and I leave her house and walk the road toward St. Jerome's. I drape my arm across her shoulders, and she pulls in close. "Thanks for scrubbing the billets, sailor."

"My pleasure, Annie Oakley. You're a dead-eye when it comes to shooting floors."

We stop at the berry patch. The air is very still, and I listen, hoping to hear the student body singing vespers, but hear only the occasional trill of a solitary bird in the trees.

The berries are mostly gone. A few linger, but they look dry. Alice picks a single blackberry, the fattest and juiciest looking of the second-growth hangers-on, and she hands it to me.

I motion her toward my open arms. She presses against me, and I lean her head back and gently crush berry juice around the bruised circle that surrounds her eye. Then I place the berry in her mouth and cup her face with my hands. A runaway bead of purple rolls down her cheek like a tear. She smiles when I intercept the stream of juice with the tip of my tongue.

I leave Alice on her couch with ice wrapped in a towel against her eye. No nooky, but maybe the promise of nooky on the horizon. I feel less lonely.

My pop is lounging in his chair when I come through the front door. "Where you been, Choirboy?"

"Out for a ride, Pop. How you doing?"

"I'll live." He holds up an empty glass. "Put a head on that for your old man."

Mr. Sako is reading at the dining room table. Mrs. Sako dries dishes. I get ice cubes and scotch and fill my Pop's glass.

"Not too much, Raymond," Mrs. Sako whispers. "He has had quite a bit already."

I tip the glass over the sink and siphon off some of the scotch. Crossing through the kitchen and dining room, I set the glass on the round wooden table next to Pop's chair. "You want the Sunday paper, Pop?"

He looks at me through red and swollen eyes, like he just woke up from a dream. He stares like it's an effort to understand what I'm saying. He raises the scotch glass, takes a sip, and closes his eyes. "I don't want to read anything. I don't want to talk. I just want to be left alone, Choirboy."

"I miss her too," I tell him. "That drinking's gonna kill you, and then where will I be?"

He waves me off, and I pull up a chair at the dining room table. Mr. Sako closes his book and folds his hands on the table. He nods toward my father and talks softly, "He will be okay. It takes time."

I'm sad to see Pop this way, yet I wonder about the peaceful mystery of Mr. Sako. What he feels about death. "You believe in God, Mr. Sako?"

"I believe in the Oneness of all things. If that is God, then yes, I do believe."

"How about Heaven and the afterlife?"

"The truth is, Raymond, I know only of this life. Of this present moment."

Mrs. Sako places a dinner plate in front of me. A pork chop, applesauce, and mashed sweet potato. "My husband talks in riddles. I warmed some dinner, Raymond. Eat real food before you try to digest the food of my husband's way of thinking."

Mr. Sako bows his head toward his wife. "She is right. You need to eat." He returns to his book, smiling as if he remembered some inner joke.

I savor the meat and applesauce and melt butter into the sweet potatoes. The warm food and the serenity of this old man feel like medicine for my loneliness.

After dinner, I excuse myself. I see my father is sleeping in the chair, and I get the elephant blanket out of the hall closet and cover him. I go upstairs and open the door to my room just as the hallway phone rings.

The receiver is cool as I touch it to my ear. "Hello?"

"Sheetsy, the Melon here."

In spite of the trouble he's caused me, I'm relieved to hear his voice. Still, I downplay my eagerness with sarcasm. "What's up, Pudgy?"

"Don't spoil my mood with name-calling, my son. I bring you great tidings."

"Yeah, what are these tidings?"

"All will unfold, once you apologize."

"Okay, Porky, I'm sorry."

"Sheetsy, Sheetsy, always the joker. I'm going to let that one go."

"Good. I've stopped trembling, and I'm deeply relieved. Now what are you calling about?"

"Two weeks from tomorrow, old buddy. Halloween. How about we have a little fun?"

"Depends."

"We pick up Alice and her friend, Melinda what's-her-name, and camp out on one of the hills behind the sem on Saturday. Halloween's actually on Monday." Melon's voice becomes more animated and raises an octave. "I want to get some evening photos of the old school as the sun's going down."

"So where's the fun?"

"Sheets, has your brain gone numb? Starlight. Two girls. We're on the outside of St. Jerome's and looking in. We commit lewd acts in the weeds under the night sky. What more do I have to say?"

"Sounds exciting. What makes you think Alice and Melinda are going to agree to this?"

"The thrill, Sheets. These are two thrill-seeking little hussies. Life's a roller coaster ride, my friend, you need to climb on."

"The last time I got on your roller coaster, my old man's truck almost got washed away into the Pacific Ocean."

"Ancient history. A few minor miscalculations on my part. I'm a new man now. No more shenanigans from the Melon."

"We got no camping gear."

"Leonard Keely from English class."

"What's he got to do with it?"

"For twenty-five bucks, he lets us borrow four sleeping bags from the army/navy surplus store where he works."

I sag against the hallway wall. The back of my neck itches. "No store is going to lend us sleeping bags."

"Not the store, idiot. We borrow them from Leonard. He slips them to us on Friday night. We get them back to him by Monday, but we do need some wheels. How much money we have to come up with to get your brother to lend us his car?"

"Donnie left for the army today. I've got the car."

"The army!" Melon yells. "How sweet is this? Your brother the patriot is off to serve his country, and he leaves us his car? What a sap!"

"He left it to me, Melon, not 'us,' and he made me promise under no circumstances was I ever to let my fat little friend drive it."

"Pretty-boy bastard. Hope the army knocks the shit out of him."

As much as I've had issues with my brother, Melon's comments irritate me. I miss Donnie, and I hope he does well in the army. "I'm tired, Melon. Had a long day with Alice. I'm going to hit the sack."

"Alice! You saw Alice today? You been holding out on me, Sheetsy. What were you doing with Alice?"

"That's for me to know."

"Sheets, you devil. You on for Halloween fun?"

This is why I'm friends with him—for all his good ideas, even the ones that aren't so good. "Yeah, I need some excitement."

On the Saturday before Halloween, Melon picks up the four sleeping bags, and we toss them in the back seat of the Ford when I pick him up from his house in the avenues. He asks me to open the trunk, where he stashes his cooler and a military duffel bag. "What's in the bag?" I ask.

"My camera case and tripod. A box of crackers."

"Crackers?"

"Yeah, to go along with the salami in the cooler."

"What else you got in the cooler?"

"I sense suspicion, Sheetsy. I tell you, I'm a reformed man. Only thing in that cooler is salami and ice. I mean lots of fresh-cut Italian salami."

We ride Melon's roller coaster toward the unknown, traveling south on the freeway. I'm still a little unhinged after Ma's death, but I'm reinforced by the two tins of liquid in my jacket pocket. I'm about to break out of my shell. Melon mentioned excitement. I'm harboring a wild idea. I almost relate it to Melon, but instead hold back, not wanting to spoil the grand surprise. "Alice is a little unsure about getting Melinda involved with you after I told her about the incident with my old man's truck. She says you're nothing but trouble."

"I resent the implication, Sheets." Melon rubs the lens of his glasses on his shirttail. "I suppose you told your little girlfriend every detail of that little adventure."

"Naw, I left out the part about you barfing. I didn't want to make her sick."

"Thanks, you're a pal. I just might withhold your share of the salami."

I crank the radio up full volume, roll down the windows. We surrender to the freedom of the sun and the wind and the deep decibels of Duane Eddy's guitar spitting out "Forty Miles of Bad Road."

Melon pops a friendly fist into my upper right arm and yells above the noise, "All right, St. Raymond! Now we're cookin', Sheets! Look out, Alice and Melinda, this is going to be one crazy night!"

We arrive at three thirty and meet on Alice's front porch, two hours before sunset. Melinda has on three sweaters, topped by a blue windbreaker that must have come from a giant's closet. Alice, recovered from the black eye, looks lost in an oversize Navy pea jacket and black watch cap. Melon fishes out the sleeping bags out of the car. "You girlies don't need all those clothes. These bags are good for below freezing."

Melinda takes an olive sleeping bag. A couple of white feather stems poke through the thin material. "I'm allergic to down. I'll start sneezing."

"A sneeze! I love to sneeze! The tickle! The release!" Melon is all grins as if he were handing out boxes of chocolate mints instead of down bags. "And when a lovely young lady sneezes, it's like sweet, incredible music."

"No, I mean I sneeze and keep on sneezing."

Alice wraps her arms around a sleeping bag, hugs it to the front of her jacket. "You can cover your legs with the bag, and I'll lend you my jacket and hat."

Melinda hands the bag back to Melon with a grimace on her face like the US military sleeping sack might be full of the bubonic plague. "But I'll be on the ground in your coat. It'll get all full of dirt and burrs."

Melon sets the bag on the entry walk and motions to Alice with an extended arm. "The lady needs a mattress. Seems that on our photo shoot, I remember a lounge chair on your parents' patio that had nice soft pad on it."

I'm getting a little pissed at the way Melon takes over. "We can't carry a lounge chair, you idiot."

"Raymond, my inexperienced friend, we don't take the whole chair, just the pad." He pats me on the shoulder. "We need the trunk open for the rest of our gear."

Here I go again, Melon's puppet. To maintain a sense of control, I almost spill the beans about what's in my pocket. Instead, I pop the trunk lid while Alice goes to get Melinda a sleeping pad.

Melon stuffs his sleeping bag into the duffel, then starts to shove the car cover into the bag. "Going to have to consolidate, Sheetsy, old buddy. Think you can manage this duffle bag?"

"I could manage it, but I'm not going to, and the car cover stays, Melon. I'll carry the cooler and my own bag. You can lug that damn duffel. You better carry Melinda's bag too. She might start sneezing."

Melinda is standing by the front door and looks uncertain without Alice's reassuring presence. Melon puts a hand on my shoulder and whispers: "She's a fragile little minx. We might have to lay the car cover over her to keep the dew off."

I brush Melon's hand away. "Anything happens to that car cover, I'll pound you into mincemeat."

It's after four o'clock by the time we amble west toward the hills. We work our way past the berry patch, then veer right along a roughly paved service road that leads to a plowed field.

I walk between Alice and Melinda as we kick our way through dirt clods and tufts of brown grass. Melon is loaded down and drags behind. Melinda has her arm around the lounge mat, balances it against her hip. She yells back to Melon, "I feel bad, you have to carry my sleeping bag."

I look back. Melon has the duffel strapped over his back, clutches the sleeping bag in front. He's red-faced but says, "Don't you worry, the Melon is a trooper. Raymond, wait for me at the fence. We need to get this bag through the barbed wire."

Past the fence line, we climb a grassy slope, drop down behind it, and traverse the hill. Melon calls for a halt. "Let's take a little rest." He wiggles the duffel bag loose and sets it down. "You girls stay low. Raymond, let's go to the top of the ridge and see where we are."

We creep low to the ridgeline. High fog begins to cool the air in the fast-moving dusk of early evening. Melon and I peer over the top of the hill. "There it is, Sheetsy, the penitentiary of our youth."

Even in the vastness of the valley that sweeps down toward the air station, St. Jerome's looks formidable. The bell tower. Four-storied buildings with their rows of windows. The place does look like a prison.

Right below us are the playing fields, and in the center of one field, a huge stack of scrap lumber and old wooden pallets is piled twenty feet high, held in place by four corner posts the size of telephone poles. The mass of debris must measure twenty feet across. "Halloween bonfire, Sheets."

"One of my better memories of the place."

"Strange how the seminary celebrates witches and darkness." Melon surprises me when he gets philosophical and shows a bit of depth. "Some religions regard Halloween as the work of the Devil. The church is strange. Look at the Black Mass."

"I didn't think you gave a shit about any of that stuff."

"Don't let my carefree exterior fool you, Sheetsy, I am a fathomless thinker."

"You're about as fathomless as a street puddle."

Melon ignores my remark, and from our vantage point, we get a bird's-eye view of gaggles of students heading up the pathway to the basement locker rooms.

"Wonder if one of those guys is Georgie.

"Who knows? The little sap. I hope he becomes Pope someday." Melon talks as he scoots down the hill. "We'll use this as our observation point. We'll make camp in the oaks behind us."

We unroll our sleeping bags and lay them in the soft duff of oak leaves. It's near darkness in the deep shade. Overhead, the silhouette of a squirrel leaps among the branches.

"Aren't there bugs in these leaves?" Melinda sounds squeamish.

Melon reaches into the duffel. "All the famous frontiersmen slept on a single blanket with a mattress of leaves. Never a bug bite! Besides,

I have a potion to keep the bugs off." Melon holds up a champagne bottle. "Anybody thirsty?"

We spread the car cover and sit in a circle, pour champagne into paper cups Melon had stashed in the cooler. We drink and feast on salami and Ritz crackers. I have to admit, the taste of salt and the tongue-tickle of champagne makes a mouth-watering dinner. I raise my paper cup. "To St. Jerome's."

Three cups meet mine. "To one crazy night!" Melon shouts, and we again touch cups.

"What else is in the duffel?" Alice asks as she sips her drink.

"My camera case and nothing else."

I reach in my jacket pocket and touch metal. "I might have something else."

"Like what?" Melon asks with a surprised tone.

"You mean fireworks?" Melinda asks.

"Not exactly." I stand up. "I think Melon and I need to take his camera to the top of the hill and get some evening shots of the old school. You girls guard the camp."

Melinda's voice raises an octave. "Guard it from what?"

Alice sprawls out on the car cover. "Don't pay any attention. Nothing out here will bother us."

I lead Melon up to the crest of the hill, and we flatten out to a prone position. He plants the champagne bottle firmly in the earth before he mounts his camera on a tiny tripod and changes lenses. Yellow light gleams from first-floor windows of St. Jerome's. "Sheets, you got a secret plan to get laid?"

"Take your snapshots of the old school, Melon, then I got a surprise for you."

"You like my new camera? No more Polaroids." He presses a button on top of the camera. Seconds pass before the shutter releases.

"Where'd you steal it?"

"I'm no thief, Sheets. Since my father sobered up, he's been a generous support of my artsy endeavors. So, what's the big surprise?"

Before I can answer, the girls have come up the hill. I motion for them to stay low and Alice drops down beside me and moves tight against my arm and hips. "We got tired of guarding the camp."

Melinda's still standing. I quickly reach up and grab her hand. "Get down! We don't want any of the beady-eyed perverts spotting us."

Melinda says in a loud whisper, "Why?"

"Melon and I aren't supposed to associate with anybody still in the sem."

"How are they gonna associate with you when we're way up here?"

Melon picks up the conversation. "It's a long story. Did you know my interest in old buildings stems from my secret desire to become a famous architect?"

Melon drones on in the darkness. Alice puts her arm across my back and presses her lips against my cheek. I move my head. Our lips meet and hold. Our moist tongues dart and glide. I feel the graze of teeth.

Alice tightens her arm around me. Grasses lean and whisper in the cool breezes that slide across the empty hills. I kiss Alice hard on the lips and break away with a whisper. "It's dark enough. We're going to have a little fun."

"What kind of fun?"

I sit up and give Melon a tap on the shoulder. "You'll see. Melon, we're going to give the old school an early celebration."

"Sheetsy, what in the hell are you talking about?"

I retrieve two narrow tins from my pocket. "Lighter fluid," I announce.

Alice is quick to catch on. She yells, "Wow! You're going to light off the bonfire!"

Melinda calls out, "I want to go home."

Melon jumps up and grabs me by the front of my jacket. "Have you lost your mind?"

"Easy, Melon." I bat his hands away. "Everybody, settle down. We're just gonna have a little fun. I need to pay back the bastards for booting me out. Besides, it's harmless. A fire tonight or on Halloween. A fire's a fire."

"Alice, let's get out of here," Melinda pleads.

"No, it'll be okay." Alice is full of excitement. "I should help you light it. I'm the one who got Melon kicked out."

"Wait a damn minute, Alice." I feel my anger rise. "Melon, I'm the one who got you kicked out."

Silence rules the darkness. Melon is the first to speak, "What are you talking about, Raymond?"

"When I first met Alice, she was practicing numerology. She asked for my room number. I lied to you, Alice. I gave you Melon's room number."

A veil of fog wisps in front of the rising moon. Melinda shudders in the cold. Alice is silent. But Melon is gleeful. "Truth time! Sheetsy, old buddy, you probably saved my life! I was never destined for Holy Orders." The champagne must be wearing off; all of a sudden Melon sounds cautious. "But now, my son, you must rethink the lighting of this fire. It could have serious consequences."

"Since when did you start thinking about consequences?"

Melon chugs champagne from the bottle. "Since right now. I'm no arsonist." He hands the bottle to Alice. She tips it back and swallows a mouthful.

Alice hands the bottle back to Melon and takes off her pea coat. She drapes it over Melinda's shoulders.

"All these months you let me think I was the cause of Melon getting kicked out." Alice takes a seat just below the crest of the hill. "You lied! You need to atone, Raymond Sheets!"

Melinda buttons up the pea coat. Turns the black collar up.

Alice begins to chant: "Atone! Atone! Atone, Raymond Sheets!"

Melinda hesitates, looks from Melon to Alice, takes up the chant, and presses the collar to her ears.

In the darkness, Melon begins a hopping war dance on the side of the hill. "Atone! Atone! Atone!"

I pry the bottle from his hands and take a long pull of champagne. The bubbles radiate and tingle my throat and nose. I almost choke as I try to swallow too fast. I raise the bottle skyward toward a sprinkling of stars and a fog-shrouded moon. "I'm guilty!" I shout. "I must atone! Let's set the fire!"

We begin to laugh and howl. I motion toward everybody down below the hilltop. "We need to stay low. We don't want to blow this little caper."

Melon takes another swig out of the bottle. "This is crazy, Sheets. I can't believe you want to do this."

For once, I feel like the joker, the trickster. "With or without you, I'm going to do it."

"Have you lost your mind?"

"I'm going to pay the bastards back for giving both of us the boot. You with me or not?"

"Against my better judgement. What's the plan, captain?"

"In five minutes, the inmates will sit down to eat. This hill is not visible from the refectory. In six minutes, you and I move out by the light of the moon. We go down the hill and through the barbed wire. We cross the field at a dead run, spray our cans of lighter fluid."

"It's more like I'll be 'dead from the run.'"

"You're not exactly a track star, but don't worry—when the adrenaline kicks in, you'll rise to the occasion. You make sure you empty that can of lighter fluid. I'll throw the match and wham! Halloween comes early to St. Jerome's."

"I want to be part of it!" Alice sounds like her voice is doing jumping jacks in her throat.

"You can hold the barbed wire for me and Melon. Your foot on the bottom strand. Pull up the center strand with your hands. Melon and I slide on through. Melinda can stand watch from here."

"No way. I'm not staying here by myself."

"All right, you help Alice hold the wire, but you better be ready to run back up this hill. Before we go, everybody close their eyes and count to two hundred. When we open our eyes, we'll be able to see better in the dark."

Melon reverts to sarcasm. "What kind of BS is that, Sheets?"

"No BS. It's an old military trick for night fighters. My uncle learned it in Korea."

We close, count, then open our eyes. I can make out moonlit silhouettes of fence posts at the base of the hill. We walk single file, trampling a path through the weeds. I lead, followed by Alice, then Melinda. Melon brings up the rear.

"What if we get caught? We could be arrested for arson." Melinda sounds agitated.

"Arson? We're not going to burn down the school. It's just a pile of wood that's waiting to be burned." I stop and turn. "Melon, you still with us?"

"Aye, aye, captain."

"Way to go, my son." I feel solid. Sure of myself. A leader in command. "Now, everybody be quiet. When we get to the fence, you girls grab the wire."

I am sweating despite the cool moist air. My breath comes fast as we crouch under the wire and make a run across the field toward the stack of dry wood. I race past Melon easily. "Don't turn an ankle, Pudgy. You're too heavy for me to carry you."

Melon doesn't answer. I nearly yell a war-whoop in wild exhilaration.

We reach the pile and begin to douse the wood with lighter fluid. We use up the fluid, and I search the inner pocket of my jacket. "Take the empty can back with you," I whisper.

"Sheets, light the damn thing. What are you doing?"

I hurl packets up high on the pile. "Seven packs of firecrackers. When these things go off, the perverts are gonna think they're being attacked by an army of commies."

Before Melon can answer, I toss a match. Blue-and-yellow flames spread low on the pile. "Run, Melon!"

We streak toward the barbed wire and slide through the opening Alice has made. Melinda is halfway up the hill and moaning. We climb the slope in record time and dive prone behind the crest of the hill. Melinda, breathless and sobbing. Melon has his arm around her. He begins to calm her in a voice I didn't know he possessed. "Easy, girl. We're okay. Everything's all right."

I'm momentarily distracted by Melon's continued effort to soothe Melinda's hysteria until Alice digs her fingernails into the palm of my hand. She whispers in disbelief: "My God. Look at that."

Down on the field, the fire chews at the backside of the lumber pile, flames rising higher into the evening sky. The fire broadens, illuminates details of the surrounding area. Goalposts show up like white sticks in the night. The concrete wall of the outdoor handball court reflects back the fiery light.

Melinda is quiet now. The four of us peer down from the hilltop. Dinner hour is finished. Someone must have alerted the student body because it now moves down the path to the playing field in a dark, gelatinous mass. Shouts go up as my firecrackers begin to pop like gunfire. Seminarians scatter back from the flames.

"Look at 'em dance, Sheetsy!" Melon is animated. Melinda's face-down, her forehead on her folded arms.

Alice grips my shoulders. Half of her torso is on top of my back as if she's trying for a better view over the top of my head. "What's making that noise? I hope it's not bullets."

"We're not that crazy!" Then I remember Alice's familiarity with guns. "It's firecrackers."

More firecrackers explode. The student body lets out a collective roar. Melon is delirious. "They won't forget this bonfire. Teach 'em not to mess with the Melon and St. Raymond. This is a good one, Sheets."

I pound the earth with the side of my fist. "You better believe it's a good one!" I'm delirious with excitement.

Suddenly, a powerful flashlight beam scans the field along the fence line. The words fall out of my mouth in a loud whisper, "Get down!"

Alice slides off my back. We slither backward down the hill. Only Melinda remains, and she's curled up like a snail. Melon crawls up to her. "C'mon, we need to get out of here." He tugs at her foot until she unfolds and skitters down the hill.

We remain under the shelter of the oaks, tucked away in our sleeping bags. We feel safe that whoever has the flashlight won't venture beyond the fence line, let alone crest the hill and come down into the woods.

Melon has the car cover pulled over him and Melinda. He reassures her that the fire is well contained and that groundskeepers live on the premises. "They're probably standing by with hoses."

Unreassuringly, Melon snorts with laughter, then he launches into a story about his conflict over whether he should become an architect or a demolition expert. "It's pulling at me like night pulls at day and up pulls at down…"

Melinda responds to Melon with a sneeze. Alice and I stifle our laughter as I reach out of my tapered mummy bag to draw her in close. I whisper, "How about like Raymond pulls at Alice and Alice pulls at Raymond?"

We're uncovered from the waist up, and portions of the sleeping bags overlap beneath us. Alice giggles into my chest. "That's the kind of pulling I like."

She places my hand on her chest. I palm her breast, feel the small firmness through her blouse. We kiss and explore, stop now and then to listen to the breeze ruffle the oaks. I don't know how much time passes, but after a while, Melon's voice tapers off and he begins to snore.

Melinda sneezes. Loud and powerful. Alice and I startle and pull apart. We recover and begin to laugh hysterically. I reach for her hand, touch the smooth polished jewels on her ring. "I feel your father's eyes."

"That's what I like about you, Raymond Sheets. You remember things I tell you."

"Actually, you told Aunt Nanette. I just happened to be there."

Alice raises her head, indicates the slope before us. "Let's go up the hill and take a peek at the fire."

We drag the sleeping bags into cooler air beyond the tree line and scramble up the backside of the hill. The half-moon has arced high and straight overhead. Gauze wisps of fog sweep across the night sky.

We boldly stand just behind the hilltop. Alice gives an audible shiver. "I wish we could get down by the fire."

The blaze has settled. I can see two dark figures at the edge of the burn. One of them pokes at the fire with a long rake or stick. Breeze-driven flames dance above a large bed of coals. "That would be nice, but let's make ourselves warm right here. Unzip your bag."

Alice runs the zipper open and hands me the bag. I splay the bag out on the ground. The bag is tapered. It unzips partially, leaving a little cubbyhole at the bottom for Alice's feet. "Get down on the bag. Slide your feet into the bottom."

Alice lies down and shudders. "I wish I hadn't given Melinda my coat and hat."

I lie down beside her, pull my open bag over the two of us. Alice clings to me. I wrap both arms around her, hug her for warmth. She nuzzles my neck. My face is pressed into the soft, clean scent of her hair. A sharp breeze taps at the outside of our nestled cocoon. "It's warmer under the trees. Plus, the ground's a little softer. Want to go back down?"

"I want to stay right here forever, Raymond Sheets." She presses her tiny body length against me. I remember Melon's gift in my wallet. *Here, Sheetsy, you'll probably use this before I ever will.*

Alice tilts her head up to my lips. My hands trace her spine down to the indentation of her lower back. Suddenly, she pulls away.

"What's the matter?"

"I want to take my ring off."

"Why?"

"I don't know why. It's like my father's in here with us or something."

"Let me have it. I'll put it in my pocket so you don't lose it."

"No. I want it outside." She lifts an edge of the sleeping bag. A brush of coolness floats into our nest, then Alice closes the gap and returns to my lips in the dark.

I detach from Alice. "I have to go outside for a minute to get some air." The condom.

"Just stick your head outside."

"No, actually I have to take a pee," I lie.

Standing in the dim light of the half-moon with my pants unzipped, under the glow of God's stars, I fiddle with the condom. I figure out how it unrolls and slips on.

Under the cover of the sleeping bag, my moves are tenuous, unsure. Alice wiggles off her pants. She begins to guide me. "You didn't have to pee at all, Raymond Sheets."

My inexperienced body soon begins to respond as if it has a knowing all its own. In the moonlit hills above St. Jerome's, Alice and I meld into one rhythm and all too soon release. I feel her beating heart and think, *Holy shit*, before I sink into the depths of sleep.

I awaken, feeling an unfamiliar deep relaxation. Our shoes out in the cold. Clothes tangled in the sleeping bag. I wonder if Alice felt the intensity as I listen to her breathe softly in her dreams.

I raise my face out into the night air. In the light of the lowering moon, I watch stars and again fall asleep under the tilt-a-whirl expanse of the sky.

I sleep and dream. I fly out of my room at St. Jerome's. I soar over the lights of the valley, leaving the warmth and security of my little niche behind the fortress of the walls.

My dream is interrupted by a bell. The dim peal of the wake-up bell sings across the dark morning sky to where I lie huddled next to Alice. I slowly awaken, the dream so real, I'm disappointed I can't fly.

I turn over and watch as windows light up at St. Jerome's. The student body opens the page of another day. I try to imagine the excited speculation and chatter about the bonfire.

Reaching down into the bedding, I find my shorts and slip them on. I step out of the bag, dragging my jeans. I slide one foot into a pants leg.

Melon emerges from the trees. "Whoa! St. Raymond, stepping into his clothes!"

With my pants half on, I motion to Melon to keep his voice down. I finish dressing. Melon grins with his elbows up and the palms of his hands on the back of his head. He bumps his hips a couple of times like some bald burlesque queen.

I direct him along the flank of the hill away from Alice. "She's still asleep."

"Not anymore." Alice's voice sounds hoarse. "Is it cold out there?"

I stand on nibbled field grass damp with dew. It scratches at my bare feet. "Yeah, stay warm. We're going to check out the fire."

We move a hundred feet from Alice, drop to our stomachs, and peer over the ridgeline. The fire has burned to ash and molten coals, with intermittent flickers of flame. A single silhouette of a man watches over the dying embers.

In the east, beyond the bell tower and the spires of the chapel, spectacular rose-colored clouds ignite the morning sky.

Melon nudges me with an elbow. "How was it, Sheetsy? Is she a hot momma or what?"

"Knock it off, Melon."

"Raymond, Raymond, confess to me your sins. I want all the lurid details."

"Melon, it was most amazing, and there was no sin."

"You penetrated a female. In the eyes of Mother Church, you have sinned against the Almighty. Did you use the rubber I gave you, my son?"

"I think Mother Church is wrong about this one. It was wonderful. I have never felt so closely connected to another human being, and the rubber is my business, bald, pudgy Melon/Father."

"Careful, Sheets, you know how sensitive I am about my anatomical shortcomings."

"About as sensitive as my knuckles are gonna feel when I bust your face. Let's get out of here. My feet are frozen."

Melon shakes his head, mutters through a smile, "St. Raymond's in love."

Alice has her head out of the bag. "What's the plan?"

"The plan is to gather up our stuff and head down off this hill." I sit in the weeds and pull on my socks. "Melon, go down to the trees and wake Melinda."

Melon reaches down and ruffles Alice's already ruffled hair before he heads down the hill. He gives a backward wave. "A night under the stars. St. Raymond, the arsonist, shouting orders like a man."

Alice fumbles with her clothes beneath the sleeping bag. "What's he talking about?"

"Who knows?" I'm tying my shoes. "It's just Melon-talk."

As we roll up our bedding, Alice and I avoid any mention of our night together. I want to ask her how she knows so much about how to do it, but I suddenly feel shy. I keep my mouth shut.

Melinda's up. She's having a sneezing fit. Her eyes are bloodshot and watery as we begin to retrace our route.

I am handing the duffel bag to Melon over the barbed wire fence when Alice blurts: "My ring. I forgot my ring."

Alice and I race through the trees and up the hill. We scan the area where our sleeping bags have matted the weeds. "I've got to find it, Raymond."

Matted weeds and one used condom. I hurriedly kick it away, get down on my hands and knees, and inch by inch scrutinize the ground.

No ring. Alice is near hysteria. "My dad's going to kill me. Do you think an animal could have carried it off?"

"I've heard of birds picking up shiny objects, but we haven't been gone that long. Maybe it got pressed into the ground. Keep looking."

We never find Alice's ring, but I do continue to see her on the weekends.

18

THE END COMES ABOUT A MONTH after the bonfire. We're necking at the El Monte drive-in, the same drive-in I used to watch through binoculars from the third floor at St. Jerome's. Going at it hot and heavy. I don't even remember the name of the movie, but at intermission, the lights come on. People in cars play games of headlight tag on the white screen.

Fabian on the radio is singing "Turn Me Loose." Alice pulls away from me and turns up the volume.

"Alice, what are you doing?"

"I like this song."

"It feels like you're telling me to turn you loose."

"Not you, Raymond."

"Who, then?"

"This guy I met. A sailor from the air station."

I unwrap my arms, gently take hold of her shoulder and push away. I feel exasperated. "You dating sailors now?"

"Maybe. What about it, Raymond?"

"I thought you and I…"

"I like you, Raymond, but I don't want to be tied to one person."

A couple of strained phone calls follow. Alice and I drift apart. I resent how casually Alice can dismiss me. I try to shed the anger, but it continues to fester. I retreat to Melon's garage more than I should. I drink beer and crush the cans, sometimes stomping them flat with my foot. Melon tries to soothe me with kind words about more fish in the sea. "And when all else fails, Sheetsy, just drink more beer."

One Saturday morning, I wake with a pounding headache. Deciding once and for all that Melon and more beer are not the answer, I retrieve Iron Jack's business card from my wallet. I give him a call, thinking maybe he can shed some light on my bad luck with women.

Jack meets me in a room off a side entrance to his house. I slump in an overstuffed chair. Morning sunlight drifts through blinds, throws linear shadows on the beige walls. I notice Jack has the same brass cannon on his desk that he had at the sem. He turns it over in his fingers while he thinks. He's dropped the formal "Mr. Sheets." "So, one lady thinks you're a creep, and you figure the other one thinks you're boring?"

I also drop the "yes, Father," "no, Father" stuff of St. Jerome's. "That's about it."

He sets the cannon down and studies me. "The under-the-tarp shenanigan was a little creepy. Let's talk about Alice."

I return Jack's gaze. "What about her?"

Jack folds his arms to his chest, leans back. "Maybe she's not bored, just feeling a little suffocated by too much attention from one guy. How are you doing after your mother's death?"

"I'm doing fine." I feel irritated that Jack is changing the subject. "I thought we were talking about Alice. What's my mother's death got to do with her?"

"May or may not have anything to do with it, but I have a hunch."

The words fly out of my mouth. "Geez, Jack, you been reading that Jung guy again?"

Jack rocks forward, elbows on the desk. He stifles a chuckle. "Maybe. How much do you miss your mother?"

"What the hell kind of question is that? She's my mother, for Pete's sake! Let's get back to Alice!"

"We will. If I make you too uncomfortable, tell me to shut up, but I think this may be important."

Once again, Jack's full of riddles. "You think Alice has something to do with my mother?"

Jack ignores my question. "What was your mother's reaction when you told her you had been expelled from St. Jerome's?"

I exhale loudly. "I never told her!"

"Why is that?"

"I didn't want to upset her."

"Was she that fragile?"

"Hell yes, she was fragile. She wanted me to be a priest more than anything. I told her I *might* want to quit the seminary, and she got all hysterical. I sure wasn't going to tell her I got the boot. As it was, she got hysterical, and that night she had a stroke." I slam my fist into the palm of my other hand. "I feel like I caused her stroke." Exasperated, my eyes well up. Tears stream my face, and it feels like a relief to shout it out. "Goddamn it, I feel like I killed her."

"Words can't kill, especially the truth. You only told her that you might want to change the direction of your life."

I dry my eyes. "How in the hell did we get from Alice to this?"

Jack's answer is blunt. "Maybe you were trying to please your mother."

My shoulders are tight. My arms feel like sticks of lumber. "Jack, what the hell are you talking about?"

"Just guessing. Were you trying to protect her? Afraid to tell her things?"

"So, what's this got to do with Alice? She dumped me."

"Maybe Alice felt a little hemmed in. She's young. Still wants to explore the world."

Or maybe she dumped me because I'm too tame and boring. Maybe I was too possessive. Maybe she did feel smothered. "The hell with it, let her explore. It was taking a lot of energy trying to get her to like me. Truth is, I don't miss her much anyway. She lives too damn far away." We sit in silence for a few seconds. My breathing slows. "So Melon was right about my mother then. She had a hold on me?"

Jack smiles. "At times, even knuckleheads have some insight."

My mind flies to the tight hug my mother gave me the last time I came home from school. I think about how I pulled away from her. How I wanted to get out from under her clammy influence. Death cut the ties. I feel guilty, yet as much as I miss her, her death has set me free. "It feels weird. You're saying maybe Alice had the same hold on me?"

"Could be. Our parents can influence us. We either become like them or at some point break away."

"I don't want to become like my parents."

"They were probably doing the best they could."

"That's not good enough." I'm nearly shouting. "My old man's a drunk, and my ma was hung up on religion."

The sun-glare in the room intensifies. Jack stands up to adjust the blinds. "Take it slow. There's a lot to digest here."

"I'm pissed! Alice dumps me, my pop's drowning in scotch, Ma was a nut! How screwed up is that?"

"Pretty common, actually. Not as screwed up as you think. Think of it this way. Some people never figure it out. You're learning early."

I look away from Jack, notice a watercolor of a charging bull and a matador on the wall. My voice grows quiet. "I feel guilty saying my ma was a nut."

"'Nut' may not be the best word. 'Fearful' might be better."

"She was afraid?"

"Perhaps. The church at one level can be steeped in boogeymen. Hell, devils, suffering for all eternity."

"You think she was afraid of going to hell?"

"Good question. I didn't know her, but I sense from what you've told me that she had a lot of fear. The church may have been her life raft."

"Some life raft. They feed you a bunch of fear, then tell you to hang on."

Jack leans on the edge of his desk, arms folded once again. "A life raft with a few holes." He smiles. "We'll have to continue this some other time. I've got an appointment to play handball."

"My old man used to play handball years ago."

Jack walks me to the door. "Maybe get him interested again. Good way to work off the scotch."

Nothing stays the same. Nothing except my old man and his drinking.

"He hasn't been home all night, Raymond." Mrs. Sako is fretting about the kitchen. It's the Saturday after Thanksgiving.

The phone rings. I answer after the second ring. The voice on the other end of the line sounds stern and loaded with authority. "Raymond Sheets?"

"Yes, this is Raymond Sheets."

"This is Sergeant Tyler down at Taraval Station. We have your father in a holding cell. A patrol car picked him up last night. He was passed out on a lawn. We didn't book him. Just brought him in to dry out. He said to call you for a ride home."

I feel sheer rage as I hang up the phone. *Damn it, Pop!* I go to the liquor cabinet and gather up the scotch bottles. One by one, I pour the contents down the kitchen sink, then take the empty bottles of Cutty Sark and slam them hard into the outside garbage can.

My pop is a mess when I go to pick him up. Grass stains on the knees of his wrinkled slacks, shirttail hanging out beneath the bottom of his windbreaker, dark stubble on his face, bloodshot eyes.

"Pop, where'd you leave your car?"

His voice is low and raspy. "I dunno, Choirboy, I'll have to think about it. Just take me home."

"We're not going home, Pop."

He's in the passenger seat of the Ford. "Look, don't give me a bad time, Choirboy. I don't feel good." His breath reeks. I start the car and open the window.

"We're gonna take a ride, Pop, and my name isn't Choirboy. My name's Raymond."

I weave the blue Ford through the avenues, eventually merging into the traffic flow of Nineteenth. I stop at a flower stand and purchase a mixed bouquet. My pop's head droops toward his chest. Through his half-opened eyes, he asks, "Who the posies for? You got a girl?"

"We're going to the cemetery. These flowers are for Ma."

The mention of my mother jolts his head upright, yet he continues to protest. "Take me home, you hear me? I need a drink."

"No more drinks, Pop. I poured the Cutty Sark down the sink. We're going to visit Ma."

He sleeps on the ride out to Holy Cross Cemetery. I pull to the curb at the foot of the grassy slope that houses Ma's remains. I shake his shoulder. "Hey, wake up. She's up there waiting for you." I hand him the flowers, which were resting on the rear seat.

He stares at me. His green eyes take on the look of a meek child. I watch him leave the car and climb the gentle slope of lawn. He drops to one knee at the gravesite. Lays down the flowers. Pounds the earth twice with his fist.

I get out of the car and walk up the hill after him. I stand behind my father and watch his body shake and convulse. Again, he hammers the sod with his beefy hand; then he goes still. I place my hand on his shoulder. "Let's go home, Pop."

Looking exhausted, he humbly follows me into the car. In a subdued tone, he asks, "You really poured the scotch down the sink?"

I turn the key in the ignition, and the car emits a throaty rumble as we pull from the curb. "You better believe I did."

He looks at me with a tired half grin. "I didn't think you had it in you, Choirboy."

"I told you not to call me that, and if you take another drink, I will personally flatten you."

"I need to taper off." He's mumbling now. "Can't quit cold turkey."

"You're not that far gone. I gave the word to Mr. and Mrs. Sako: no alcohol in the house. You come home from work with liquor on your breath, I'll tell everyone in the office that you got a drinking problem."

"You stay away from the office. You got no business there."

I knew this would get to him, but I'm angry and relentless. We're stopped at an intersection, and when the light turns green, I accelerate. "I'm making it my business."

"When did you become such a mean bastard?"

"It came full on this morning, but it started the day I was born." I glance at my father. He has his chin to his chest, and I think he's smiling. I ask him, "You ever think about taking up handball again?"

"I'll think about it. Too busy. Just get me home. I'm dead tired. Need to sleep."

I change lanes, make a right turn on Ocean Avenue. "I'd like you to meet my friend Iron Jack."

"Who the hell's Iron Jack?"

"Friend of mine. He was in Korea. Hell of a handball player. Probably whip your ass."

19

I SHOULD TAKE MY OWN ADVICE WHEN it comes to drinking. I hang around with Melon. Drink more beer than I should in his garage.

One Saturday past midnight in early December, after too many Hamm's, I'm still feeling the sting of Alice's rejection. Melon and I borrow his father's sleek-finned Plymouth. We cruise Nineteenth Avenue, cross through the park, north on Park Presidio, circle a block, and head west on Geary toward the beach. The misty night air seems to magnify the city lights along the boulevard. I feel nearly immortal as we approach the curve near the Cliff House. Melon guns the Plymouth. Both of us hooting and hollering, I shout, "Alice is a bitch!"

Melon accelerates. At this empty hour, the vacant sidewalk and the seawall fly by in a blurred rush. The speedometer reads seventy as we hit the flats of the Great Highway. Melon shouts, "If it makes you feel any better, I've got her ring!"

The speedometer needle tilts toward eighty miles an hour. The mist has turned to a downpour. Windshield wipers frantically try to erase the rain. Wet pavement glares under the blast of headlights. I lash out at Melon, "What are you talking about?"

"That morning on the hill. I picked up her ring!"

"You asshole!" I scream these last words to Melon a split second before the right front tire of his father's elegantly polished black car slams a concrete abutment that juts into the roadway near the south end of the seawall. Upended, I flash on my sister as metal screeches, rolls, and tumbles. Blackness.

I open my eyes. Dim light. Hum of machines. My father hovers over me. I try to speak but lapse into sleep. Time seems to stand still as I alternate between waking and sleep. At one point, I remember Donnie saying, "You're going to make it, little brother." His wide eyes suggest he's trying to convince me. He has his hair in a military buzz cut. *You'll never score with the ladies looking like that.* From somewhere in a dreamscape, I'm inwardly laughing.

Faces come and go, peering down into a well of darkness.

I surface into distorted time. My head hurts. I try to reposition my clumsy body to relieve pain, but I can't move. A woman at the foot of the bed writes on a clipboard.

"Where am I?" I ask.

"Well, well," she replies, "welcome back. Looks like you're going to make it."

I repeat my question.

"UC med center. You were in an accident. Lucky to be alive."

"I'm confused. What day is it?"

"It's Wednesday. I guess you could call it day. It's three in the morning."

"Where's Melon?"

She moves toward me from the foot of the bed, wrinkles her forehead, "Melon…?"

My eyes close tight and heavy. I sink into the underworld and dream. Melon and my mother play ping-pong. I'm frustrated they won't acknowledge me. They lay down their paddles and leave through a window. I follow them down a hill where an old man in an Eskimo parka sorts garlic bulbs. The man speaks to them of large black dump trucks that get smaller with time until they are no bigger than a toy.

I wake to Iron Jack and my father standing at my bedside.

"Hey, buddy, going to sleep your life away?" My father forces a tight-lipped grimace. He bends over the bed to study my face.

"Hi, Pop, you know Jack?"

"We met three days ago when you were in the ICU."

"You're now on a nursing floor," Jack chimes in. "Which means you're gonna get well soon."

"What's the matter with me? I can't move my head." My throat hurts when I try to speak. My words sound hoarse and feeble. "Feels like I'm nailed to the bed."

My old man turns to Jack, then looks down at me. "You had severe head trauma and some fractured vertebrae. Seems you broke your neck, son."

"I saw Melon with Ma. They were playing ping-pong. There was some black dump trucks." I recall the dream that seems so real I'm not sure it was a dream. My body convulses with grief. I rasp out a question. "Where's Melon? How come nobody can tell me where Melon is? Melon's dead, right, Pop?"

My father gives an almost imperceptible nod. My head throbs. I let out a groan and tumble back into the safety of darkness.

My dreams, quick, feverish, jumbled, and full of dread. I awaken intermittently; faces come and go. My brother. My father. And always nurses hurriedly moving through. A nurse adds tape to a tube in my arm.

"The pain is bad," I utter. "God, it hurts to talk."

"I'll speak to the doctor about more meds, but we're pumping all we can into you, hon."

I nod off and waken to Mr. and Mrs. Sako. He leans toward my ear and whispers, "Breathe slow from stomach, Raymond. Breathe to pain. May be helpful."

I lose track of time. Only alternating light and darkness through the hospital window signal night from day.

Then the telephone rings, waking me from sleep, or was I asleep? A cloud-filtered pearly light floods the room. I blindly reach for the bedside phone. Pain shoots down my arm. I nearly drop the receiver as it brushes against bandages wrapped just above my ear. "Hello," I rasp.

"Raymond, it's Alice. Are you all right?"

Alice. My eyes flood at the sound of her voice. "Melon," I blurt out, "Melon's dead." Suddenly the room becomes cold. My right hand presses the phone to my ear. My left hand pulls the edge of a blanket toward my chin. "Melon's gone, Alice." My voice squeaks as I try to hold off pain and a surge of emotion.

"I'm sorry," she says in a hushed whimper. "Oh my God, Melon! I'm so sorry." My eyes clamp shut to dam the flow. Alice sounds like she is crying. The last thing I hear is her tearful whisper, "My father's in the brig," before I nod off to the buzz of a dial tone in my ear.

"Let me have that, son." A bespectacled man takes the phone out of my hand. A black-and-chrome stethoscope is hanging against his white coat. "I'm Dr. Splint, and, yes, that's my real name."

My head hurts too much to acknowledge his humor. The doctor's silver hair is thinning, he looks lean and fit, and a gray mustache fans out over a benevolent smile. "I operated on your head. We retrieved a couple of bone fragments. Seemed touch and go for a while, but it appears you're going to be okay once the neck heals."

"My dad said I have a broken neck."

The doc folds his arms as if he's about to deliver a lecture. "Seven vertebrae in the neck. You managed to fracture three of them. Luckily, no damage to the spinal cord."

"When can I get out of here?"

"Hope to have you out before Christmas. You'll be in a back-and-neck brace for some time. At least you fared better than your buddy."

I bolster up my voice. Try to sound tough. "How'd he die, Doc?"

"Ejected from the vehicle. Dead at the scene. You boys were apparently traveling at a high rate of speed."

My last words to Melon nesting dormant for days now awaken to flood my body. I recall an anger rush that springs like a snake. "Melon is an asshole!" Words spew out of my mouth as if I'm disconnected from my brain. "He was driving too fast just like the asshole that killed my sister!" Feeling disjointed, I continue to rage, "I want out of here, Doc!"

Dr. Splint, ready to leave the room, turns back toward my bed. "Easy, Mr. Sheets, I'll have one of our psychiatrists look in on you. Mind has to heal along with the body. We're working to get you out of here as soon as you are well enough to leave."

"I'm not nuts, Doc. I don't need a psychiatrist! I just need out of here!" I struggle to lift myself from the bed but succumb to a piercing pain and the tumble-screech and clang of metal, then darkness.

Emptiness. The horrific split second of the accident is imprinted in my body cells. My head pounds. I want to scream. Part of me has died along with the fucking knucklehead. Asshole Melon. Sleep. I dream of running barefoot, my feet slapping white foam along the surf line. Salt-splash stings my eyes.

～

I'm awake but weak and depleted when a sturdy old woman appears at the foot of my bed. "Mr. Sheets, I'm Maja Litwak. I'm a mental health doctor here at the hospital. How are you feeling?"

Large glasses magnify her soft and direct gaze as she studies me. Her full lips, slightly parted, seem on the verge of a friendly smile. "I see you have been in a most unfortunate accident." She enunciates clearly and exactly as if she has spent many years practicing English. "How are you feeling?"

"My head hurts, and I can't turn my neck."

She moves to the right side of the bed, lightly touches the back of my wrist with her warm hand. I notice her thick, silver hair brushed back, strong and willowy, unlike my grandmother Nona's stiff, wizened coils. Discreet pearl earrings, matching the color of her hair, dangle from her ears.

I add, "I'm hungry, and I want out of here."

She leans in so I can better see her face. "They've been feeding you through a tube. I can talk to the nurse about possibly getting you some soup. Sometimes with a neck injury, the swallow reflex gets affected."

"My throat does hurt. Where are you from?"

"If you mean my speech, I am of Polish ancestry." With a slow dignity and stature, Maja Litwak returns to the foot of my bed and faces me.

"My friend Alice is Irish." I want to pull the sheets over my head and hide from this woman's kind, probing eyes.

"Does Alice know you've been in an accident?"

"She called me. Her father's in the brig."

Maja Litwak scribbles on a clipboard. "This Alice sounds like a close friend."

"She came to my mother's funeral," I inform her. My throat aches as I try to talk. "Everybody's dying." I spit the words out.

Dr. Litwak returns to the side of my bed. "Who else has died?" Her voice, calm, soothing, again a whisper.

"My sister died," I croak. "She was in a rollover accident just like me and Melon. Melon's dead. He was driving too fast. I'm pissed at Melon." A blowtorch scorch in my throat. Suddenly, tears flood my face. "I'm sorry," I rasp.

"You are grieving, Mr. Sheets. Anger and sadness become part of the process. Talking helps. Do you wish to tell me more about Melon? Talk only as much you feel comfortable."

"Not now," I whisper.

She hands me a tissue. "Maybe later then. Meanwhile, you and I need to figure out how to best get you through this. I have a couple of suggestions that may help. Would you like to hear them?"

I want to nod my head, but it's locked to the pillow. Instead, I raise my hand, signaling her to continue.

"Imagine yourself in a place that makes you feel joyful. For me, it is sipping a cup of tea in my garden."

"I like to run the beach from the Cliff House to Sloat."

"Excellent. A very strong image. Imagine the sound of the waves, the smell of salt air. Feel the sunshine. You're running without worry." She pauses. "As you think of this, breathe slowly through your nose. Breathe from your stomach. Long exhale through your mouth."

I open my eyes. Maja Litwak is back at the foot of my bed. "That's the same thing Mr. Sako told me to do. Breathe slowly from my stomach."

"This Mr. Sako sounds like a very wise man."

"He's a Buddhist."

Maja Litwak nods. Her smile involves her whole face, her forehead, and the skin around her eyes. "Interesting. I'm going to leave now. Any questions about what we've discussed?"

My eyes feel heavy. I breathe slow and deep. A sense of calm sweeps my body. "No," I answer.

"Get some rest, Mr. Sheets. Remember to breathe consciously. Practice running the beach. I'll speak to the nurse about soup, and we'll talk again very soon."

~

I'm fed chicken soup through a straw. It *does* hurt to swallow, and the salty liquid flows dull and metallic across my tongue. I scrunch up my face at the lack of flavor.

"It's the pain meds. Messes with your taste buds." An older nurse leans over me and fusses with the bandages on my head. She's sturdy with graying hair pulled severely tight. A smooth wooden stick spears a coifed bun on the back of her head.

I try to break through her abrupt manner. "What's the weapon for?"

She positions herself where I can see her face. "Anybody gets feisty with me, I reach up, grab my dagger, and stick 'em." She suppresses a grin. "So don't mess with me."

"Wouldn't think of it." My anger and sadness take a back seat. "When you think I'll be out of here?"

She unhooks a clipboard from the end of the bed. "Depends on how fast you heal. One of your visitors asked the same question this afternoon. Older gentleman."

I wonder about my old man. "What'd the guy look like? Did he smell like liquor?"

She replaces the clipboard. "Big guy. Slightly bald. Maybe a hint of alcohol. He's been here a lot. Sometimes plays cribbage with a younger good-looking guy built like a weight lifter. While you're snoozing, they're having fun. I tease 'em about being high rollers. At a penny a point and a nickel a game, they'll never get rich."

"Anybody else been here?"

She washes her hands at a sink. "Not on my watch, but I'm only on for eight hours." She pulls paper towels from a dispenser. "Got work to do. You know how to get me if you need anything."

"You mean I'm not your only patient?" I enjoy her spunk. Don't want her to leave.

"Don't I wish," she calls over her shoulder. Then she's gone.

Damn. My pop's back into the Cutty Sark. I nod off holding a cup of soup against my chest.

I startle awake.

"You're supposed drink the soup, not spill it," the old nurse grumbles as she snatches the thin white blanket and top sheet off the bed. "You got a visitor in the hallway. I'll let him in soon as I clean up this mess."

Crisp and efficient, she replaces the bedding and ushers Jack into the room. He drapes a topcoat over a chair. "Cold out there. How are you doing?"

"Frustrated I can't move. Feel guilty, dark and depressed about Melon. Called him an asshole just before he died."

"What brought that on?"

"He pilfered a ring that belonged to Alice. I flew off the handle. Then the car flipped. We'd been drinking."

Jack settles in beside the bed. "'Guilt' is pretty strong. 'Regret' might be a better word."

"Whatever. Mr. Sako told me the same damn thing. I feel shitty. Melon's dead." My eyes flood. "I hate these damn tears."

"Mr. Sako is telling the truth." Jack pulls a chair to the side of the bed and sits. "You're sad Melon died. Tears are part of the work of getting better."

I wipe my eye with the back of my hand. "I had a dream about Melon and my mom."

"I know. I was here with your dad when you mentioned the dream. Something about dump trucks and ping-pong. Want to tell me about it?"

I relate the dream like it was vivid reality. "The dump trucks were black like sin."

Jack stretches his back. "Black like sin…interesting. Sounds like there was some fun involved. Your mom and Melon playing ping-pong. Perhaps they're in a happy place."

My head and neck are throbbing so much, it's difficult to think. "What do you make of the Eskimo in the parka? What about the garlic?"

Jack looks wide-shouldered and formidable in his blue dress shirt. "Let's see…garlic is a healing herb in some cultures. Many Eskimos live close to nature. I'm not sure. Maybe garlic for the body, and nature for the mind? What do you think?"

"Maja was talking about her garden. I told her I like to run on the beach."

Jack is curious about this new name. "And who is Maja?"

"Dr. Litwak. She likes sipping tea in her garden. She's told me to picture running the beach. Feel the sun. Breathe slowly from my stomach."

"Ah, she's teaching you meditation."

"I guess. She's only been here once. Said she'd be back."

"Sounds like you're being well taken care of. What about the dream? What do you make of the shrinking dump trucks? You mentioned they were black like sin."

"You know. Like the milk bottles in Catholic grammar school. Black bottle's mortal sin. Half-black bottle's venial sin. Die in the state of mortal sin, you go to hell."

"Pretty scary stuff, if you believe it. Toy dump truck. Toys. Maybe a child's way to look at worship and religion?"

"What do you mean, Jack?"

"We talked before about God as love. Maybe love drives the universe, not some angry god. Maybe it's time to put that version of God to rest."

My mind is in a tug-of-war. If God is love, what about Melon? What kind of god kills off Melon? Something inside of me whispers that Melon killed himself. I'm lucky he didn't kill me too. "I got a headache, too much to think about now. How'd you know I was here, anyway?"

Jack dismisses any notion of some special notice. "The picture and news of the accident were all over the morning papers."

"You save the paper?"

"I did, but maybe you don't want to look. Pretty gory."

"I want to see it."

Jack stands. "Suit yourself." He picks up his overcoat. "Have to go. I'll try and get back to see you in a few days. I'll bring the paper."

I call after him: "I think my dad's drinking again."

"He's had little relapses, but I talked to him about AA meetings." Jack stands at the foot of my bed. "Your accident really shook him up. He's actually gone to a couple of meetings. Let me work with your dad. We play cribbage and handball. You just heal up."

My old man appears at my bedside later that evening. He's wearing his McGregor jacket. "How you doing, tough guy?"

"I dunno, Pop. They say I'm going to live. Understand you're going to AA."

He pulls a chair to the edge of the bed and sits. "That's between me and a Higher Power. It's not your concern."

"What's this Higher Power? You making friends with God? Ma would like that."

"Never mind what your mother would like, and the Higher Power could be nothing more than the wind breathing through the trees." My pop rubs at the bristle on his chin with his thumb and forefinger, then reaches into his jacket pocket. "You know who belongs to this ring?"

The sapphire. "It's Alice's ring, Pop. Where'd you get it?"

"Your buddy's father gave it to me. Poor guy was pretty shook up. Said the cops found the ring in his son's pocket. Thought you might know something about it."

I clutch the ring in my hand. It's good to hold something so solid. My pop stays for a while, and we talk. When it's time for him to go, I notice a tear in his eye when he says, "We're going to get you out of here soon, tough guy." He softly places his hand on my bandaged head. "You be good, he says. "You have nice people taking care of you. Don't give them any trouble."

Days flicker by. Nurses tilt my bed up each morning. One morning, in the middle of the week, I'm surprised. Uncle Tool drops in for a visit. He carries his guitar.

"Tool, you're a long ways from Seattle. You here to sing me some songs?"

Wave of black hair above his forehead. Wide Italian smile under his dark eyes. "I'm here to teach you a song or two. I talked to a nurse on your medical team, and she talked to a therapist. Both agreed a little music might do you good." He hands me the guitar. "Your dad says you're making progress. Sorry I haven't made it down here sooner, but I've been thinking of you. How you doing?"

"Neck's messed up, but I guess it could be worse." My arms and hands feel sore and heavy as I run my thumb over the strings. The guitar gives off high to low echoes. "I don't know the first thing about music."

The deep grain polish of the guitar reflects the fluorescent lighting as Tool picks up the instrument. "Don't worry, I'll teach you some chords if you like. Might be a way to help you pass time." Tool begins strumming and singing. "My mind is such...I pretend too much."

"Remember that night in North Beach? You, me, and Donnie?" He asks.

He hands me the guitar. Turns my left wrist, wraps my fingers around the strings. "The left hand works the fingerboard. The right hand picks and strums."

"Can't move my head, Tool. Can barely see what I'm doing."

"That might be good. You can learn by feel."

Tool spends the day with me. Nurses come and go. At lunchtime, I struggle with soup through a straw. Share my Jell-O with Tool. By late afternoon, I make it through the first three chords of "There Goes My Baby" by The Drifters. I feel elated for the first time since I've been in the hospital. Tool keeps egging me on. "Look at that. My nephew's a rock and roller."

Over the next few days, I fixate on the guitar, running my hands over the wood and listening again and again to the deep, hollow reverb as I pluck the strings. Tool returns twice to update my lessons.

I'm saying good-bye to Tool when my phone rings. "Thanks for everything, Tool. I'll get the guitar back to you."

He waves good-bye and says, "It's yours, buddy. I got another one."

Tool disappears out the door as I reach for the phone. He needs to get back to Seattle. The phone call's from Alice. She wants to know how I'm healing. The sound of her hushed voice in my ear reminds me of the closeness, the tenderness I felt with her that night on the hill.

"I'm learning to play the guitar. Also, I got a surprise for you," I tell her. "I'll get it to you soon as I can drive again."

She tells me her father's out of the brig. "Busted down to seaman for drunk and disorderly. Maybe this time he'll learn," she says.

We're trading stories about drunk fathers when the physical therapist comes into my hospital room and interrupts our phone conversation.

The therapist fits me into a neck–and–back brace and gets me up and walking. My legs feel weak, and I'm glad when she helps me back into the bed.

Maja Litwak and her clipboard become almost daily visitors. I show her the news clipping and a picture of the accident that Iron Jack has dropped off. I was noncommittal when I first saw it. It's like I don't really want to look too close.

Then, with Maja in the room, the enormity of what happened hits me hard. The upturned car pancaked on the wet street. The partial view in the lower left-hand corner. A covering over something on the pavement. Melon. The knucklehead. A storm rages deep inside. Then a howl climbs to the surface as I come unhinged. Maja grips my hand. With my other hand, I pound at the mattress.

The storm passes. Little storms continue to percolate over the weeks, small fits of depression. I continue to breathe and meditate. My sessions with Maja become more and more intense as we delve into Melon and the accident. We also talk about Lucas Foyt, and always St. Jerome's. Each time, before she leaves the room, together we close our eyes and she guides me into deep breathing.

Maja comes into the room on December 24. "It seems you won't be leaving the hospital by Christmas, but I have a tiny present for you." She hands me a sitting Buddha. It's small and metallic, fits in the palm of my hand. "I saw it in a shop window and thought of you."

"Thanks." I chuckle. "He's fat and bald, just like Melon." Thoughts of Melon are getting easier to deal with, yet sometimes they still unsettle me. I quickly change the subject. "I sure would like to get out of here."

"I have met with your medical team. Perhaps by New Year's, but no promises."

"I'm a little disappointed."

"I know. It is difficult." She folds her arms. A grandmotherly clinician in a white coat. "Time probably feels at a standstill right now, but you will be running the beach very soon. I will be off duty tomorrow."

"Merry Christmas, Doc."

"A very merry Christmas to you." A thought occurs to her, and she shares it with me. "Perhaps I should tell you. In English, my name is Maya. Do you know what one of the origins of Maya is?"

"Don't have the slightest idea."

"Maya was the name of the mother of Buddha."

I know the doc well enough to tease her. "Sounds like you may have some connections, Doc."

"Who knows?" She smiles, and every little line on her face lights up before she leaves the room.

Christmas comes with roast turkey and mashed potatoes. I take small bites, still having trouble swallowing. Elderly carolers go from room to room singing "Silent Night" and "Little Town of Bethlehem."

My pop stops by. Donnie follows him in. The bandage wrap is off my head, replaced by two smaller bandages where Dr. Splint did the cutting. One side of my head is shaved. "You are one ugly brother," Donnie remarks. "At least they could have shaved your whole head so you looked balanced."

"You're pretty ugly yourself, and you weren't even in an accident."

"Yeah, the army destroyed most of my hair."

My pop and Donnie pull chairs to the side of my bed. That's how we spend Christmas. Pop's mostly somber and silent. Donnie tells me about the army. "I start advanced infantry training after the first of the year."

"They going to turn you into a killer?"

Donnie flexes his arms in a mock Charles Atlas pose. "After completing basic training, I'm already a double badass."

"If I wasn't a semi-invalid, I could still whip you."

My father's arms are folded. "You're a full-on invalid, sonny boy. You won't be whipping anybody for a long while."

"Thanks for the encouragement, Pop."

He stands and grins apologetically. "That's what fathers are for. Think you two can stay out of trouble while I stretch my legs?"

Donnie pipes up, "Don't go harassing the pretty nurses, Pop."

"Naw, I leave that to you, Romeo," he calls as he leaves the room.

"Tool trust you with that thing?" Donnie points to the guitar standing up against the wall near the head of the bed.

"More than trusts me—he gave it to me. You think Pop's going out for a drink?"

"Don't think so. I been home two days, and I'd say he hasn't touched a drop. He's just a little down with the holidays and no Ma. It's up to him, little brother."

I walk Donnie through some of the guitar chords while he fiddles with the strings. He seems to want to linger by my bedside. I show him the news photo of the accident. "Damn Melon." Donnie pulls hard at a deep-sounding string. "What was going through his mind, driving that fast? Let alone in the pouring rain?"

"Don't know. We both had quite a few beers. I was yelling and cussing out Alice, and Melon was being his usual raucous self. Then wham!"

"What was the deal with Alice?"

"She dumped me, but she's been calling on the phone lately, just to talk." I show Donnie Alice's ring. "Cops found it in Melon's pocket."

Donnie turns the ring in his hand. "Nice stones. How'd Melon get it?"

I'm starting to feel drowsy. "He stole it," I mumble.

"Stole it?" Donnie hands me the ring. "I never did trust the little shit."

"Not as bad as it sounds. I'll tell you sometime." Talk about lack of trust. My mind flashes on Denise. The way Donnie bullshitted her, and the way I tried to deceive her. I quickly shake the thought. "Say, my neck hurts, and I'm tired. I gotta sleep now."

I wake up to find Donnie gone and Mr. Sako sitting in a bedside chair. Don't know how long I've been asleep.

"Hi, Mr. Sako, what time is it?"

"Four in the afternoon. How are you, Raymond? You are looking much better than the last time I was here."

I squeeze my eyelids open and shut a couple of times to clear my head. "Mostly fine, Mr. Sako, but I miss my mom, and now Melon's gone."

He leans his weathered face in close. "Yes, losses very difficult. All things change. Most hard time for you now."

"I feel sad. Then I feel angry that I was so stupid with my drinking."

"Yes, a mistake, but now present moment most important. Angry thoughts like unwanted visitors. Accept but don't entertain them. Need to let go. Don't ask them in for tea."

Present moment most important. With Mr. Sako's words tucked in my memory, I slowly walk the corridor. The on-duty physical therapist notes my progress. She's short, toned, and gray-haired. "You're on your own, Mr. Sheets. We're finished with you here. I'll give you a phone number to call for outpatient rehab."

Dr. Splint examines my injured head and releases me on the last day of the year. I wince as his gloved hand presses the tender wounds. "Looks good. You have a follow-up appointment in two weeks."

My pop appears with a change of clothes, and the old nurse with the stick in her hair helps me into a pair of khaki pants. She is tying my shoes when Maja Litwak enters the room. "You look most healthy."

The old nurse finishes up with the shoes and ushers Pop out of the room. The psychology stuff is all very confidential. "A very exciting day, yes?" Maja asks, standing in front of me as I sit on the edge of the bed.

"Happy to be getting out, Doc. I'll miss the people here, but not the place. The corridors, the rooms, the restrictions and limitations, remind me of my old school."

"St. Jerome's seems to have left a mark on you."

"The church, my mom, and St. Jerome's. I guess I been branded. With half my head shaved, I must look like I been literally branded."

Maja smiles widely. "The hair is already starting to grow, and remember the positives we talked about."

"I know. Iron Jack. Mr. Sako. Even Melon the meathead."

"Teachers come in many forms."

"Sure do." I lower my eyes in a moment of bashfulness, then refocus on her pleasing face. "You been a teacher, too, Doc."

"Thank you for saying so. It feels good to hear that. How would you feel about a follow-up appointment in a couple of weeks?"

I feel relieved I won't be breaking all my ties. Much as I don't like the hospital, I feel a sense of security here. "I would like that."

"Here's my card." She turns to leave. "My office hours are generally late afternoons."

The Buddha and the sapphire are in my pocket. An orderly wheels me out to my pop's waiting car. It's a cold, sun-dappled morning. I can't turn my head to the left or the right. I feel confined and restless.

I look straight ahead, track the white disc of the sun as it seesaws in the clouds.

In a way, I'll miss the hospital. I feel a homesickness for the attentiveness and kindness of people. Kindness. Maybe that's the God Jack talks about.

Sunlight. Clouds. Kindness. A personal, angry God feels far away as if long ago he died with Melon in the wreckage. I retrieve the smiling Buddha from my pocket, slowly thumb his belly.

My father's ham-like hands grip the wheel as we motor down Parnassus. I'm uneasy as we merge with city traffic. It's my first time in a car since the accident. I concentrate on my breathing, thankful my father is silent now, less provoking, less turbulent. Maybe he's tuned to a Higher Power.

My doubts, anger, and sadness will return, but for now I'm certain: love drives the universe. In the present moment, the bearded angry god with a stick is a myth. That god is not real. That god never existed.

I've traded my mother's fearsome god for my father's Higher Power, the source of the wind, breathing through trees.

Buddha belly. I think of Melon's sardonic grin, voice of a joker: "Sheetsy, Sheetsy, my old friend St. Raymond," he says, "your father's right." Melon, the clown, the knucklehead. For once in my life, I believe him.

Acknowledgements

Thanks to fellow writers Donna Emerson, Helen Heal, M.A. Rasmussen, and Patti Trimble for their honest critiques, support, and encouragement.

Special thanks to my Monday writing partner, Devika Brandt, for her poetic eye, honest critiques, and sapphire wisdom. Also thanks to Pete Callander for giving me a kick when I needed it, to Joe Cutler for scouting pathways through a forest of dreams, to Bruce Fortin for opening the door to the middle way, to John Paine and Katrina Robinson for their keen editorial diligence, to my brother, Jerry Thomas, for his sustained interest and doses of humor, and a huge thanks to Judy Thomas, the love of my life, for her infinite patience in correcting my computer glitches and calming my threats to throw the machine out the window.

Belated thanks to Frs. Gregoire, S.S., and Hillman, S.M. Both of whom encouraged me at an early age to write.

About the Author

Ron Thomas's poetry and prose has appeared in the *Texas Review*, *Wisconsin Review*, *Sanskrit*, *Quiddity*, *New York Quarterly*, *Cimarron Review*, *Willard and Maple*, *Fourteen Hills*, *Meridian Anthology of Contemporary Poetry*, *Poet Lore*, and many other journals. He used to run marathons until his left knee got older than the rest of him. Now he bicycles and lives with his wife and their dog in Sebastopol, California.

I Want to Walk You Home is Thomas's first work of fiction.